the debt collector

BOOK FIVE OF THE
SYDNEY HARBOUR
HOSPITAL SERIES

CHRIS TAYLOR

LCT Productions Pty Ltd
18364 Kamilaroi Highway, Narrabri NSW 2390

ISBN. 978-1-925119-32-9 (Paperback)

The Debt Collector is a work of fiction. Names, characters, places, brands, media and incidents either are the product of the author's imagination or are used fictitiously. Any resemblance to actual persons, living or dead, events, or locales, is entirely coincidental.

Published in the United States of America.

BOOKS BY CHRIS TAYLOR

THE SYDNEY HARBOUR HOSPITAL SERIES
(in order)

The Perfect Husband
The Body Thief
The Baby Snatchers
The Final Bullet
The Debt Collector
The Lab Test
The Stolen Identity
The Cliff Top Killer
The Likeable Fraudster

THE MUNRO FAMILY SERIES
(In order)

The Profiler
The Investigator
The Predator
The Betrayal
The Deception
The Negotiator
The Christmas Vigil
The Ransom
The Defendant
The Shooting
The Maker

Find out more about all of Chris Taylor's books, including the hugely popular Munro Family series by visiting her website at: www.christaylorauthor.com.au/about/books

Dedication

*This book is dedicated to my sister, Catherine,
for having the courage to follow her dreams.*

And as always, to my rock: my husband, Linden. I love you.

Acknowledgments

As usual, no book comes into being without a lot of help and support by my friends and family. A world of thanks must go to my wonderful editor, Pat Thomas. Thank you for everything that you do to make my stories even more amazing than I could ever dare to dream. To Detective Superintendent Michael Kilfoyle and Scott Pearce of the New South Wales Department of Forensic Medicine, thank you for lending my story credibility. Any mistakes are wholly my own.

To Alisha and all of the staff at damonza.com, thank you for yet another fantastic cover. To my sister, Nicole Guihot and to my friend, Ally Thomson, thank you for your excellent editorial comments, proof reading skills and suggestions. I hope you like the final result.

To Amy Atwell and her dedicated staff at Author EMS who are so much more than book formatters. Amy, once again, thank you for your magic.

To the fantastic writer organizations such as

Romance Writers of Australia, Romance Writers of America and Romance Writers of New Zealand for all the help, support and encouragement they offer new and aspiring writers, including me.

To my readers, thank you for your support and love for my stories. Your encouragement and enjoyment make this journey all worthwhile.

And lastly, to my friends and family, especially my husband and children. Thank you for putting up with late dinners and even later conversations as I've emerged day after day from the sometimes scary but always enthralling world I've created on my computer.

PROLOGUE

Dear Diary,

It's taken years of patience, but finally I've been able to put my plan to the test and boy, has it paid off! My preparations were meticulous. I left not the slightest thing to chance.

His final moments were beautiful. Everything went to plan. He succumbed to death with a slight look of fear, but mostly confusion, probably wondering where he went so wrong...

I feel not the slightest bit of sympathy or regret. I gave him more than he'd ever had. No one can provide charity indefinitely. Not even me.

What can I say? It was time to collect on my debt...

Chapter 1

With a nod to the smartly dressed doorman of the Hilton Hotel, Hannah Langdon smoothed her long blond hair over her shoulder and straightened her spine, anticipating the usual stir caused by her arrival. Stepping inside the entryway of the luxurious hotel, she kept her head down and crossed the foyer quickly to avoid the collection of curious glances she invariably attracted in public.

It wasn't her fault she looked like a younger Charlize Theron and was often mistaken for the model and actress—even though the woman had been born in South Africa and now lived in the US. Hannah had never stepped foot outside Australia. She'd barely been out of Sydney, the city of her birth. It was laughable she could be mistaken for the globe-trotting actress who left everyone gaping in her wake.

The reality was, Hannah had been blessed with a body women envied and men drooled over, and a face that was every bit as beautiful as her shape. That didn't mean she welcomed the attention. In fact, she much preferred the quiet and solitude of her place of employment at the Max Grace Funeral Home.

She loved the peace and serenity the funeral parlor afforded and she loved her job as an embalmer even more. Her boss was pushing eighty and wasn't at all interested in her or how she looked. As long as she got the job done with a minimum of fuss, Max Grace was a happy man. As for the people she worked over... Well, they were the most affable of all.

She never got curious stares from the corpses she lovingly restored to a more appealing sight and it was Max's job to deal with the grieving relatives. It was normal for Hannah to spend the entire day inside the building, out back in the embalming room. If it weren't for the fake tanning cream she applied in the summer at the insistence of her best friend, Samantha Wolfe—Samantha Coleridge, now—Hannah's skin would be as pale as freshly churned butter.

"There you are, Hannah! I'm glad you've arrived!"

Hannah turned and looked into Samantha's smiling face. Dressed in a low-cut, black silk dress that hugged her curves, Hannah's best friend looked stunning.

"Sam! How are you? I can't believe you found me in this crowd!" Hannah said, smiling back and giving her friend a hug.

"Are you kidding? All I had to do was look for the horde of men who'd halted mid-stride and mid-sentence to ogle and marvel at your beauty! It didn't take me long to find you!"

Hannah looked away, embarrassed, though she knew there was no malice in Sam's teasing.

"Hey, I'm joking," Sam hurriedly added, noticing Hannah's discomfort. "I'd die to look the way you do! Where did you get that dress, by the way? It looks sensational."

Hannah grinned. "You won't believe it; I bought it on eBay. I got it for the grand sum of fifty-five dollars, including postage. I wasn't sure if it would look as good on me as it did on my computer screen, but I just couldn't get past the color and of course, the price."

Samantha gave her a once-over. "I'm green with envy. You must be thrilled with the results. And I know what you mean by the color. Crimson looks so good on you. The dress alone is enough to capture the attention of every man in the room." She softened her comment with another smile.

Hannah glanced down at the strapless, fitted bodice and the silk skirt that flared out gently over her hips. The filmy fabric swirled around her legs and ended just above her ankles in a flurry of movement and light. Knowing she looked good, filled her with confidence. For the first time in a long time, she felt fun and flirty. Just the right kind of mood to be in for a night at the Sydney Harbour Hospital's Annual Charity Ball.

"There's a good turnout. The numbers bode well for the auction later tonight. Where are we sitting?" she asked Sam as her friend led the way through the crowd.

The ball was the major fundraiser for the hospital and tickets usually sold out within days of becoming available. Hannah had attended with Sam more than once, but this was the first time she'd come since Sam's marriage. It wouldn't be quite the same for her as when the two of them were single, footloose and fancy free, but she liked Rohan and hadn't seen Sam for ages and she was looking forward to catching up.

"We're sitting at a table not far from the dance floor, which should suit you perfectly," Sam replied with a cheeky wink.

Hannah chuckled. It was no secret she loved to dance. In some respects, her affinity for the dance floor was in stark contrast to her reticent, almost shy nature, but she couldn't help it. She'd been born with rhythm flowing through her veins.

"Where's your husband? I thought you two were still attached at the hip."

Sam turned back to her and rolled her eyes then followed with a smile. "Hey, it's been three months since the wedding," she protested. "Give us a break!"

Hannah laughed. "Ha! You can't fool me. If there ever comes a time when you're not glued to his side, I'll know something's up. He's at the bar, right, getting drinks? It's the only reason why he wouldn't be here by your side. Truth be told, your togetherness is a little nauseating."

Sam pulled a face. "You're jealous."

Hannah smiled and shook her head. "Not in the slightest and I mean that from the bottom of my heart. I couldn't be happier for you, Sam." Hannah glanced around her and then added, "I just hope I know at least some of the other people at our table. No doubt you and your husband will only have eyes for each other. Neither of you will likely be capable of normal conversation."

This time, Sam poked out her tongue, but her eyes sparkled with mirth. Her black hair, piled high on her head, gleamed beneath the light. In her mid-thirties, Samantha was five years older than Hannah, but her looks belied her age. Her skin glowed with a youthful vitality much younger women would envy.

"For your information," Sam replied tartly, "my sister, Ava, and her boyfriend, Lachlan Coleridge, are here. You know them. I told you she's dating Rohan's younger brother, didn't I?"

"Yes, Sam. The same night you vacillated back and forth about whether it would be cool or annoying for two of the Wolfe sisters to marry brothers. Are they getting *that* serious? Do you think marriage is on the cards?"

Sam stopped and turned back to Hannah. Her eyes sparkled with excitement. "You know, I think it is. Even though he's still technically, married, I've never seen Ava so besotted. It's Lachlan this, and Lachlan that. He moved back to Sydney from the country for her, you know. Isn't that so romantic?"

Tears glistened in Sam's eyes. Hannah started in surprise. It wasn't like her friend to become so emotional over something as trivial as her sister's love life.

"Are you feeling all right, Sammie?" she asked in sudden concern.

Sam's cheeks reddened and she averted her gaze. "Yes, of course. Why do you ask?"

Hannah shrugged and then swept her gaze over Samantha's body. Sam's normally flat stomach looked slightly distended, as if... All of a sudden, it hit her.

"Oh, my goodness! You're *pregnant!*"

Sam's eyes widened in surprise. Her mouth opened, but no words came out. Hannah didn't need any more confirmation.

"You're having a *baby!* How fantastic! Why didn't you tell me?" She frowned in mock hurt.

Sam was quick to reassure her. "Don't be upset, Hannah. We decided to keep it from our friends until we knew everything was all right. Only our immediate families know."

"How far along are you?"

"Twelve weeks," Sam said, beaming.

"So you're through the danger period."

"Yes, just. Although it hasn't been easy; I've been sick every day since I conceived. I keep hoping the nausea will ease, now that the first trimester has passed."

Hannah squealed, filled with delight. "I bet it's a girl! They say you always get sicker with girls."

Sam shook her head and smiled. "I never had you pegged as someone who'd believe old wives' tales, Hannah Langdon. Rohan and I decided not to press to find out. Boy or girl, it doesn't matter. We'd be happy either way."

"Oh, stop! Please! You're about to say 'as long as it's healthy, nothing else matters,' aren't you? You must have a preference, one way or the other!"

Sam laughed. "No, I don't and what they say is true. Just you wait until you're pregnant. You'll see what I mean. The sex of the child is irrelevant. All you want is a healthy baby."

Hannah stared at her friend, at the happiness that beamed across Sam's face, and forced back a rush of yearning. She wanted so much to be a mother, to feel what Sam was feeling. There was still time. She was only twenty-nine. She hadn't given up hope she'd find Mr Right and make it happen. She only hoped he was also on the lookout for *her*.

"Oh, look, there's Rohan and Lachlan. I'm not sure where Ava is. She might have gone to the bathroom. And there's Lane Black. He's a friend of Rohan's. Lane's a detective at the State Crime Command in Chatswood. He's married to Zara. They have the cutest set of twins. Come on, I'll introduce you. Zara's a lawyer and she's gorgeous, inside and out. You'll love her!"

At the mention of Lane Black, Hannah frowned. It was a name that conjured forth old memories and feelings that belonged firmly in her past. She gave herself a mental shake. *Surely it couldn't be the same Lane Black she'd gone to school with? The one whose brother she detested with all her heart?*

Sam took Hannah by the hand and dragged her through the crowd toward the group of men gathered at a nearby table, leaving her with no more time to dwell on the possibility of that connection. All tall and broad shouldered, dressed as they were in tuxedoes and bow ties, the men were a formidable and appealing group. Even with the rest of the males in the room similarly attired, there was something about their group that commanded particular attention.

With Sam still tugging her forward, Hannah had no choice but to follow. As she drew nearer, her heart gathered speed.

"Hannah, it's nice to see you again," Rohan said, stepping forward to peck her on the cheek. She murmured a suitable reply.

"And this is Lachlan, Rohan's brother," Samantha added. "You met him at the wedding. He was Rohan's best man."

Hannah recognized the younger Coleridge brother and held out her hand. Lachlan shook it in casual greeting.

"Hannah. Yes, I remember. You were in the wedding party. We were seated across from each other," Lachlan replied. "I have very fond memories of that wedding," he added with a smile and then glanced around at the crowd.

Hannah spied Ava heading in their direction about the same time Lachlan did. Hannah watched as Lachlan's smile widened and love and tenderness filled his eyes. She swallowed a sigh and ignored the pang in her heart. She yearned to have a man look at her like that. She'd only been in love once in her life and that had been a long, long time ago...

Hannah's thoughts were interrupted as Samantha continued the introductions.

"Lane and Zara, I'd like you to meet my best friend, Hannah Langdon. And this is Lane's brother, Jacob. He's a doctor at the Sydney—"

At the mention of Jacob's name, the rest of Sam's words were blocked out by the pounding of Hannah's heart and the rush of blood through her ears. Her chest constricted and her mouth went dry. *It couldn't be him. Please, God, don't let it actually be* him.

He was turned slightly away from her. As if in a dream, she went through the motions of shaking hands with Lane and Zara. All the while, her thoughts were focused on the man who had haunted her nightmares. And then he turned and faced her, mere inches away and there was no place left to hide.

It was *him.*

Jacob Black. He was here, at the ball, with his brother. The same Jacob Black who'd been responsible for the death of the only man she'd ever loved. Anger, hot and fast, rushed through her veins, leaving her lightheaded. She gasped and reached out blindly for support.

Her fingers skimmed over the fabric of Sam's dress. She clutched at it in her desperation. Sam turned and smiled. Hannah saw Sam's lips move, but she was deaf to what her friend said. Oblivious to her distress, Sam continued to nod and chatter, unaware of the fact her best friend's world had just disintegrated.

And then Jacob, of all people, was steadying her with a solemn look and his hand was big and warm around hers. She shook it automatically, but couldn't manage any words. His eyes were as she remembered from more than a decade ago, though she spied a trace of weary cynicism in their blue depths that hadn't been there before.

Crows' feet crinkled the corners of his eyes and frown lines were etched into his forehead. He was the same age as she was, and yet, it appeared life had taught him some harsh lessons. She twisted her lips at the thought. It served him right if the road he'd traveled since high school had been rocky. She refused to feel sorry for him.

"You look as beautiful as you did ten years ago, Hannah," he murmured.

She narrowed her eyes at him. Though he appeared sincere, she didn't want compliments from him. Aware that the other members of their group were watching, she forced the briefest of smiles.

"Thank you. You're looking…well."

He grimaced and shook his head and then muttered a reply. "How kind of you to say so."

Standing beside Hannah, Samantha looked from one to the other and then back to Hannah, a quizzical expression on her face. "Don't tell me you two know each other?"

Panic gripped Hannah's insides. She opened her mouth to reply, but words escaped her. She drew in a breath and did her best to ease the band of steel that had tightened around her chest.

"I… We… That is, I…"

"We went to high school together," Jacob supplied, his casual tone at odds with the bitterness that now glinted in his eyes.

Sam laughed and clapped her hands in delight. "How amazing! Rohan, did you hear that? Hannah and Jacob went to school together!" She turned back to Hannah. "How long has it been since you saw each other?"

Hannah gulped another mouthful of air and managed a reply. "We... We haven't seen each other since graduation."

Sam's eyes widened. "Wow! That long! What a coincidence that you meet again at the Sydney Harbour Hospital Charity Ball!"

Jacob's gaze remained fixed on Hannah's. "Yes, it is. Quite amazing," he murmured.

Hannah felt the tension reverberating from him and wondered at its cause. She was the one who had the right to feel upset. Every moment of the last time she'd seen him had been seared into her memory. In an instant, her dreams were shattered; her future disintegrating like dust. It had been eleven years since it happened, but if her feelings meant anything, it could have been yesterday.

CHAPTER 2

Jacob stared at the beautiful woman before him and tried desperately to get control of his heart rate. Her stunning looks had only improved with age—and she'd been gorgeous at eighteen. Tonight, her long blond hair hung loose around her shoulders, kissing her pale bare skin. The neckline of her dress dipped low enough to showcase her generous cleavage—something else that had been in evidence when she was young.

The silence between them lengthened and his gaze remained fixed on hers. A furious blush crept across her cheeks and her eyes sparked fire. Her anger irritated him. It was obvious she hadn't forgotten—or forgiven. And there was nothing he could do about that.

The proper thing to do would be to excuse himself and leave the ball immediately. It would save them both the discomfort of spending time together when it was clear it was the last thing she wanted to do, but something inside him rebelled at the thought of turning tail and leaving. He'd paid his debt to society. They'd taken two years of his life. As far as he was concerned, they were square.

A surge of feral anticipation flooded through him. He was damned if he would run. If she felt so uncomfortable, let *her* be the one to leave the ball before it had started. He smiled at the thought.

"I'm glad you're so amused at seeing me again," Hannah hissed.

He tamped down his instinctive urge to protest and smiled even wider. "Of course. Who doesn't enjoy catching up with old high school friends? It really has been way too long." He deliberately swept his gaze over her, taking time to note the ring finger on her left hand was bare.

Her eyes flashed dangerously and her mouth tightened, indicating her displeasure, but short of informing everyone in their party about the nature of their relationship, she was left with no choice but to respond with a modicum of courtesy. The look she shot him told him she was far from happy with being backed up against a wall, but her reply was surprisingly polite, provided he ignored the frosty tone.

"You're right. I can't think of a better way to spend the night."

She favored him with a brilliant smile and Jacob felt the full impact of her stunning beauty. His heart skipped a beat and then pounded erratically. It was all he could do to suck in a breath and respond.

"Great," he managed and held out his arm.

"Why don't I escort you to our table? It looks like the evening's about to begin."

———

Quietly seething, Hannah took the proffered arm and walked through the milling crowd toward their allocated table. Sam had told her they were seated close to the dance floor, however the polished Italian tiles seemed miles away.

She'd had no choice but to take Jacob's arm, unless she wanted to cause a scene. She was at a ball with her friends. This wasn't the time or place. *And Jacob darn well knew it.* A fresh wave of anger rushed through her and she threw him another narrow-eyed glare.

What the hell was he playing at? He had to know she wanted nothing to do with him. *Did he think the passing years had dulled her memory? That she'd forgotten the devastating thing he'd done?* It was never going to happen.

She'd sit beside him and swap casual chit chat because she'd be damned if she'd waste her two-hundred-dollar ticket and she didn't want to ruin the evening for her friends—but once it was over, that was it. He'd be lucky if she even bid him goodnight.

"So, how are your parents?" Jacob asked solicitously as he pulled out her chair and waited for her to sit.

"They're fine," Hannah managed through gritted teeth.

He took the chair beside her and lowered himself into it. The sleeve of his tux brushed her bare arm and she tensed. Her gaze shot to his, but his expression was bland, as if he hadn't even noticed. Surreptitiously, she moved as far away from him as her seat allowed.

Their table quickly filled with the members of their party and Hannah was relieved when Sam took the vacant seat next to hers. She shot her friend a look half-filled with desperation, but Sam appeared not to notice. She merely offered Hannah a smile and then turned to Rohan, who had seated himself next to his wife.

"What are you drinking? There are bottles of red and white on our table. I assume they're included with our ticket." Jacob's voice sounded way too close and once again, Hannah tensed. With her thoughts in a turmoil, she turned slightly in his direction.

"I'd rather have a beer, if you don't mind," she replied. She needed to put some distance between them.

She'd noticed, on her way across the room, that the queue to the bar was satisfyingly long. It should take him quite awhile to make it there and back. With a bit of luck, he might even get lost and half the night might pass before he managed to find them again. She could only hope.

Unaware of her thoughts, he smiled at her in surprise and then nodded and pushed back his chair. "A beer it is. He looked around at the others. "Does anyone else want something from the bar? I might as well take an order." He smiled.

Hannah was struck by his good looks and manners. He'd been pleasant to look at in high school too, but back then, she'd only had eyes for her boyfriend. His best friend had gone largely unnoticed.

After murmured requests for drinks, Jacob left the table and headed in the direction of the bar. Hannah turned immediately to Sam, taking hold of her arm in an effort to catch her attention.

"Sam! Why didn't you warn me Jacob Black was attending?"

Sam's eyes widened in surprise. "I had no idea you knew him, Hannah. Is there something wrong?"

Hannah stared at her friend. Once upon a time, she wouldn't have hesitated in regaling Sam with a blow-by-blow account of the dramas associated with the man seated at their table, but something about the paleness of Sam's cheeks and the tautness around her mouth stopped her. The words died on Hannah's lips.

"Are... Are you all right, Sam?"

"D-do you mind coming with me to the bathroom? I think I'm going to be sick."

Pushing away from the table, Samantha stood and headed in the direction of the bathrooms on the far side of the room.

Rohan half-stood, his face filled with concern. "Sam? Are you okay?" he called after her.

"It's all right," Hannah quickly reassured him. "I'll go with her. She... She isn't feeling well."

"Damn!" Rohan cursed softly. "I thought we'd seen the last of it."

"I'm sure she'll be fine," Hannah replied. "I'll go and check on her. We'll be back in a moment."

Rohan sighed with relief. "Thanks, Hannah. I appreciate your help."

"No problem." Hannah gave him a brief smile and then turned and headed toward the bathrooms. With thoughts of Jacob now pushed to the furthest recesses of her mind, she quickened her stride and soon after, found herself in the powder room. All but two of the stalls were unoccupied.

"Are you all right, Sam?" she called softly.

"I… I think so, Hannah. I'm right down the end. It's just another bout of morning sickness. Nobody told me it can go all day and night. I was hoping by now, the nausea would have lessened, but the passage of time doesn't seemed to have made any difference."

Hannah nodded in understanding and then grimaced as she heard the sound of retching. "Is there anything I can do?" she asked.

"No. I'll be fine, just as soon as I stop vomiting."

A moment later, Hannah heard the toilet flush and the door to the stall opened. Samantha emerged looking frail and wan, but as she leaned over the sink and splashed her face, a tiny bit of color returned to her cheeks.

"How are you feeling?" Hannah asked.

Sam gave her a strained smile. "Better now."

"Are you certain you're up to staying? I'm sure Rohan would be happy to take you home."

"And ruin his evening? He's been looking forward to catching up with his police buddies for weeks."

"I can take you home and stay with you until he comes home later," Hannah offered, suddenly warming to the idea.

Sam shook her head. "Then I'd be spoiling *your* evening!"

"Well, I'm sure Rohan will leave if you're not feeling up to it. He loves you. He won't sit around having a good time while you're suffering."

Sam straightened and reached for the paper towel Hannah offered and dabbed it across her face. "I agree and that's why I'm staying. Besides, now that it's over, I feel so much better. It's weird how everything feels almost normal again after a vomit. Thank you for offering though."

Hannah pulled a face. "Yuck."

Sam smiled. "Oh, come on, Hannah Langdon! You're not going to stand there and try and convince me you have a weak stomach. Not when I know what you do for a living. And how much you love it!" Sam added.

Hannah grinned unashamedly. "So? I'm an embalmer. Why does that mean I can't have a weak stomach?"

Sam rolled her eyes and grinned back at her. Hannah was relieved to note her friend looked almost as good as usual. They both turned and headed toward the exit. Without warning, Sam came to a halt and eyed Hannah curiously. "What's going on with you and Jacob Black?"

The question hit her from out of the blue. She searched around for something to say. "Um...nothing. We knew each other in high school. That's all."

Sam looked unconvinced. "Don't give me that nonsense, Hannah Langdon. I saw the way you looked at him. Was he an ex-boyfriend? Did he break your heart? Or, maybe you broke his? Come on, spill! I want all the gory details."

She smiled as she said it and Hannah did her best to respond in kind, keeping her tone light.

"As much as I'd like to appease your curiosity, it was nothing like that. He was... He was my boyfriend's best friend."

Sam nodded. "Okay, but there's more to it than that; I can tell. You're flushed and on edge. It isn't like you."

Hannah closed her eyes and drew in a deep breath. Sam knew her too well. They'd been friends for a long time. It was time to come clean.

"You're right, there *is* more to it."

Samantha pounced, her eyes gleaming with triumph. "I *knew* it!"

Hannah chuckled. "Well, I'm pleased the issues regarding my personal life have taken your mind off your nausea woes."

"Ah, so he *did* mean more to you than what you're saying? Don't tell me you were secretly in love with him the whole time you were dating his best friend?"

Hannah's mood sobered. "No, Sam. It was nothing like that. I loved Luke with every fiber of my being. I thought I'd marry him and be the mother of his kids. I thought we'd grow old together."

Sam's expression turned serious. "What happened?" she asked quietly.

With another fortifying breath, Hannah began to speak.

"We were eighteen. I was in love with the captain of the rowing team and he was in love with me. Luke Parker was all I ever dreamed of. I couldn't wait to become his wife. My days and nights were filled with fantasies of white picket fences and three kids who looked like their dad—two girls and one boy. I'd even named them." She paused.

Sam's expression remained sober. "Go on," she quietly encouraged.

Hannah drew in another breath. She might as well get it over with. "We were in our final year of high school. Our future was looking bright. Then the night of November eighteenth happened and our world was turned on its end."

"What happened?" Sam whispered, her eyes filled with fearful anticipation.

"Luke was killed in a car accident. Jacob Black was behind the wheel, drunk."

Sam's face lost some of its newly restored color. "Oh, my goodness! Hannah! How awful. What happened to Jacob? Was he charged?"

Hannah nodded. Memories bombarded her from every which way, but she forced herself to finish the story.

"Yes, he was charged with drunk driving and dangerous operation of a vehicle in a manner causing death. He said... He said they'd been arguing and that Luke had made a grab for the wheel. The judge gave him two years in jail."

Sam shook her head slowly back and forth, her

eyes wide with shock. "Wow, I had no idea. Rohan met Lane through work. We've all gone out together a few times and attended police functions every now and then. I've heard Lane speak about his family, but I hadn't heard anything about Jacob spending time in jail."

Hannah grimaced. "Yes, well I can't imagine it's the kind of thing that gets bandied about at dinner parties, especially given a number of the guests would likely work in law enforcement."

"And to think Jacob's now a doctor, and a well-respected one, from what I hear," Sam mused. "He's head of the Emergency Department at the Sydney Harbour Hospital."

Hannah started in surprise and then recalled Sam saying something about Jacob being a doctor when she'd first introduced them. "Well, it doesn't sound like he was held back by his stint in jail," she replied tartly and immediately felt ashamed of her spiteful comment.

Sam frowned. A flush heated Hannah's cheeks and she averted her gaze. In silence, they left the bathroom and headed toward their seats. Guilt surged through Hannah's veins and she reached out and touched Sam's arm, bringing her to a halt.

"I'm sorry, Sam. I shouldn't have said that. It was mean. It's just that, where Jacob Black's concerned, I lose my head. I feel so...so..."

"Cheated?" Sam offered.

"Yes! Cheated! Angry! Annoyed! He killed my boyfriend! The man I loved and planned to marry. He stole my future. He stole my *life*." Hannah's voice cracked on the last word. Tears filled her eyes. She stared at Sam in desperation, hoping to make her friend see.

Sam stepped forward and hugged her. "Hey, it's all right. I understand. You're right to feel the way you do, but honey, it was more than a decade ago. The man spent two years in prison. He repaid his debt. Okay, he's alive and your boyfriend's not and that's a sad and disappointing fact, but that's the thing—Luke is dead. He's never coming back. It's time you stopped punishing yourself and Jacob for his death."

Hannah continued to stare at Sam as she tried to take it all in. *Had she been punishing herself all these years?* Is that why she hadn't allowed herself to get close to another man? Hadn't risked being hurt again?

"There you are! I was beginning to worry."

Hannah blinked to clear away her heavy thoughts and spied Rohan descending upon them, his arms outstretched toward his wife. Sam smiled.

"Hi, honey. I'm fine. Just another bout of morning sickness, but I'm all good, now. We were on our way back to the table."

Rohan kept his gaze on his wife, his brow furrowed in concern. "Are you sure you're feeling up to it? We can always go home. These nights never end early and if you're not feeling the best—"

"No, I'm fine, I promise," Sam replied, laying a hand on Rohan's arm. She gave him another reassuring smile and the concern on his face eased.

"You're sure?"

"Yes, darling, I'm sure. Now, let's get back to the table before everyone starts wondering where we've all disappeared to. It looks like they're serving the starters."

Resting her hand in the crook of Rohan's arm, Sam gave her husband a quick kiss and together, the three of them headed back through the crowd. Hannah stared at the couple walking side by side, taking support and love from each other, and sighed, considering what her friend had said.

Was Jacob Black the reason she'd been sabotaging her love life these past ten long years? Perhaps it was time to find out.

CHAPTER 3

Jacob looked up at Rohan and Samantha's approach and spied Hannah following close behind. He stifled a sigh of relief that was tinged with disappointment. As much as he wanted to spend more time with her, every moment reminded him of a past he'd rather forget. On a warm night in November, he'd made a fatal decision that had irreparably shaped the rest of his life. *Would he ever forgive himself, or ever be free of the guilt?*

With a murmured thank you for the drink that now sat near her place at the table and a swish of her dress, Hannah returned to her seat. The faintest scent of her perfume wafted past his nose. It smelled spicy and exotic—like vanilla and cinnamon and something else. His body tightened reflexively and he cursed silently. She'd made it clear she despised the very sight of him. It wouldn't do to draw her attention to the fact that he found her attractive—more than attractive... He'd been in love with her for most of his life.

He hated the fact he'd had to keep his love a secret through their long and tumultuous high school years. She'd only ever had eyes for Luke. Jacob wasn't one to think ill of the dead, but even in life, Luke hadn't deserved her. Not that Jacob had ever told her. He hadn't found the courage to do it more than a decade ago and then the accident had happened and that was the end of it. She'd hated him from that moment on. Still did.

"How's Toby?" Hannah asked quietly.

Jacob started in surprise. He'd expected her to make some polite chit chat and then get the hell out of there. The last thing he'd anticipated was for her to enquire about his twin.

"He-he's fine," Jacob replied hastily and was immediately filled with guilt. If there was one thing his brother wasn't, it was fine, but he could hardly tell Hannah the truth. She probably didn't care, anyway.

"Really?" she answered, raising one perfectly shaped eyebrow.

He stared at her. "You sound surprised."

She lowered her gaze to her hands, where her fingers tangled in the napkin. A faint blush stole across her cheeks. "No, I... I mean, I'm glad to hear he's doing okay."

Jacob's gaze narrowed on hers. He wondered if she knew. "Why would you think otherwise?"

Hannah's flush deepened and once again, she avoided his gaze. "No reason. I just heard...after the trial...when you went to prison... He...he didn't take it well."

Jacob's heart thumped hard against his chest.

Any mention of that time brought with it a rush of memories, none of them good. His hands clenched into fists and he fought to keep his breathing steady. She didn't appear to know the truth about Toby's current state of health. It was best they keep it that way.

"I didn't see him much after the sentencing. My visitors at the jail were few and far between. Toby didn't have a car. He relied on our mom to transport him to and from the prison. It wasn't easy for him to come and see me. He wrote a few letters and I always wrote him back, but even those dwindled over time. It was like he forgot."

Hannah stared at him, her eyes dark with emotion. "What about your mom? I thought you were close?"

Jacob drew in a deep breath and eased it out on a heavy sigh. "We were."

"Were?" Hannah asked quietly.

"She died two years ago, not long after Lane and Zara's wedding. Breast cancer. She battled it for many years. It was one of the reasons she couldn't visit me in jail as frequently as she wanted to. She often wasn't well enough to make the trip. And of course, my father died when I was young."

"Which meant Toby couldn't go, either," Hannah finished.

"Right. Anyway, that was a long time ago and we've managed to put it all behind us. It's funny that you ask because I reconnected with Toby almost a week ago. He's about to start a new job."

Hannah looked surprised and Jacob

understood her reaction. He'd been out of prison for eight years. More than enough time to meet up with his twin again. It still pained him to think about the turmoil Toby experienced when Jacob went to jail, but there was nothing he could do about it—then, or now.

"Do you mean you haven't seen him all this time?" Hannah asked.

Jacob cursed under his breath. He shouldn't have used the word "reconnected." It had given her the wrong impression, even if it had been the truth.

"No. Yes. What I mean is, it took a long time for me to find him after I got out of jail. He just kind of disappeared. It isn't hard to do in a city."

"But what about your family? Your mom and your brothers? Didn't they know where he was?"

"No. Toby left without a word of good-bye to anyone. No one had a clue where he was. At the time I was sent to prison, Lane was already enrolled in the Goulburn Police Academy. He was a young constable when I was released. He was stationed here, there and everywhere, including two stints in the country. My youngest brother, Rusty, was still in high school when I was arrested. I think he probably did it even tougher than my twin."

"But what about more recently? Lane's a detective. Surely he'd have access to databases which would make it easier to find him?"

Her tone had taken on an accusatory note and Jacob's defenses rose. His fists clenched beneath the table. She knew nothing about him or his family. She had no right to judge.

"Toby disappeared without a trace. He wasn't on anyone's database. He had a provisional driver's license in high school, but it had never been renewed. He'd never bought a house and unlike me, he'd never been arrested. Lane did everything he could think of, but it was like our brother had simply vanished. We guessed and hoped he might still be in Sydney, but no one knew for sure and I don't know if you've noticed recently, but we live in a city of more than five million people. It's not easy to find someone who doesn't want to be found."

His breath came faster and his body was tense. Hannah must have seen some of the pain and turmoil in his eyes, because her face went blank then relaxed into a soft, conciliatory smile.

"I'm sorry," she said quietly. "I shouldn't have said that. It wasn't fair. Besides, it's none of my business."

Her apology seemed genuine and Jacob was reminded how she and his twin used to get along so well. Toby had been deprived of oxygen during his birth and was ever-so-slightly developmentally delayed. Hannah had always shown him kindness.

Toby looked at the world through eyes that remained as innocent as a child's. It was often his undoing. Less honorable people took advantage of his disability and his simple view of the world. Jacob had been helpless to protect his brother from inside the walls of the prison and that knowledge had killed him. It was even worse when his mother had eventually told him Toby had disappeared and no one knew where he'd gone.

Blinking back a surge of emotion the old memories brought forth, Jacob forced a semblance of a smile. "Apology accepted. It was a difficult time for us all. I'm grateful it's now behind us."

Hannah nodded, her expression somber. "I'm glad to hear Toby's found you again. He loved you very much."

This time, a lump lodged itself in Jacob's throat and he swallowed but barely managed to nod.

"You said he's about to start a new job?" Hannah asked, reaching for her beer.

"Yes, he's going to be working at a funeral parlor in Balmain," Jacob replied, watching the movement of her throat as she swallowed.

Hannah's voice was filled with surprise. "Really? I work at a funeral parlor in Balmain and it's one of only a few there. I work for the Max Grace Funeral Home. Do you know where Toby's going to be working?"

It was Jacob's turn to be surprised. He turned to her and sat forward in his seat. "I'm almost certain that's the name of it. Toby only mentioned it briefly, but he's very excited about getting the chance. It's not easy for him, as I'm sure you understand. Not everyone has the time or inclination to employ someone like him."

Hannah nodded. "I know what you mean and it sounds just like something my boss would do. Max Grace has a very kind and generous heart. He often extends a hand, in the form of employment, to those less able to obtain work elsewhere. His only family is a thirty-year-old nephew and Bobby

Grace doesn't go out of his way to endear himself to his uncle, or anyone else. He's supposed to be employed full-time at the funeral parlor, but we're lucky if he shows half the time. That makes it hard on the rest of us. If Max were less supportive, I'm sure Bobby would find himself out on the street. It's nothing less than he deserves."

"Well, if Toby is working with you, I'm glad. He's... He's done it tough these past years. It will be good for him to have a friend, and one who knows him from way back when he was young, is even better."

He gently smiled at Hannah and was pleased when she smiled back. Her earlier animosity seemed to have been set aside—at least for the moment.

Throughout the rest of the meal, they traded stories and caught up on people from their old neighborhood. The charity auction came and went and Jacob bid on and won a sixty-inch curved screen TV. Hannah confessed she'd stumbled upon her career as an embalmer after watching a television series. She told him how the world of death and funeral parlors intrigued her and she'd felt an odd kinship with the dead. When he asked her to explain, she shrugged and said, "I was raised a Catholic. I believe wholeheartedly in the afterlife and everything that comes with heaven. I want people to look their best when they meet God, face to face." She glanced at him from under her lashes, as if to gauge his reaction. He gave her an encouraging nod and she continued.

"Working over the deceased, preparing them for the hereafter, brings me deep satisfaction. It's hard to explain, but it kind of feels like it's my parting gift to the dead." She blushed and kept her eyes averted, as if embarrassed by what she'd said and then added softly, "I only hope someday someone else treats my body with as much love and respect."

Jacob shook his head, though he wasn't surprised at the depth of care and concern and love she had for the deceased. She'd always been kind and caring. It was one of the reasons he'd fallen in love with her so many years ago.

He reached over and refilled her glass with the table wine. Somewhere between the main meal and dessert, she'd switched to drinking red. The alcohol appeared to have relaxed her—either that, or she'd chosen to let her anger slide—and regardless of the reason, he was enjoying this much-more-mellow Hannah. In fact, he couldn't get enough.

He finished refilling her glass and she smiled her thanks. Topping up his own, he set the bottle back down on the table and then picked up his glass. Savoring the rich taste of the wine on his lips, he glanced across at the girl who'd haunted his dreams.

"So, are you married, Hannah, or seeing anyone?"

She frowned and he cursed silently, damning himself for breaking the mood, but then she surprised him by smiling at him lopsidedly and shaking her head.

"No, not married and not seeing anyone, either. The truth is, I don't know many men who are keen on spending time with a woman who works with the dead. The whole idea kind of creeps them out."

She offered him a shrug and continued. "Most men I date turn tail and run the moment I mention I'm an embalmer. Occasionally, one of them will quiz me about my work with a kind of morbid fascination, but their interest is only fleeting and it usually doesn't take long for even the curious to beat a hasty retreat. I spend a lot of time at work. I feel most at peace there. Sam teases me about becoming a hermit. She's sure I'll never find a prospective husband. Not that I'm looking," she hurriedly reassured him, a darker blush staining her cheeks. "I'm not even thirty. Young by anyone's standards, right?"

She winked at him and giggled and he laughed. Joy and delight at her uninhibited behavior surged through him. He'd never known her like this. During their high school years, she'd treated him like her boyfriend's mate and afterwards... She hadn't even been able to speak to him. The memory sobered his mood.

"Hey! What's the matter?" she teased and he could tell she was a little tipsy. "Why the sad face? Surely you agree? After all, we're the same age, right?"

Jacob stared at her and then forced the sad memories away. They were here now, together, enjoying each other's company. It was enough.

"Would you like to dance?" The words were out

before he could stop them, but there was no way he was going to take them back. To his relief, a smile of delight lit up her face.

"I'd love to!" She pushed away from the table.

He stood and helped her from her chair, his heart pounding double time. He couldn't believe, at long last, he was going to take Hannah Langdon in his arms.

Hannah took an unsteady step toward the dance floor, wobbling on her five-inch heels. She normally stuck to beer when she drank and the unaccustomed red wine had gone straight to her head. She'd become so engrossed in her conversation with Jacob, it had seemed a good idea to switch to what was readily available on their table, rather than send him back to the bar—but she was now paying for it.

Her head felt slightly fuzzy and the world around her was a little out of focus. She wobbled again and reached out in an effort to steady herself. Jacob was there in an instant, his arm warm and strong around her. She leaned against him, momentarily setting aside her decade-long animosity.

In fact, for the last hour or so, she could barely remember why she'd been so angry at him for so long. He was warm and kind and interesting. He was smart and funny and wickedly good-looking. In fact, he was the perfect package.

It didn't mean she was interested in him, although she couldn't deny how nice it felt to lean into his warmth and strength. He guided them to the dance floor and then took her in his arms.

She was taller than the average woman and dancing with men was often made awkward by the height difference, but Jacob made it easy. Even with her heels, they were equally matched, almost looking eye to eye. It was a nice change and she relaxed against him, feeling the rhythm in his feet. The song changed its tempo from fast and frantic to slow. He drew her even closer against him and her heart picked up its pace.

He smelled warm and spicy and oh so male. The muscles beneath her hand were taut. She looked up at him and noticed there were tiny flecks of navy in his bluer-than-blue eyes. They darkened with emotion under her gaze. Her breath caught.

"You have beautiful eyes," she murmured without thinking and then blushed.

"Thank you," he responded and then swung her around in his arms.

"Oh," she gasped and clung to him, her world also spinning momentarily. She glimpsed his tender smile before he spun her around again.

"Jacob, please!" she gasped. "I-I... I'm a little dizzy."

Immediately, he slowed his steps and his hand tightened on her hip to steady her. "I'm sorry, Hannah. Are you all right?"

She drew in a deep breath and eased it out and then gave him a nod. Now that they were barely moving, things had righted themselves.

"Yes, thank you. I'm fine. I guess I've had a little more wine than I'm used to," she confessed. "It's gone to my head."

Jacob stared at her. Hannah's heart skipped a beat. The music, the muted chatter, the crowd—all of it receded until there was nothing and no one but him. His head lowered as if in slow motion and a moment later, his lips were on hers, warm, gentle, seeking. The shock of it held her momentarily immobile. And then reality came crashing back.

With another gasp, she wrenched her mouth from his and pushed away from the circle of his arms. Without pause, she turned and abandoned him on the dance floor.

Chapter 4

Hannah tugged off her sandals and threw them on the floor. She was still trembling with anger at the audacity of Jacob taking advantage of her when he knew she wasn't thinking straight. *He'd kissed her!* The conceit of the man! How *dare* he? He knew how she felt about him, how much she hated him, how much she blamed him for Luke's death. Did he think all of that could be forgotten in one night of comfortable conversation and a generous amount of alcohol? Had that been his plan all along?

That horrible thought struck her and she was filled with renewed anger. *Perhaps that was the reason he'd kept plying her with wine?* He'd wanted to soften her up, charm her with his looks and gentle smile. As if that would be enough to erase her memory and wipe the slate clean. Nothing he did could ever change the fact he was responsible for her boyfriend's death, and no amount of alcohol and sweet talk would change that.

She reached around and unzipped her dress and then shrugged it off. The silky fabric slid down her body and pooled at her feet. Stepping away from it, she stalked into the bathroom and removed her makeup and then brushed and flossed her teeth. It was way past late and she was tired, but her mind was in overdrive and she knew from experience, it would be a long time before she'd lose herself in sleep.

Staring into the mirror, she narrowed her gaze at her reflection and wondered at the woman who looked back at her. She looked about as happy as she felt. In fact, she felt like she needed to cry. Luke had been dead more than a decade and yet, she still mourned his loss, and perhaps even more, the loss of her promised future. A future that had been stolen by Jacob Black. The same Jacob Black who had tried to kiss her.

No, not tried. He *had* kissed her and it was nice, really nice—until she came to her senses. And then it was horrible.

No, that wasn't fair. The kiss hadn't been horrible. It was the fact Jacob Black was on the other end of it that had ruined it. For so many years, he'd been like an infected sore and the wound he'd caused remained untreated. Most people thought he'd repaid his debt by spending two years of his life in jail, but nothing would bring Luke back and even knowing Jacob had been punished hadn't brought Hannah peace.

The intervening years had lessened the pain, but nothing could erase it from her memory. Coming up close and personal with Jacob again had brought it all rushing back—and more. His easy manner, clever conversation and liberal amounts of alcohol had served to distract her from her memories, but there was no denying in the harsh, cold light of her bathroom, that she hadn't forgiven, or forgotten.

In the deep recesses of her closet, she still had the scrapbook she'd kept, filled with cut-out pictures of wedding gowns and bouquets and table arrangements and all other manner of wistful dreams of a girl who looked forward to her marriage. It was hidden behind a box of childhood memories and no matter how many times she'd told herself to get rid of it, she couldn't bring herself to do it. She couldn't bring herself to forget about the past.

Her chest tightened and tears burned behind her eyes. She wished she could call on her Catholic upbringing and her belief in turning the other cheek. She wished she could find it in her heart to absolve Jacob and let the pain and anger go. Her mother, Mary Langdon, a staunch, Irish-born Catholic, had urged her to do just that, claiming it wasn't healthy for Hannah to store up so much hate, but try as Hannah did, she couldn't.

Perhaps it was a good thing that she'd run into Jacob again? Perhaps it was time to confront him and get answers to the how and the why that had eaten into her soul for so long? Jacob had pleaded guilty at the trial, so she hadn't been given the opportunity to listen to the evidence and even though he'd written to her from the jail in the early days of his sentence, she'd returned the letters to him unopened, not willing or ready to read what he had to say.

She wondered again if her knot of anger and resentment had caused her to hold herself back in the few relationships she'd endured since graduation and if that was the real reason she hadn't found love. Until now, she hadn't considered the fact that she was still single could have had anything to do with Jacob Black.

It wasn't like time was running out. A lot of people her age were still single. Besides, she didn't need a significant other in her life. She had her parents who loved her deeply and her cat, Pepper, who loved her just as much. And she had her job. She lived her life the way she wanted to and took solace from her ability to restore dignity to the dead and the comfort she brought to their families.

With a heavy sigh, she switched off the bathroom light and padded across the carpet toward her bed. After disposing of her underwear, she pulled on her pajamas. Collecting Pepper from the corner chair, Hannah sat the cat on the vacant side of the bed and climbed under the covers—all the time trying to convince herself it was enough.

———

Jacob scanned the faces in the crowd, searching for his twin. Toby had said he'd meet him outside the bus station on Broadway. Jacob had promised his brother he'd drive him to his place of employment on his first day of work. They'd agreed that being late wasn't an option.

Pushing his way past the hordes of people, all mindlessly hurrying to work, Jacob made his way over to the part of the bus shelter where it was common for homeless men and women to sleep. Toby sat in the far corner, a bundle of possessions at his feet. When he caught sight of Jacob, he smiled.

"Jacob! You remembered!" he called out over the din of traffic and pedestrians.

Jacob came up to his brother and gave him a brief hug, ignoring the stench of filth and unwashed body that rose up to meet him.

He'd stumbled across Toby one night, nearly a week earlier, in the Sydney Harbour Hospital Emergency Department. His twin had been attacked by an unknown assailant and had suffered a knife wound to his hand. Jacob had been stunned at Toby's appearance. He'd barely recognized him under the dirt and grime and stench that enveloped him.

"Good-morning, Tobes. Did you sleep here again, last night?" he asked, looking around at the filth of trash and food scraps and other detritus that littered the small area.

Toby merely offered him a smile. "Of course. It's like I told you at the hospital. This is where I live. See, under the brightest light."

Jacob shook his head, once again dismayed at his brother's circumstances. "I wish you'd come home with me. Like I told you last week, I live in a nice apartment within walking distance to the hospital. We could shop for some new clothes for you or I could give you money to buy them yourself. I have two spare bedrooms. You could take your pick. It would be perfect."

Toby kept smiling. "Perfect for you, maybe. I like living here and soon I can buy my own new clothes. Like I told you, this is my spot, right near that light. I'm still not fond of the dark. Carrie lives over that way and Michael's just down there. We keep each other company. We look out for each other."

Jacob tamped down his impatience. He was still shocked to discover his brother lived on the streets. It was inconceivable when Toby had a loving family who would be more than happy to help out. Jacob was only relieved their mother wasn't alive to see it.

But now wasn't the time to get into it with his twin. It was already eight-thirty-six and Toby had told him he needed to be at work by nine. They still had a ways to drive to Balmain, especially in the peak-hour traffic. Jacob was just grateful he wasn't rostered on until the evening and that he had been available to drive his brother to his job.

Jacob wasn't sure what Toby intended to do on the days when his brother wasn't available to transport him. Curious, he hefted his twin's meagre possessions off the ground and as they walked toward Jacob's truck, he put the question to him.

"How do you normally get around the city? Do you catch a bus from here, or the train?"

Toby smiled and shook his head, his blue eyes

twinkling. "No, Jake. No buses or trains. I use these." He pointed to his bare feet, black with filth and dirt. Jacob suppressed a shudder.

A wave of urgency surged through him and it had nothing to do with the time. He needed to sit down with his brother and talk to him, *really* talk to him, and find out where Toby's life had gone off the rails.

In the back of his mind, he recalled Hannah saying that his twin had taken Jacob's imprisonment hard. He couldn't bear the thought that Toby's current circumstances had anything to do with him.

Weaving through the heavy traffic, Jacob followed his in-car GPS directions to the Max Grace Funeral Home. Though he'd been through the inner west Sydney suburb of Balmain a few times, he wasn't overly familiar with its streets. Pulling up outside a tastefully restored terrace house that was bordered by equally stylish neighbors, Jacob killed the engine and turned to look at his brother. "We're here."

Toby looked out the window and Jacob drew his attention to a metal sign that hung from a black painted pole outside the building. Printed on the shiny surface of the sign, were the words: Max Grace Funeral Home.

Toby turned back to him and grinned, his expression filled with equal parts nervousness and excitement. "I guess you're right."

Jacob's gaze drifted across his brother's dirty long-sleeved shirt and equally filthy pants and he frowned. "Are you sure you know this guy?"

Toby nodded his head enthusiastically. "Yes! He came up to me in the bus shelter the day before I was attacked. He asked me who I was and how long I'd been living there. He gave me twenty dollars and told me to find myself a hot meal. He was nice."

"How did that turn into a job offer?" Jacob asked, curious.

"Mr Grace—that's the guy who gave me the money—offered to come with me to the diner. He ordered a huge amount of food. And he paid for it out of his wallet. He didn't even ask about the twenty. I ate until I was bursting." Toby lowered his gaze. "It had been awhile since I'd had such a good meal."

Anger and frustration once again surged through Jacob. "Toby, I told you at the hospital—you're more than welcome to come home with me. It isn't right that you're out living on the streets. We're brothers. Why do you find it so hard to accept my help?"

Toby stared at him solemnly. "I know that you care, Jacob and it makes my heart smile, but you've already sacrificed so much for me. It's time for me to stand on my own. I don't need your help. I'm happy the way I am."

"How can you be happy?" Jacob exploded, his temper getting the better of him. "You're living on the streets! Okay, we didn't exactly grow up in the lap of luxury and Mom worked at least two jobs to keep us all alive, but we had a decent roof over our heads and we never went to bed hungry. How can you dismiss all that and live like a homeless person? I don't get it. I really don't."

Toby shook his head sadly. "I don't expect you to get it, Jacob. We might be twins, but we've been apart a long time. Let's just leave it at that."

Jacob opened his mouth to protest again, but closed it when Toby's mouth thinned into an immoveable line. Jacob had seen it before. The stubborn set of his twin's mouth, the clenched jaw. He knew exactly what Toby was thinking and there would be no budging him, at least, not at this time.

With a sigh of defeat, Jacob opened his car door and climbed out. Toby followed suit. Together, they climbed up the concrete steps that led to the small front porch. Jacob rang the old-fashioned doorbell and then stood back. He turned to his brother.

"You still haven't told me how you came to be offered a job."

Toby smiled and shrugged. "That's easy. After we'd finished eating and Mr Grace had paid the bill, he told me how much he liked me. He said he was looking for someone to help out at the funeral home and wanted to know if I was interested."

Jacob regarded him slowly, still feeling a little dubious about the whole thing. Despite Hannah's assurances that offering Toby a job was just the kind of thing her boss would do, Jacob wasn't too sure. Just then, the panelled oak door opened and his contemplation over the situation came to an abrupt halt.

Hannah stood in the doorway. She was clothed in plain green shapeless surgical scrubs and her face was free of makeup. Her long hair was concealed under an unflattering cloth cap, but nothing could disguise her beauty. It took him a moment to gather his thoughts and he stammered when he spoke.

"H-hi. I... I wasn't expecting to see you."

She looked at him with a quizzical expression, one eyebrow cocked upwards. "I told you at the ball I worked here. Did you think I was making it up?"

Embarrassment spread up from his neck and heated his cheeks. "No, of course not. It's just that... You said you were an embalmer. I assumed you worked...out back."

Though her expression remained solemn, her eyes twinkled with laughter. "You're right. I do, but we're a little short-staffed at the moment. Max's nephew still hasn't shown up for work and Max is tied up with grieving relatives in the front room." She shrugged. "Which leaves me as the only one available to answer the door."

Her gaze drifted to Toby. The slight widening of her eyes was the only indication she gave to his much-altered appearance. With a friendly smile, she put out her hand.

"Hi, Toby. I'm Hannah Langdon. We went to school together a long time ago. Do you remember me?"

Toby frowned and then his face broke into a wide smile. "Hannah? Is it really you? What are *you* doing here?"

I work here." She laughed. "And now you do, too."

With a shout of joy, Toby threw his arms around her and hugged her. After a slight hesitation, Hannah relaxed into the embrace. Jacob's admiration for her ratcheted up another notch.

"So, it's true," he said in an effort to bring the embrace to an end, "Toby has a job here?"

Hannah stepped away from Toby and nodded. "Yes. I spoke to Max about it this morning. Apparently he met your brother at a bus shelter last week and offered him employment. Like I told you before at the ball, Max is like that. He has a heart of gold."

It was the second time she'd referred to the ball and he tensed, remembering how they'd parted. From the narrowing of her gaze, she was recalling the moment, too. He cleared his throat and looked away.

"I'd better get going. I have a few things to do. Will you be all right, Tobes?"

His brother turned to him and gave him an enthusiastic smile. "Yes, Jake! Of course! I was excited before, but now that Hannah's here, I'm going to have the best time ever!"

Jacob glanced at her and found her smiling fondly at his twin. His heart clenched. She'd never looked at him like that. And then he told himself not to be stupid. How the hell could he be feeling envious of his twin? It was ridiculous.

"I'll take care of him," Hannah assured him and linked her arm through Toby's.

Jacob nodded. "Well, all right, I guess I'll come back at five and collect you. Is that right?" He directed the last question to Hannah.

"Yes, we close at five, but I can drop him home. It wouldn't be any trouble."

"It's fine. I don't have to be at work until six. I don't live far from the hospital. Dropping Toby...home won't be a problem. At least, not today."

"You do shift work?" Hannah guessed.

"Yes, but I'm pretty flexible with my roster. There have to be some perks for being the senior resident of the emergency department."

She stared at him, but her expression didn't alter. Whether his position impressed her or not, remained a mystery. Feeling the need to put some distance between them, he dragged his gaze away from hers, turned and jogged back down the stairs.

"I'll see you later, Tobes," he called over his shoulder. "Have a good day."

CHAPTER 5

Dear Diary,

I love it when a plan comes together and this one's working out just fine. It might have taken a little longer than I thought, but my meticulous preparations and patience have finally been rewarded. Once, twice... And now I have taken steps toward securing yet another ticket to a better life. I can hardly wait...

Hannah glanced over to where Toby worked quietly refilling the supplies stored in the overhead cupboards and wondered what had happened to him in the intervening years since she'd seen him. It was obvious he'd fallen on hard times and during their tea break, he confirmed he was living on the streets.

She wanted to ask him what happened and

whether it had anything to do with Jacob, but she was afraid to know the answer. The events of that night in November were forever seared upon her mind. Her life had been destroyed and it had taken her years to recover. A therapist would argue she still hadn't fully recovered and they'd be right. She didn't want to think that others might have suffered similar awful consequences. When she looked at Toby, she couldn't help but wonder if he was another casualty of that horrible time.

"How long have you been working here?" he asked her, curiosity bright in his blue eyes. Eyes that reminded her of his brother.

"Almost six years."

Toby nodded. "Did you go to college?"

Hannah thought back to high school and the days she'd spent by Luke's side, dreaming of nothing more than a future as his wife.

"Yes," she replied. "It wasn't something I planned on doing, but after graduation..." She gave him a tiny shrug. "I guess my plans changed."

His beautiful eyes shadowed with pain and Hannah immediately felt bad. She hadn't meant to remind him of that awful time. She was sure his memories of it were just as horrible as hers. She hurried to soothe him.

"I'm sorry, Toby, I didn't mean to drag that up again. It was a long time ago. It's time to put it to rest."

"I still dream about it, Hannah," he whispered, his voice low and rough with pain. "It was so awful. I was so scared. And when they took Jacob away and put him in jail... He was in handcuffs, Hannah!

I couldn't bear it! I tried so hard to accept what had happened, but in the end, I had to run away. I didn't tell anyone. Not even my mom."

Sadness surged through Hannah at the anguish on Toby's face. She put down the instrument she'd been cleaning and peeled off her gloves. Moving over to where he stood, she patted him awkwardly on the arm. "It's all right, Toby. Don't think about it. I'm sorry, I should never have said anything. I didn't mean—"

"I know you didn't," he interrupted. Tears glinted in his eyes. "I wanted to tell you. You were there. You understand. It's been horrible holding it all inside. And then, when Jacob told me Mom had died..." He hiccupped on a sob. "I didn't even get to say good-bye."

Hannah felt awful. Toby's life had been hard enough in the years since high school. It wasn't fair for her to make it worse now by dredging up old, ugly memories.

"How are you going with those cotton swabs?" she asked lightly in a desperate attempt to distract him.

Gradually, his gloomy expression cleared and she breathed a quiet sigh of relief. The last thing she wanted to do was upset him. He'd been working quickly and efficiently all day and she was grateful for his help. It had been more than a month since Max's last assistant, Christopher Lowery, had sadly passed away and his replacement, Edward Sutton, had lasted only three weeks before he up and disappeared. Hannah's workload had doubled as a result.

Christopher Lowrey and Edward Sutton were two other examples of Max's charity. Both were men who'd fallen on hard times. Max had offered them employment and for Christopher, even a place to stay. He'd been given an area off the freezer room where Max had previously stored unused equipment. Though small and rather cramped, it still had an edge over sleeping under the railway bridge in the park.

Though both men were in their forties and suffering signs of malnutrition and general neglect, they'd been good workers. Christopher had confided in Hannah that he'd once been a wards man in a large city hospital. He hadn't minded the sight of dead bodies and he'd been a great help to her in the embalming room. It pained her to know he'd come to such a sad end. She could still remember the shock she'd felt when Max told her the news.

Apparently, Christopher had been drinking heavily, as he sometimes did and had stumbled out into the road. He'd been hit by a fully laden semi and had been killed on impact. The truck hadn't stopped at the scene. The police surmised the truck driver hadn't even been aware of what he'd done.

For Edward, things had worked out differently. One day he was there, going about his usual duties, and the next, he was gone. It had been over a week since she'd last seen him. Hannah had spoken to Max about him and had even queried Bobby about his whereabouts, but neither man knew where Edward was or where he could have gone. In the end, they simply put it down to the fact that he'd moved on and had chosen not to say good-bye. After all, working with the dead wasn't for everyone.

She hadn't yet introduced Toby to the deceased people they worked over. Better to let him get used to the idea of being in a funeral home before she presented him with the reality of the job. She didn't want him running for his life when he'd barely just begun. It was nice having him around.

She'd always enjoyed his company in high school. As Jacob's twin, more often than not, he could be found by his brother's side. As best friends, Jacob and Luke spent a lot of time together and by default, that included Toby. Hannah hadn't minded. Toby always wore a friendly smile and had time to say hello. His childish delight in everyday things was endearing and she was never irritated to have him around.

Some of her high school girlfriends used to wonder out loud whether she ever got sick of Jacob's brother hanging around.

'He's soft in the head, Hannah.'

'How can you stand to waste your time talking to him?'

'He doesn't understand. He's stupid.'

Hannah would immediately take umbrage at their mean and nasty words and would defend Toby long and loudly. She didn't care what the others thought. He was a nice guy and always treated her with courtesy and respect. She didn't care about anything else.

In fact, she probably spent more time talking with Toby than she did his twin. Jacob and Luke had often been training or doing practice runs on the river. As champion rowers, they spent many hours with their coach and crew and Hannah and Toby were often left on the riverbank as spectators.

"Does Jacob still row?" she asked without thinking.

Toby shook his head. "I don't think so, but I haven't seen him for years. I don't know what he does."

"When did you meet up with him again?" she asked, feigning ignorance. Not that she doubted Jacob, but she was interested to hear Toby's side of the story.

"He came across me in the emergency room last week. I'd been taken to the hospital. I got cut."

He lifted his left arm and for the first time, Hannah noticed the white bandage that covered part of his hand. She frowned.

"What happened?"

He lowered his gaze. "I was asleep in the bus shelter, in my usual spot. Minding my own business. I wasn't bothering anybody. The next thing I knew, some guy was coming at me with a knife. I put up my hand to stop him and he got me across the fingers. A bystander called an ambulance. I ended up at the Sydney Harbour Hospital."

"Where you found Jacob," she finished. "Did you know he was a doctor there?"

"No. I hadn't seen him since… Well, a long, long time ago. I didn't know where he was."

Hannah shook her head slowly, back and forth. "Wow, Toby, that's amazing. I mean, it's awful that someone stabbed you, but to find your brother as a result. That's wonderful."

Toby smiled softly. In that moment, despite the dirt and grime, he looked so much like his twin, it snatched her breath away. Of course, they'd been close to identical in high school and from a distance, it was hard to tell which was which. It was only when you got closer, or spoke to them, that it became clear which one you had.

The years of neglect and living on the streets had widened the gap between their physical appearances but every now and then, she caught the slightest hint of the good-looking man Toby Black had once been—and could be again with a decent bath and some regular, nutritious meals.

Earlier, he'd told her both Lane and Jacob had invited him to stay with them. Apparently, Rusty would have extended the same invitation, but he was already sharing a tiny apartment with three others and there simply wasn't room. But Toby had turned both his brothers down and she couldn't help but wonder why, and whether he'd feel the same way about an invitation from her.

Her condo overlooking Bondi Beach was sleek and modern and large. With three generous bedrooms, it had plenty of space, particularly because she lived there on her own. The apartment had once been owned by her maternal grandmother. As the only grandchild on her mother's side, Hannah had been fortunate enough to inherit the place and she loved it. With glorious views all the way down the coast, she sent a little prayer of gratitude heavenward to her grandmother every morning when she woke to the sound of the surf. She decided to sound Toby out.

"It's been so lovely having you around to help out today, Toby. I hope you've enjoyed it."

He nodded enthusiastically. "Yes, it's been great, but I'm wondering when I get to see the bodies. Isn't that what you do here? Take care of dead bodies?"

She laughed at his frankness. "Yes, that's exactly what we do here. I've kept the bodies in the fridge today. I didn't want to scare you off on the first day!"

Toby smiled and shrugged. "It's okay. I don't mind dead people. It's not like I know them—and they're not really there, anyway, are they?"

"What do you mean?" she asked softly, intrigued.

"My mom always told me when you die, your soul goes up to heaven. It's only your body that's left to rot in the ground and a body without a soul is nothing but an empty shell."

A lump of emotion clogged Hannah's throat and tears burned behind her eyes. Toby's simple explanation touched her heart. It was exactly how she felt about the people who found themselves on her table. She cleared her throat and responded.

"Your mom was probably right, Toby, but I still like to spend time over each body. I like them to go to their final resting place looking their best."

She looked across at him and found him frowning. "What's the matter?" she asked.

"So, you believe the soul *and* body go up to heaven. Is that what you're saying? Is that why you want them to look their best?"

Now it was Hannah's turn to frown. "No, I don't think the body goes up to heaven. I think the bible's quite clear on that. I guess… I guess I like to think the dead are looking down on me and I want to do my best. I want to give them that gift. I want them to know they departed this life looking great for those they leave behind. To remember them that way. Do you know what I mean?"

He smiled and nodded. "Yes, I know exactly what you mean!"

One look at his beatific face and she was certain he did.

"Would you consider coming to stay with me for a while?" she blurted, wanting so much to help him out.

He fell quiet and appeared to consider her question. She tried again.

"I know you told me you said no to your brothers, but you didn't tell me why. Besides, I'm not your family. I'm a friend. I wouldn't interfere in your business. You'd be free to come and go. It's just that I've really enjoyed the time we've spent together and I'd like to help you out. You need a place to live and I have plenty of room. I also have a cat. Her name's Pepper and she's the sweetest thing. What do you say?"

It took him awhile, but finally he turned to face

her and nodded, a smile slowly spreading across his face. "I love cats! Do you mean it?"

"Yes, of course."

His smile widened. "I think I'd like that, Hannah. You always were a good friend."

A surge of pleasure rushed through her and she smiled back. "So were you."

The door to the embalming room swung open and Hannah and Toby looked up from what they were doing. The owner of the funeral home strode inside, his thick white hair all askew. Upon spying Toby, his rounded face and rosy cheeks became wreathed in smiles.

"Toby! How lovely to see you again! I'm so glad you took me up on my offer."

Toby looked pleased at Max's comments. "Of course. I'm very grateful for the job, Mr Grace."

"I'm sorry it's taken me all day to come and greet you. I've been stuck for hours in the front room with grieving relatives. It's been a treacherous weekend on our roads, with several unexpected deaths. That makes for a busy week."

Hannah acknowledged her boss' comment with an understanding nod. "It's all right, Max. I've shown him the ropes."

"Good, good. I knew I could rely on you. Unlike someone else I might mention." Max's expression darkened. "Where *is* that lazy, no-good nephew of mine?"

Hannah shrugged. "I'm not sure, Max. I haven't seen Bobby since lunchtime Friday."

Max's frown deepened and he shook his head. "I don't know why I keep him on. I've done everything I can to help him. I gave him a job when he had nothing; I paid him above what I have to. I even found him an apartment close by and helped him with the rent. And how does he thank me? By not bothering to turn up to work. He's probably sleeping off another big weekend, like he did the weekend before."

Hannah remained silent. It wasn't her place to speak ill of Max's nephew. Besides, she didn't have to. Max knew exactly what Bobby was all about. Her boss might have the kindest heart in the world, but he was no fool. It was to Bobby's detriment that he underestimated his uncle's insight and clarity of mind.

"So, how has your first day gone?" Max asked in a more cheerful tone, turning back to Toby.

"Great, it's been great," Toby smiled. "Hannah's been showing me what to do."

"She's a lovely girl, isn't she? And so pretty!" Max followed his declaration with a cheeky wink, gazing at Hannah with fondness.

She laughed back at him. Max might be well into his seventies, but he was still an outrageous flirt.

"Yes!" Toby shouted. "Beautiful."

"It's nice of both of you to say so," she replied with a grin. "And on that note, it must be time for us to clean up and get ready to leave." She looked across at Toby and gave him a smile. "Our time here is done."

"For today, anyway," Max added.

"I'll show you to the showers, Toby," Hannah said. "You can get out of those scrubs and clean up."

A look of embarrassment washed over him and

she frowned in concern. "What is it, Toby? What did I say?"

He stared at his feet. "I... I don't have anything else to wear. Only the clothes I arrived in and they're...dirty."

Understanding dawned on her and she was quick to reassure him. "Don't worry about it. We have plenty of scrubs. I'll find you another pair. You can put them on after your shower. We'll take your clothes home with us and put them through the wash."

Max gazed at them quizzically. "What's this? You're moving in with Hannah?"

Hannah nodded. "Yes. Toby and I have known each other for a long time. We went to high school together. He's...looking for a place to stay." She shrugged. "I have plenty of room."

"You could always stay here," Max offered. "There's room out the back." He shot a glance in Hannah's direction and murmured, "Christopher won't be needing it anymore."

Toby looked from one to the other, appearing a little overwhelmed. Once again, Hannah hurried to reassure him.

"It's all right, Toby. I have more than enough room and it would be fun to have some company. That's if you still want to come."

Toby smiled widely. "Thank you, Mr Grace, you're very kind, but I think I might stay with Hannah. She's a good friend." He turned back to Hannah. "I really want to come."

She shrugged off his gratitude, a little embarrassed by his eagerness. "It's no problem,

Toby. I'm happy to help." Turning away, she headed in the direction of the showers.

"What about Jacob?"

Toby's words halted her in her tracks. She'd forgotten that his brother had promised to collect him after work. She turned back to face him.

"Do you have his cell number?"

"No. There's no need. I don't have a cell."

Hannah bit her lip in indecision. They couldn't leave without waiting for Jacob to arrive and explaining to him about the new arrangements. It would be plain rude, especially when he was going out of his way to stop by and collect his brother. She could try and reach him at the hospital, but if he intended to collect Toby on time, he'd more than likely have already left. There was nothing for it but to stay put.

As much as the thought annoyed her, her heart skipped a beat. She was still angry at him, but after spending the day with his twin, she'd come to realize she wasn't the only one who'd suffered because of that night.

"It's all right, Toby. We'll wait for Jacob to arrive. It's a pity he'll make the trip for nothing, but if he lives near the hospital like he said, he doesn't have to come too far out of his way. I'm sure he'll understand."

Once again, Toby's face lit up with a smile and his handsome looks were clear to see. "Thank you, Hannah. See, I said you were a good friend."

She smiled and nodded her head in acknowledgement of the compliment and then headed toward the showers.

Toby was still in the shower when Jacob arrived right on the dot at five. At the sight of him dressed in a suit and tie, Hannah's heart picked up its pace. Nerves fluttered in her stomach at the thought of telling him his brother was coming home with her. She wasn't sure how he'd react—whether he'd be angry or pleased. She sucked in a quick breath and blew it out. In a moment, she'd find out.

"Hi," Jacob murmured, his blue eyes cool and assessing.

"H-hi," she stammered and blushed. Cursing under her breath, she got straight to the point.

"I'm sorry you made the trip out here, because I've invited Toby to come and stay with me in my condo. I live near Bondi Beach and have plenty of room. He... He's agreed."

Jacob's gaze narrowed. "What do you mean, he's agreed to stay with you? I asked him a week ago to move in with me and he refused. Why would he want to go with you?"

Hannah suppressed the urge to snap back at him. He hadn't meant his comment as an insult. He'd just discovered his twin preferred her company to his. It was understandable that the idea might upset him.

"It's no big deal, Jacob. Let's just be happy for Toby—that he's not going to spend another night out on the streets."

She stared at him, silently pleading with him to understand. Any minute, Toby would be out of the shower and bounding into the room.

Jacob's cheeks flushed and she could see he

was struggling to hold back his words. She was sure he was happy his brother had found somewhere to stay, but he was likely also irritated and probably even hurt that Toby hadn't wanted to live with him.

"What's he going to do for clothing? Shoes? Everything else he needs?" Jacob demanded.

Hannah shrugged. "We keep plenty of spare scrubs here, including disposable shoes. I'm sure we'll figure something out."

Jacob reached into his back pocket and pulled out his wallet. "I'll give you some money," he said, offering her a wad of bills.

She took a step back. "No, please, I don't need any money. I can see to his needs. But thank you," she added, seeing the protest forming on his lips.

"Where is he?" Jacob asked, reluctantly stowing his wallet away.

"He's still taking a shower. A good thing."

Jacob's lips compressed. He nodded. "Well, I guess that's it then. He doesn't need me hanging around now that he has you."

And with that, he turned and left. Hannah watched his departing back until the door closed and hid him from view. She was sorry it had ended like that. She didn't want it to be a competition for Toby's affections. She hadn't made him the offer of a place to stay to make herself feel needed. All she was doing was looking out for a friend. There was no harm in that. Jacob would have to deal with it.

CHAPTER 6

Trying to stay focused, Jacob tied off another suture in an effort to pull together the gaping leg wound of the young boy who lay on the bed in the emergency ward. His evening shift had started less than an hour earlier and he was out of sorts, still irritated about Toby going home with Hannah.

Jacob had made the effort to collect his brother from the funeral home after his first day on the job only to discover his services were no longer required. Toby had gone home with Hannah. Was moving into her condo, no less. He was glad his brother wouldn't be sleeping on the streets and it warmed him to know Hannah cared enough about Toby to offer him a bed, but it irked him that his twin had accepted Hannah's invitation after declining his own. The truth was, he was jealous.

"Is everything okay, Doctor?"

The soft query issued by the nurse assisting him, penetrated his dark thoughts and he rapidly blinked them away.

"Of course, Bridget. I was... Never mind. Can you hand me another packet of sutures? We're going to need a few more."

The nurse moved to do his bidding. She looked down at the boy who lay on the bed and shot him a wry smile. "You certainly did a job on this leg, Braydon. What did you do again?"

The woman who'd introduced herself earlier as Braydon's mother stepped closer and replied. "He was racing his older brother on his bike at my parents' place. Unfortunately, the bike didn't have any grips on the handle bars. He hit a bump the wrong way and the handlebars twisted, tearing a hole in his leg."

"Ouch," Bridget said.

"I bet it was fun beforehand, though, right?" Jacob waggled his eyebrows at the boy and received a grin in return.

"Yeah, it was so cool," Braydon replied. "We've built jumps in the backyard and Jonty and I spend hours riding over them again and again. I got unlucky, that's all."

His mother rolled her eyes. Jacob chuckled. "Boys will be boys, Mom. You ought to know that by now."

"Oh, I know it all right," Braydon's mother replied with a wry smile. "I'm surprised we're not at the emergency room more often."

Jacob laughed again, recalling the antics he and his three brothers had gotten up to in their youth. Despite the fact they'd grown up without a father, they'd had plenty of good times and, much to their mother's despair, it hadn't stopped them from doing all that they could to injure one another through foolhardy, but oh-so-funny pranks.

"I remember a time when my oldest brother, Lane, found a collection of old forty-four-gallon oil drums," he told Braydon's mom. "Together with some planks of wood we'd found in a dumpster, we constructed an impressive bike jump. We wedged the drums between two pine trees. Lane assured us the drums wouldn't move and it was perfectly safe for us to use. He was the oldest. We looked up to him. We trusted he knew what he was doing."

"Uh oh, this doesn't sound good," Braydon's mom said with a smile.

Jacob grinned and continued. "I was always keen for a challenge, always feeling the need to prove I was as tough and brave as Lane, so I was the first to attempt the jump. Unfortunately, Lane had miscalculated. When I hit the boards on my BMX, the drums moved sideways and I ended up smashed on the ground. Eight stitches later, I was good to go." He tied off the last suture and grinned down at Braydon. "Just like you are. We're all done."

The boy stared up at him, his eyes wide with admiration. "Do you still have the scar?"

"Yes, I do. After all these years."

"Will I have a scar?"

"Probably. A small one, at any rate."

"Cool! I'll be able to tell everyone about how I got it! Thanks, Doctor!"

"No problem," Jacob laughed. "But I don't

want to see you in here too often. It's not good for your mom's stress levels and you need to take care of her. Who else is going to bring you into the emergency department when you need patching up?"

Braydon grinned. "I'll look after her, I promise." He turned to stare up at his mom. "Won't I, Mom?"

Braydon's mother ruffled his hair and pressed an affectionate kiss on his cheek. "You sure will, honey."

Jacob's heart clenched at the loving glance that passed between them. His father had been killed in the line of duty when Jacob and Toby were three and their mother had now been gone two years. *Two years...* The same amount of time he'd spent in prison...

The memory of his mother waving good-bye as he was escorted away by the corrections officers flooded his mind. He'd seen the tears coursing down her cheeks and it had been all he could do to hold back his own. He'd bitten his tongue until he tasted blood, unwilling to let her see how upset and scared he was as the first day of his sentence began.

Virginia Black had been just thirty-two when she was widowed. Her husband had been a decorated police officer, high up in the DEA. He'd been responsible for putting many a drug dealer behind bars, before he was fatally wounded by a bullet from an addict high on cocaine.

Overnight, Jacob's mom lost her husband and was faced with the reality of raising four kids on her own. Jacob's youngest brother, Rusty, was barely six months old at the time. Still, they might have been deprived of a father, but there had never been a shortage of love. As a single mom, Virginia had worked hard to raise her boys and provide for them as well as she could. He was forever grateful for the sacrifices she'd made. He missed her even more at times like this.

"What do you say to the doctor, Braydon?"

The gently voiced question jolted him out of his memories and Jacob smiled at the mother and son.

The boy sat up on the bed. "Thank you, Doctor."

"No problem, Braydon," Jacob replied. "Take it easy, and be careful, okay?"

With another nod of gratitude, Braydon's mom helped him from the bed and together, they left the ward. Turning back to the tray containing the used dressing pack, suture material and disinfectant, Jacob couldn't hold back a sigh. Bridget eyed him curiously.

"That sounds awfully heavy, Doctor Black? What's the matter?"

Jacob glanced across at her and forced a smile. "It's nothing."

"It didn't sound like nothing."

His gaze strayed to her face and then skimmed over her body. Even wearing the shapeless uniform, it was clear the nurse had a nice figure. The bodice of her dress stretched over her breasts, revealing a generous cleavage before falling loosely over rounded hips. Her eyes were clear and friendly and with a start, he spied a spark of interest in their blue depths. He'd worked with

Bridget for nearly a year and had never noticed her before. Now, when he'd finally taken the time to really look at her, he realized all he could think about was Hannah.

Hannah reached for the jar of formaldehyde and refilled her syringe. She glanced at Toby, gauging his reaction. "How are you doing?" she asked.

"I'm good. Don't worry about me. I find all of this really fascinating."

She smiled, glad that he hadn't freaked out when she'd introduced him to their latest client. "You don't mind the smell?"

Toby scrunched up his nose like a child would, but then grinned. "I've smelled worse."

Hannah laughed and was sure he spoke the truth. Though he was now looking cleaner—after another shower at home and one that morning before he left for work—there was still a residual odor clinging to his skin. He probably wasn't even aware of it. She was sure it wasn't his own body odor he referred to.

"Why are you injecting that stuff into her?" he asked, breaking into her thoughts.

"The formaldehyde is a preserving agent. It also gives the body a more lifelike appearance. It plumps out the features and helps them look less drawn. It's worked magic on this woman, don't you think?" She grinned.

Toby nodded. "It sure has. Is there anything I can do to help?"

"Yes. See that trocar on the counter? I need it over here, along with the pump and tubing under the sink."

Toby looked in the direction she pointed and quickly moved to where the equipment sat. Picking it up, he brought it to her.

"Thanks, just leave it on the table, there."

"What do you do with it?" he asked, pointing.

"This drains the body fluids from our lady's nooks and crannies. I insert the trocar just here, under her ribs, and then we start the pump. Make sure the end of the tubing is hanging in the sink, or we'll have a mess everywhere."

She grinned at him and he grinned back. A surge of pleasure went through her. It was so nice sharing her day with someone who found her work as enjoyable and interesting as she did.

"There, that should do it," she murmured and then bent down to start the pump. The quiet hum of the aspiration machine filled the room. A moment later, dark, viscous fluid began to drain into the sink.

"Now, that's what I call a stink!" Toby laughed and pinched the sides of his nose together.

She winked at him. "You're right. It's not entirely pleasant, but you get used to it."

The door to the embalming room swung open and Max filled the opening. "I'm looking for that no-good, lazy nephew of mine," he said without preamble. "Has anyone seen him?"

"Good morning to you, too, Max," Hannah said dryly.

Her boss flushed with embarrassment. "Yes, good morning, Hannah and you, too, Toby. It's good to see you back."

Toby looked puzzled. "I thought you gave me a job, Mr Grace? Why wouldn't I be back?"

"I'm sorry, I didn't mean it like that," Max hastily apologized. "And of course I gave you a job. It's yours for however long you want it. We must sort out your pay. Do you have a bank account?"

Toby lowered his gaze and slowly shook his head. "No, I don't."

"Not to worry," Max said cheerfully. "We'll work something out."

"I could take you down to the bank on our lunch break and open an account for you," Hannah offered Toby. "Do you have any ID? They'll need at least a driver's license and a Medicare card, or something of that nature."

"I don't have any of those," Toby replied, concern now shadowing his eyes.

"That's all right," Max assured him. "I'm happy to pay you in cash. I've done it before for some of my other employees in your situation. It won't be a problem."

Relief flooded Toby's features and Hannah felt tears burn behind her eyes. Her boss was the kindest, most charitable soul ever. The only person she'd ever seen him have harsh words with was his nephew and from what Hannah had seen of Bobby Grace, he pretty much deserved it.

"Now, as I asked before, have either of you

seen my nephew? I sent him over to the hospital early this morning to collect a body from the morgue and I haven't seen him since."

"Perhaps he's been delayed?" Hannah suggested kindly.

Max grimaced. "Yes, delayed by his girlfriend, no doubt. Or perhaps he's with his bookmaker this time? Or worse, his dealer. He always has some excuse and it's never anything to do with what he's being paid to do."

Hannah remained silent and returned to finalizing her preparations for the woman on her table. The aspiration process had been completed. Removing the trocar and tubing, she handed both to Toby who took them and the pump back over to the sink.

"What's next?" he asked curiously.

"Now we inject another kind of fluid between the thoracic and abdominal cavities," she explained. "It will saturate all the organs and eliminate any residual odors."

Toby absorbed her response and nodded. "Good."

Max smiled. "It sounds like you're going to fit in just fine here, Toby. I'm so glad our paths crossed."

"Me, too," Toby replied, ducking his head shyly. "And thank you, Mr Grace. You don't know how grateful I am that you were willing to take me on. Apart from my family and Hannah, no one's ever been so kind to me before. I... I don't know what to say."

Max beamed with pleasure and came over and patted Toby on the shoulder. "Don't think anything of it, son. I do my best to help my fellow man. It's the reason we're all put here on earth, isn't it?"

Hannah smiled at the pair of them, her heart filling with contentment. What Max said was right. They could all try a little harder to extend the hand of friendship and kindness to their fellow man. It would surely make the world a better place to live. She thought of Jacob and how he'd told her about searching long and hard for his brother and though she didn't doubt his sincerity, she couldn't help but feel sad about how long it had taken him to find his twin—and the missed opportunities they'd never have again.

"Now, Toby," Max added, clearing his throat. "As a new employee of my funeral home, I'd like you to stop by and visit my doctor, if that's all right. His offices are only a few blocks away."

Toby frowned. "Do I look sick, Mr Grace? I don't feel sick."

Max laughed. "No, son, you don't look sick. And please, call me Max. It's just that I like to have my workers checked over and given a good bill of health. It's standard procedure with new employees. I'll make an appointment for you in the morning, if that suits?"

Toby glanced in Hannah's direction. She shrugged and nodded. She couldn't remember Max requesting she undergo a medical, but then, she hadn't been living on the streets.

"I could drop you off at the medical center on my way to work, if you like?" she offered.

Max nodded. "That sounds like a good plan. I'll

give you the details as soon as I've made an appointment. Is that all right with you, Toby?"

Toby smiled enthusiastically. "Yes, of course, Mr Gr—Max. Whatever you say."

"Good. Then that's settled. "Now, where is my nephew?"

It was more than an hour later that Hannah spied Bobby's large form slipping into the funeral parlor through the rear door, pushing a gurney. On it was a body wrapped in a plastic sheet. He nodded a brief greeting and then his gaze fell on Toby.

"Who do we have here?" he asked, halting mid-stride, a look of confusion taking over as he studied Toby.

Hannah made the introductions. "This is Toby. Toby, meet Bobby Grace."

"Are you Max's nephew?" Toby asked.

"That's me," Bobby responded with a grimace. "And believe me, some days that feels more like a curse than a blessing."

Hannah frowned at his comment. The man was way too rude. The way she'd heard it, his uncle had taken him in and gotten him clean and given him a house and a job when Bobby's immediate family refused to have anything to do with him. The man ought to show his uncle a little more gratitude and respect.

"You shouldn't talk about your uncle like that," she replied, eyeing him balefully.

"What are you going to do?" he sneered. "Run and tell on me?"

"You're really tall," Toby said. "How tall are you? I'm tall, but not as tall as you."

Bobby's confusion faded to narrow-eyed irritation. "Why the fuck would you care about my height, you idiot?"

Hannah's temper simmered just below the surface. It was only her sure knowledge that her anger was wasted on the likes of Bobby Grace that kept her from exploding. Ignoring her, Bobby turned his sneer on Toby.

"I see my dear old uncle hasn't tired of dragging in hobos off the street. Where did he find you? Central Station? You look a little familiar. Perhaps I've seen you under one of those fig trees in Hyde Park. I hope you fare better than the last hobo who worked here. Has my uncle told you what happened to Christopher?"

Toby's face reflected his hurt and shock and confusion. In an instant, Hannah's anger found its head.

"For your information, Toby has a very nice family. He has three brothers and all of them live in Sydney, so keep your nasty assumptions to yourself." She folded her arms across her chest and continued. "Get out, Bobby. Don't you have work to do? We don't need the likes of you here. Take your spitefulness elsewhere."

Bobby's sneer turned uglier and a calculating gleam entered his eyes. He sauntered toward her, crowding her space. She backed up and found herself against the wall. He reached out and traced a finger down her cheek. She froze and a menacing chuckle turned up his lips.

Apart from very infrequent once-overs, he'd never before shown any interest in her as a woman, but all of a sudden, she wasn't sure if his disinterest had been an act. His hand slipped lower and skimmed her breast. She gasped. The scars that criss-crossed his face stood out against his skin. Fear made her heart beat faster.

"Not so brave now, are you, little Miss Goody Two-shoes," he smirked. "I know what you're trying to do—turning my uncle against me. It isn't going to work. Blood's thicker than water, sweetheart. There's no way my uncle will give this place to anyone else but me."

Hannah gasped again, shocked at the direction of his thoughts. He wasn't trying to come onto her at all. He was trying to scare her. She'd been working at the funeral home for six years, but it never occurred to her to even consider Max might leave the place to her. It was obvious the possibility had been playing on Bobby's mind.

"You're crazy!" she said. "Max would never leave this place to me and I wouldn't want him to. You're his only family and the sole heir. It's only right that he leave it to you, but I suggest you start earning your right to it rather than slouching off all the time. Max has done so much for you already. A little gratitude wouldn't go astray."

Bobby eyeballed her in silence, his breath coming fast. With a muttered curse, he backed away from her and spun around on his heel. He stalked out of the room and a moment later, she heard the sound of the front door slamming.

So much for her pep talk.

CHAPTER 7

Jacob took a sip from his mug of coffee and thought about his brother. He wondered how Toby and Hannah were getting on. He hadn't seen or heard from either of them for a few days.

With a sigh, he turned the page of the newspaper and did his best to put his brother out of his mind. Knowing Hannah was looking out for his twin should be enough to ease his worry. With a determined shake of the paper, he skimmed the headlines and took a moment to catch up on the happenings around Sydney and the rest of the state. He'd found the newspaper in the staff tea room. It was more than a week old, but the date didn't matter. It had been at least that long since he'd caught the six o'clock news.

With the advent of digital devices, newspapers and television news services were almost redundant these days, but he hadn't even had time to pull out his iPad. The emergency room had been inundated with a rush of children suffering fevers and gastro bugs and a three-car pile-up on Parramatta Road had kept everyone on their feet.

A busy Friday night the week before, dealing with the usual assortment of assaults and alcohol-induced accidents, had spilled over into Saturday and apart from the handful of hours he'd spent at the hospital ball, it felt like he'd barely drawn breath. He had two rostered days off starting the next day and couldn't wait.

A small headline in the bottom half of the opened page caught his attention: Dead Man Linked to Balmain Funeral Home.

The story went on to say a man in his mid-forties had been found dead at the foot of the stairs inside a city hostel frequented by people living on the fringes of society. An autopsy revealed that the man had an extremely high alcohol level and it was surmised by the police that he'd tripped and fallen down the stairs. The man suffered a broken neck and it was the coroner's opinion that he'd died instantly. He'd been identified by a pay packet found in the pocket of his pants—Edward Sutton had been employed by the Max Grace Funeral Home.

Jacob frowned. Ordinarily, the article wouldn't catch his interest, but the mention of the same funeral home where Toby now worked, intrigued him. He'd been hired right after the man had been found dead. *Perhaps that employee's death was the reason Toby had been offered the position?* It was a sad way for a job vacancy to open up.

Glancing at the clock on the wall of the tea

room, he folded the paper and tossed it back onto the table and then finished the last of his coffee. His break was over. It was time to climb back into the trenches and deal with whatever needed to be done.

———————

Toby took his time to carefully wash and comb the hair of the man laid out on the steel gurney. He glanced across at Hannah.

"What's life insurance, Hannah?" he asked, his tone full of quiet curiosity.

Hannah paused midway through drying the man's feet and looked up at her assistant. "It's something you pay for to help out your family in the event of your death. An insurance company charges you a premium and, in return, if you die before a certain age, they pay out a sum to your estate. Why do you ask?"

"No reason, it's just the doctor I went to the other day said something about a life insurance policy. I didn't know what it was."

Hannah frowned. She had no idea why Toby's doctor had talked to him about life insurance. As far as she knew, Max had sent Toby for a medical for the purposes of ensuring he was healthy and free from disease. There should have been no reason to mention life insurance. She'd believed the appointment had been a purely precautionary measure and an act of kindness. *Perhaps Toby had misheard?*

"There! How does it look?" he asked, interrupting her thoughts.

She glanced up and was pleased to see Toby had done a good job of styling the man's hair in the same manner he'd worn it prior to his death. It was important to her to get it right, and that was the reason she always asked the relatives for a recent photograph of the deceased. It helped when applying the makeup, too. Some women wore very little makeup in life and others had it caked on thick. It could be an unpleasant shock to the relatives if the embalmer didn't get it right.

She smiled at Toby. "He looks just like he did when he was still alive. You've done a marvellous job."

Toby blushed beneath her praise. "Thank you, Hannah. It's very kind of you to say so."

"It's not kind at all," she protested. "I'm merely stating the truth. You're a quick learner and you listen well. What's more, you care about these people as much as I do. I can see it in the respectful way you handle them and in the care you put into your work. I'm so pleased you decided to come and work here. It's a real pleasure to have you around."

His blush got redder and spread right across his cheeks, but a shy smile of pride and satisfaction filled his face. "Do you really think so?" he asked, hope shining in his eyes.

"I *know* so," she said in a tone that brooked no argument.

"I can't wait to tell Jacob. I haven't spoken to

him since I started. I wasn't sure if I'd like it here or if you'd like having me here. I didn't want to have to tell him the job hadn't worked out. He was so happy for me when I got it. Now that I know I'm going to be allowed to stay, I want to tell him how well things have worked out."

At the mention of Jacob's name, Hannah's heart skipped a beat. She hadn't been able to stop thinking about him and having daily reminders of him with his twin less than a few feet away for most of the day and night had only made it more difficult.

"Do you know how to reach him?" she asked, keeping her tone casual.

"I guess I can call the Sydney Harbour Hospital. He works in the emergency department."

She smiled faintly. "Yes, he told me."

Toby looked at her, his expression filled with curiosity. "You've been talking to him?"

"No, not since he dropped you off here the other day. We... We met at the hospital ball the weekend before."

"That's when he told you he was a doctor," Toby guessed, smiling.

"Yes. We were seated at the same table. We managed to catch up. I hadn't seen him since...high school."

Toby's expression sobered and the light in his eyes dimmed. "Yeah, I remember." When he looked at her again, his eyes were tortured. "I'm so sorry, Hannah. I'm so sorry about Luke."

"Don't be, Toby. It's all right. Please don't get upset again. It wasn't your fault."

Tears glinted in his eyes. "But it wasn't Jacob's fault, either. He—"

"Toby," she gently interrupted. "I get that you feel bad for Jacob and that, as his brother, you feel the need to come to his defense. I admire your love and your loyalty. It's a rare thing, these days. But if you don't mind, I'd rather not talk about it, okay?"

He stared at her a moment longer and looked like he might say something further, but finally he swiped at his tears with the back of his hand and slowly nodded. "Okay."

"Now, if you like, you can borrow my cell phone to call Jacob. I'll find the hospital number for you."

"Thank you, Hannah. That would be great."

The genuine gratitude that shone in his eyes touched her heart. "No problem," she managed, her voice husky with emotion.

Heading into the small kitchen at the back of the house, she found her handbag and pulled out her phone. Doing a quick online search, she found the number for the emergency department of the hospital where Jacob worked. She returned to the embalming room and handed Toby her phone.

"Thank you," he said. "I promise, I won't be long."

"It's fine. Talk as long as you want."

A look of panic suddenly passed across his face. "What if he's not at work?"

"Then we'll find some other way to reach him. He's friends with some of my friends. I'm sure we can track him down."

Relief filled his expression and his shoulders

slumped on a sigh. "Okay, I'll try the hospital and we'll see what happens."

He began to dial the number and Hannah turned away to give him a little privacy. She heard him ask for Doctor Jacob Black and was pleased when he said he'd be happy to wait. It was a good sign. A moment later, it was obvious Jacob had come to the phone.

The simple pleasure on Toby's face as he spoke with his brother pulled at Hannah's heartstrings. Not only were they flesh and blood, but they were identical twins. It was well documented that identical twins had a special bond and it appeared the one between Toby and his brother was no different. She was saddened by the thought that for a whole decade, they'd been out of touch.

Choosing to give Toby a little more privacy, she pulled open the door that led out of the embalming room and wandered into Max's office. Her boss sat in his usual spot behind his large, cluttered desk. His white hair was slightly mussed and a frown creased his forehead. He looked up at her in surprise.

"Hannah! What is it, my dear? Is everything all right?"

She smiled. "Yes, of course. Toby's speaking on the phone with his brother. I thought I'd give him some privacy."

Max's eyes widened. "He has a brother? Why on earth was the boy living on the streets? I assumed he had no family."

"Three brothers, in fact. They've been apart for

ten years. They've only recently reconnected."

"I see. I guess that explains it."

Hannah suddenly recalled the conversation she'd had with Toby about his appointment with the doctor. Max had arranged for the medical. He was the perfect person to ask about it.

"Toby told me the doctor he saw the other day said something about a life insurance policy. It struck me as odd. Do you know what he's talking about?"

Max frowned. "Life insurance? Are you sure?"

"Well, not really. Toby thought that's what the doctor said."

Max lifted one shoulder in a half-shrug. "I don't know why. I sent him there to undergo a full medical, but it was only because I was concerned for his overall health. I'm not sure how long he's been living on the streets, but it's obvious it's been quite awhile. I just wanted to make sure he was...okay."

Hannah nodded. It was as she'd expected. Toby must have simply misunderstood. She told Max as much.

"Yes, well, I guess it's easy enough to get confused about things like that, especially someone like Toby. He's a lovely boy, but he does seem a little limited in his understanding of things."

"You're right and it was very kind of you to get him medically assessed. Not many bosses would have bothered."

Max's cheeks turned pink with pleasure, but he waved her praise away. "You don't need to say things like that, Missy. I like you well enough already. Now, get out of here and get back to work."

Hannah shot him a fond smile and turned and left the room. Easing open the door to the embalming room, she found Toby cleaning the counter. He handed back her phone.

"How did you do?" she asked, tossing it back into her handbag.

His face lit up with a smile. "Great. He was there. I told him about my job, how much I was enjoying it, working here with you. He told me to say hi."

Hannah started in surprise. She hadn't expected Jacob to offer such a courtesy. They hadn't exactly parted on friendly terms at the ball and she hadn't been overly affable when he'd arrived at the funeral parlor that first afternoon to collect Toby. No matter how much time had passed since high school, she hadn't forgotten and she wasn't ready to forgive.

"He wants to take us to dinner," Toby added.

Hannah blinked, not sure she'd heard right. "Excuse me?"

"He invited us to dinner. He asked me if you'd like to come along. He has a couple of days off, starting tomorrow. He's happy to do it whichever night suits."

Panic took hold in Hannah's stomach and her hands clenched. She didn't want to spend time with Toby's brother. He was dangerous to her equilibrium. For so long, she'd borne a grudge against him—she'd sometimes even dreamed of getting revenge and now he was here, back in her life and doing his best to prove she was being churlish and petty to hold on to her rage.

Was it possible he *wasn't* the devil incarnate who'd gotten away with murder? Maybe he *was* just a guy who'd made a mistake and had taken his punishment. At least, that's what he probably wanted her to think.

"I-I don't think that's a good idea, Toby."

Toby's face fell. "But it would be fun, Hannah! Just like old times! Don't you remember how we used to hang out together—you and Luke and me and Jacob? We spent most afternoons together, down by the river, eating sandwiches and cake we brought from home... Don't you remember?"

At her continued silence, his voice drifted off. Looking bewildered, he slowly turned away and picked up his cleaning cloth. His movements were slower, heavier, as if the job had suddenly become harder. Anguish burned inside her.

She didn't want to spend time with Jacob. She didn't want to forget what he'd done and how she felt about it. But she couldn't stand the thought of disappointing his brother and removing the smile from his innocent face. With every bath and shower, he became more like the Toby she'd once known and the similarity to his gorgeous twin was heartbreaking.

She'd told Toby earlier, it wasn't *his* fault Luke had lost his life and if her words were sincere, Toby shouldn't be punished for someone else's deeds.

"All right. I'll come," she said quietly and was rewarded with a loud *whoop* and a cheer. Toby spun around to face her.

"You mean it? You really *mean* it? You'll come?"

The excitement on his face was contagious. "Yes," she laughed. "I'll come."

"Can I borrow your cell phone again? I want to call Jacob and tell him right away."

She laughed again. "He's at work, Toby. He probably won't be able to come to the phone again. Surely, it can wait. The day's only half over; it's not like we're ready to leave."

His face fell. "*Please*, Hannah? I've got to at least try."

She looked at him and found herself relenting. What did it matter if he tried to call Jacob again? If his brother was busy, Toby would be advised accordingly. Surely there was no harm done, either way. She tugged her phone out of her bag again and handed it to him.

"Be my guest."

"Oh, I forgot to tell you. Jacob gave me his cell number. I saved it to your phone." He grinned. I put it under 'Jacob.'"

Hannah's belly did a flip flop, but she remained silent. It wasn't Toby's fault that she disliked his brother—and Toby probably remembered when it hadn't been like that. There was a time when they'd enjoyed each other's company. Toby was no doubt oblivious to how things had soured between her and his brother.

Once again, Toby dialed a number and listened as it rang out. This time, she heard Jacob's voice tell the caller to leave a message. Toby happily confirmed Hannah was able to join them for dinner. He finished by asking Jacob to call him back on Hannah's phone to confirm the arrangements.

For the rest of the day, Hannah felt unsettled. Every time she thought of the pending meal, her stomach twisted with nerves. Her thoughts flitted from the moments of pleasantness at the ball, to the kiss that had ended their night—and underpinning it all was the knowledge that he'd as good as gotten away with killing her boyfriend.

He'd been sentenced to two years. *What was that compared to the loss of someone's life?* The sentence had been a pittance, a farce and it annoyed her every time she thought about it. Not exactly the best frame of mind to be in as their dinner companion.

She sighed heavily. The continuous burn of anger and resentment low in her belly was doing her no good. She'd give herself an ulcer if she kept it up. There was nothing for it. She'd do the best she could to keep her animosity in check for Toby's sake, and for her own.

Chapter 8

Dear Diary,

I find myself facing an interesting dilemma, one I haven't come across before. I located my next victim and did the usual things. All was going well. But this time, I seem to have miscalculated. Unlike the others, this one isn't alone.

I've made some discreet enquires. He has a family and at least one friend. He's not a nameless, faceless drifter living on the streets. Someone might miss this one if he were to disappear. I'll have to ponder it further before making a decision...

Jacob ran a comb through his thick dark hair and then set the comb down on the vanity. Staring at his reflection in the bathroom mirror, he checked that there was nothing caught in his teeth and then gargled a second time. He glanced at his watch and noted the time. He still had thirty minutes before he was due to meet Hannah and his brother for dinner.

He'd offered to collect them, but Hannah had politely declined and told him they'd meet him at the restaurant. He couldn't help but wonder if she wanted to be able to escape him if things went pear-shaped. Again.

Still, he was willing to take his chances. He'd been given the opportunity to spend some more time with her—and for that, he was grateful.

———————

Hannah knocked gently on the door of Toby's room and waited for him to answer.

"Come in."

She pushed open the door and found him smoothing out the wrinkles on his recently laundered clothes. With Max's permission, he'd added to his meager wardrobe by bringing a couple of sets of scrubs home. One set had been put to use as pajamas.

"I have a present," she said, handing him the shopping bag.

He smiled lopsidedly. "It's not my birthday until next week."

"Really?" she replied in surprise. "What date?"

"May sixteenth."

She made a mental note and then urged him to open the bag. He frowned at the clothes in his hand.

"What's this?"

"I stopped by the menswear department during my lunch break. I bought you some new clothes." She watched him—a little on edge—uncertain how he would react to her gift.

A smile slowly grew on his face. When he looked back at her, tears glinted in his eyes. "You bought me new clothes?"

She smiled tentatively. "Yes. I hope it's all right?"

"Of *course* it is!" He grinned and strode over to her and enveloped her in an enthusiastic hug. Lifting her off her feet, he swung her around.

"Nobody's ever bought me new clothes before, except, maybe my mom. But she's my mom. It was her job to buy me clothes."

Hannah laughed, pleased that he'd accepted her gift in the manner it was intended. "There are a few new shirts and pants and a couple of pairs of jeans. And there are a pair of boots in a box on the kitchen counter. I kind of guessed at the size. I'm sorry, I didn't think about a suit, but you should be okay. The restaurant doesn't stand on formality. Pants and a shirt will be fine. We'll leave in fifteen minutes."

Toby's grin widened. "I'd better hurry, then. I'll need to change."

She closed the door behind her and headed down the hall. Her heart felt lighter than it had all week and suddenly she looked forward to the night ahead.

———————

Jacob spied them the moment they entered the restaurant, although his brother's appearance almost made him do a double take. Toby was smartly dressed in a long-sleeved, white shirt that was tucked neatly into a pair of navy-blue pants. The last time Jacob had seen him, his feet had been filthy and bare. Now he wore shoes that shone as if recently polished—either that, or they were new. *Hannah must have gone shopping.* The knowledge that she cared enough about his twin to do something like that warmed him through, although it still irritated him a little that she hadn't accepted his offer to pay for it.

He stood and motioned them over. Hannah acknowledged him with a nod and a quick smile. His heart somersaulted. She wove through the other tables, Toby following close behind. The eyes of every other man in the room followed her progress. She was dressed simply in a white dress with a fitted bodice that flared out gently over her hips and ended just below her knees. She wore open black sandals, with at least three-inch heels. Her thick blond hair was pulled back in a ponytail, the simplicity of it making her look younger than her twenty-nine years.

The hairstyle might have appeared severe on some women, but not on Hannah. It emphasized her perfect bone structure and the luminescence of her skin. He wondered vaguely how she appeared so healthy and wholesome when she spent most of her time inside, away from natural light... But then she was beside him and her light perfume filled the air. His thoughts scattered like dandelion seeds on the wind.

She held her hand out in greeting. "It's nice to see you again, Jacob. Thank you for inviting me along."

Jacob took her hand in his. Her skin was soft and her bones felt small and delicate, even though her handshake was sure and firm and exuded confidence.

"It's good to see you, too, Hannah. I'm pleased you were able to join us."

"Hey, Jake," Toby said and gave Jacob a quick hug.

Taking their seats, Jacob ordered a round of drinks. Hannah picked up the menu. "The food is so good, here. It's always tough to make a decision."

Jacob looked at her in surprise. "Do you eat here often?"

Hannah smiled. "As often as I can, although most of the time I do takeout. I love Thai food. Sam and I have spent many a night solving the problems of the world over May-Ling's green coconut curry chicken."

He frowned. "Sam?"

"Yes. Samantha Wolfe. My best friend. You met her at the ball. She married Rohan Coleridge a few months ago. He's a detective, like your brother."

Jacob nodded, filled with relief that she hadn't been referring to a man. The memory of Rohan's wife came back to him. "That's right. She wasn't feeling so well that night. You went with her to the bathroom."

"Morning sickness," Hannah explained. "Or in Sam's case, morning, noon and night sickness."

Jacob nodded sympathetically. "That's tough."

Hannah smiled. "Yes."

"It sure smells good in here," Toby commented, looking around at the quaint Thai-inspired décor. I can't remember the last time I ate restaurant food."

Hannah turned to him and smiled, a teasing look in her eyes. "Don't tell me you're complaining that my cooking isn't restaurant quality?"

Toby grinned back at her and Jacob couldn't help but notice the obvious closeness between them. It was like when they'd been young. The two had always had a special friendship. Now, even after all the years apart, it had taken less than a week for their friendly camaraderie to re-establish itself. Jacob felt a pang and once again, realized he was jealous. The recurring feeling annoyed him.

His brother had been living on the streets for who knew how long. It was obvious he'd been doing it tough. Although the physical reminders of the life he'd been living had been removed with hot water, soap and clean clothes, Jacob couldn't help but wonder about the emotional reasons behind the way Toby had been living his life. It scared him to think it might have had everything to do with him and what had happened on that night in November.

"It's good to see you looking so well, Tobes," he said quietly and meant it.

Toby nodded and flushed. "Hannah's been

taking really good care of me, Jake. And I'm really loving my job."

Jacob nodded, his heart filling with contentment. He looked at Hannah. "I'm grateful for everything you've done for my little brother," he told her.

She frowned. "*Little* brother?" A moment later, comprehension flooded her face. "Oh, yeah. Little brother. I remember that dig."

Toby rolled his eyes, but amusement glinted in their depths. "He's only older than me by three minutes. Three minutes shouldn't count."

"Of course it does," Jacob protested good-naturedly. A lot can happen in three minutes."

Hannah joined in the fun. "You're right. In three minutes I can boil water and make a bowlful of noodles. Add a few herbs and spices and, hey presto! You have a meal!"

"And here I thought you only served restaurant-quality food at home!" Jacob teased.

She smiled at him, taking the jibe in the spirit intended. "You ought to come over one night and decide for yourself."

––––––––––––––

Hannah stared at Jacob and snapped her jaw shut, unable to believe what she'd just said. *What the hell was she doing, issuing an invitation like that?* It was one thing to accept a dinner invitation to a restaurant in the city, surrounded by other people. It was another thing to invite him into her home, with the implicit intimacy that suggested—even with his brother in attendance.

She'd been lulled into a false sense of contentment, trading comfortable conversation across the table. The drinks had arrived and she'd already taken several sips from her beer. She was secretly impressed that he remembered her choice of beverage from the ball—not all women enjoyed beer. The yeasty taste of it had slid down her throat all too easily, relaxing her, making her vulnerable.

She'd arrived at the restaurant and was lucky enough to secure a parking spot not too far away, all the while, second-guessing her decision to come to dinner. She'd been more than a little nervous about seeing him again. Toby's chatter on the way had helped distract her for a while, but the moment she spied Jacob smiling at her from across the room, her nerves had doubled in intensity.

But the comfortable mood at the table and sense of relaxed familiarity that came back to her in the company of the two attractive men had served to ease her tension and she'd been enjoying the evening. So much so that without thinking it through, she'd invited him home to dinner. Now, all she could do was hope he turned her down.

"You're probably too busy," she started in an effort to dissuade him. Jacob opened his mouth, but his twin beat him to it.

"What a great idea!" Toby exclaimed. "It's our birthday next week! We could celebrate it together, with Hannah. It would be just like old times, back when we were kids." He turned to his brother, his eyes pleading. "Please say yes, Jake. Talk to your boss. Change your roster. It's been so long since we were together on our birthday." His voice lowered. "It would mean so much to me if you could make it."

The tension that had gripped Hannah the instant she issued the invitation dissipated. The longing in Toby's eyes tugged at her heart. *How could she try and dissuade his brother from attending?* Toby needed this. He needed to reconnect with his twin. And what better way to do it than at their joint birthday? Surely, she could do it for Toby's sake?

Jacob's gaze burned into hers. "Are you sure? I mean... Just because you're friends with my brother, doesn't mean I expect anything from you. I know how you feel about me. I wouldn't want to—"

"It's all right," she interrupted him. "I wouldn't have said anything if I didn't want you to come around. And after all, Toby's staying with me. It would be easy to share a birthday dinner with the two of you. In fact, it sounds like fun."

The more she thought about it, the more she realized that was true. She didn't want to soften her heart toward Jacob, but she had a sneaking suspicion it was happening without her say-so. A wave of guilt went through her. *Was she being disloyal to Luke?* He'd died because Jacob had climbed drunk behind the wheel. There was no arguing against the facts.

A surge of sadness went through her. Nothing would bring her boyfriend back, no matter how long she stayed mad at Jacob. Even so, the thought of letting her anger go and accepting what had happened made her feel panicky. For more than a decade, her anger had sustained her, had been the thing that got her through the grief and loss. *Was it even possible to give that up?*

"All right. I accept," Jacob said.

His words jolted her from her increasingly frantic thoughts. *He'd accepted. He was coming over for dinner. Oh, God. What was she going to do?*

The arrival of the waitress, brandishing a pen and notepad, brought her thoughts to a sudden halt.

"Are you ready to order?" the woman asked with a friendly smile.

Jacob nodded in Hannah's direction. "Please, you go first."

Once again, his good manners warmed her. She offered him a smile of acknowledgement and then turned to the waitress.

"Yes, um… I'll have the mussaman beef curry and some special fried rice, please." She turned to Toby. "What are you having, Toby?"

After taking their orders, the waitress collected their menus. Reassuring them the food wouldn't be long, she turned away and headed back toward the kitchen.

"I saw an article in the paper yesterday about one of your coworkers," Jacob said, glancing across at her as he took a sip from his beer. "It sounds like he met a sad end. Did you know him?"

Hannah grimaced and nodded. "Yes, I did. Christopher Lowrey worked as my assistant for more than a year. He was a good worker. He'd had some tough knocks in life, but he was a survivor. I liked him. I was very saddened to hear he'd died so tragically. The police said the truck driver didn't even realize he'd hit him."

Jacob frowned. "What are you talking about? The story didn't say anything about a truck. This guy was found dead in a stairwell and I'm sure his name was Edward something. It's my middle name; that's why it stuck with me."

Coldness gripped Hannah's insides. She stared at Jacob in shock, trying to make sense of his words. *Edward? Dead? How could that be?* A sense of urgency tinged with panic surged through her and she leaned forward.

"When did this happen?"

"The paper was more than a week old. I guess it happened sometime around then."

Hannah's heart thumped. "What else did the article say?"

Jacob shrugged. "Not much. It was brief on detail. Something about the fact he'd been found in the stairwell of an inner city hostel with a broken neck. An autopsy revealed his blood alcohol level was high. The police have surmised he stumbled and fell down the stairs and met an unfortunate end. It only caught my attention because it mentioned the Max Grace Funeral Home. I'd never heard of the place until Tobes started working there. A week earlier and the story would have escaped my notice."

Thoughts swirled through Hannah's mind. Christopher had met with an accident a little over a month ago. Now a second work colleague had died. *What was going on? Was it merely a coincidence?* She couldn't help the shiver of premonition that trickled down her spine.

She wondered if Max knew about Edward's death, and if so, why he hadn't mentioned it? Thinking about how Edward had died, she was flooded with sadness. Nobody deserved to die like that, alone and in pain. She prayed he'd died quickly.

Bobby Grace picked nervously at a scab on his forearm. Old scars and new criss-crossed his hands and arms, the permanent evidence of a violent life. He thought he'd put it all behind him the day they released him from jail, but somehow, his past kept coming back to haunt him, no matter how hard he tried.

Not that he'd tried too hard. He wanted to be strong, but the truth was, he was weak. The lure of sweet oblivion at the end of a needle was too strong. It blurred the nightmares of his years in jail like nothing else could. His uncle just didn't understand.

Max Grace had lived an easy life. He'd never known what it was like not to be wanted, not to fit in. Bobby's father had hung around just long enough to get his mother pregnant and his mother... Well, he guessed she'd done the best she could in the circumstances... Too bad it wasn't enough.

Meanwhile, Uncle Max had gotten rich off the business of dying and Bobby and his mom were left to struggle on the streets. It killed Bobby to see his uncle extending charity to men down on their luck. His uncle hadn't bothered to extend the same kind of charity to his sister and her bastard son when it might have mattered the most.

Bobby was sure the man expected him to be grateful. Like he should thank him or something, for throwing him a tidbit of generosity—like a grateful dog would slobber over its master for tossing it a bone. It made him sick. Still, the old man couldn't live forever and Bobby was his only family.

Surely he'd have the decency to leave the business to his nephew? Bobby wasn't certain he could hang around long enough to find out. He needed money and he needed it fast. Rat didn't go easy on anyone who was in his debt. The last poor bastard who'd failed to come up with cash had been found floating in the Harbour. Bobby sure as hell didn't plan to end up like that.

Five male figures appeared in the darkness, all wearing dark colored hoodies that concealed most of their features, but Bobby knew who they were. He tensed. Doing business with dealers always made him nervous. There was something wild and animal-like about them and he could never predict their mood. Right now, he didn't have the money he owed them and the knowledge made his gut go weak.

"Where is it?" Rat demanded as soon as he was close enough.

Bobby dug into his pocket and handed over a wad of cash. "Here." He thrust it into Rat's filthy hand and waited, shifting nervously from foot to foot.

Rat made a show of counting it. "You're three hundred short," he snarled.

"Yeah, I'm sorry. I-I'll have it next time. I promise."

The glint of a knife blade caught Bobby's eye. He swallowed. He outweighed Rat by at least fifty pounds, but the guy hadn't come alone. Flanked by four hefty bodyguards, Bobby didn't stand a chance. Besides, he was tired of fighting. All he wanted was the drugs. The hit of sweet oblivion. Nothing else came close.

"You'd better," Rat growled, his sharp, pointed teeth glimmering in the faint light. "Next time, I won't be so understanding." Rat stared meaningfully at his bodyguards, his message clear as they narrowed their eyes at Bobby.

Bobby managed a jerky nod before stumbling away from them. He hurried down the alleyway, finally breathing a sigh of relief when he turned the corner and disappeared from their sights.

CHAPTER 9

Hannah heard the door to Max's office open. Setting aside the jar of formaldehyde, she glanced across at Toby.

"Do you mind finishing this off? I just heard Max come in. I need to speak with him."

Toby grinned. "Sure." Taking the syringe from her, he picked up the jar.

"I won't be long," she assured him and peeled off her latex gloves.

"No problem. I know what to do."

She smiled softly. "Yes, you do. You're a quick learner, Toby. We're lucky to have you."

He blushed, but happiness shone in his innocent blue eyes. Her heart clenched. He looked so much like his brother.

"I'll be back soon. Give me a yell if you need any help."

"I will."

Hannah made her way across the hall to Max's office and knocked gently on the closed door.

"Come in."

Turning the knob, she greeted him with a trembling smile. Max glanced up briefly and greeted her.

"Hannah! Good morning! I hope you had a good weekend. What can I do for you?" he asked and then returned his gaze to the papers in his hand.

Now that the moment was upon her, she was suddenly at a loss for words. She opened her mouth, but to her horror, tears welled up in her eyes.

Max looked up again and frowned. "Hannah? Are you all right?"

"I… I discovered on Friday night that Edward was found dead more than a week ago. Did you… Did you know?"

Max remained silent and Hannah's apprehension increased. "Max…?"

He sighed heavily. "I'm sorry, Hannah. I guess I should have told you, but coming so soon after Christopher's death, I didn't want to upset you."

She shook her head in disbelief. "When did you find out?"

Max averted his gaze. "The police came to me the morning after he was found. Apparently he had a payslip in his pocket. They tracked him back here."

Her jaw gaped open. "You've known all this time and didn't *tell* me? I came to you the first morning he didn't show for work. You knew how concerned I was. I asked you if you knew where he'd gone. You told me you didn't know anything. You told me he'd probably decided to move on. Why did you lie?"

A flush spread up Max's neck and moved across his rounded face. With his white hair haloing his head, he looked like a guilty angel. When he looked up at her, his eyes pleaded with her to understand.

"I'm sorry, Hannah. I truly am. I didn't know back then. When the police told me... I wanted to spare you the pain. Edward hadn't been here as long as Christopher, but the two of you were friends. The whole tragic business was just so sad. I... I couldn't tell you."

Hannah bit her lip and nodded. She understood. Max had been doing what he always did—thinking of others and acting accordingly. She could hardly blame him for wanting to spare her. He thought he'd been treating her kindly by keeping her in the dark.

"It's all right, Max," she said quietly. "You did what you thought was best. I guess it doesn't matter, now. It's not going to bring Edward back, or change the way he died. Did the police find any family? Is that why he wasn't brought back here?"

Max bowed his head. When he looked up at her again, his expression was troubled. "I'm... I'm not sure. I guess so. I... I hate to change the subject, but something else has kept me sleepless all weekend."

Hannah frowned. "What is it, Max?"

Max's thin shoulders slumped on another heavy sigh. "It's about the life insurance thing. After you spoke to me about it last week, I couldn't stop thinking about it. It seemed like such an odd thing for Toby's doctor to say. I phoned the medical center and spoke to the doctor who carried out the physical exam." His tone grew heavier.

"He told me my nephew had called him shortly after I'd arranged the appointment and explained the exam was for the purposes of an application for life insurance. There are certain other tests that are carried out when an examination is done for that purpose," Max explained.

"Yes, I understand," Hannah said. "What I don't understand is why Bobby would request it. It doesn't make sense. Why would Toby need life insurance?"

Max compressed his lips and his expression turned grim. "It might have something to do with this."

He pushed some papers toward her. She glanced down at them. General & Life Insurance Company was written in bold black type across the top of the page. Skimming through the small print, she came to the details of the insured and her eyes widened. The policy insured the life of Edward John Sutton, forty-three, for the sum of five hundred thousand dollars. The policy was owned by Robert Grace.

In disbelief, she looked up at Max. "Bobby took out life insurance on *Edward*?"

Max's lips tightened and his expression grew somber. "Yes."

"Where did you find this?" she asked.

"After I spoke to the doctor, I went through Bobby's desk. I wasn't exactly sure what I was looking for, but I had an awful feeling. I've owned this business for close to fifty years. I've had a lot of staff come through my doors. Before Bobby got here, none of them left in a box. And now, two former employees have met unexpected deaths in a short space of time."

He drew in a breath and continued. "I found the policy in the bottom drawer of Bobby's desk, beneath an old phone book. It wasn't exactly hidden, but if I hadn't been searching for something suspicious, I might not have found it. I've also noticed large sums of cash missing. I can only guess he's been using it to pay the premiums."

Hannah shook her head in disbelief. "You can't possibly mean...?" She couldn't even bring herself to say it.

Max's expression was heavy with sadness and regret. Deep lines cut into his face. He'd aged before her eyes.

"I think my nephew's involved in something unthinkable. I don't want to believe it, but what else am I to think? He's the beneficiary of a life insurance policy worth half a million dollars for a man he barely knew; a man who recently turned up dead."

"But the police reported it was an acciden—"

"Yes," Max interrupted, his expression grave. "But, what if they're *wrong* about the cause of death?"

His words sunk in and Hannah gasped at their implication. "We have to talk to the police. We have to tell them what we know."

Max sighed heavily. Tears welled up in his eyes. "Yes, we do."

"Would you like me to come with you to the station?" Hannah asked quietly.

With his shoulders bowed, Max shook his head. "No, but thank you. I appreciate your offer. It's very kind of you."

"Are you sure? Because I'd be happy to—"

"No, Hannah, but thank you again. He's my nephew. This is something I have to do on my own."

Hannah returned to the embalming room just as Toby withdrew the trocar and suction pipe from the woman who lay on the table. He looked up as she entered.

"How did you do? Did you speak with Max?" he asked.

Hannah tried to return his polite smile, but failed. Her lip wobbled. Almost immediately, he noticed her distress.

"Hannah! What is it?" he asked, his brow furrowed in concern.

Pulling all her strength forward, Hannah drew in a deep breath and forced herself to regain control. She'd suffered several shocks in a short space of time, but now wasn't the time to fall apart. She was at work and it wasn't fair to Toby to offload her baggage onto him. With an effort, she controlled her emotions and offered him a strained smile.

"I'm sorry, Toby. I just received some...unexpected news. I'll be all right. I promise."

He continued to look at her doubtfully. "Are you sure?"

"Yes, I'm sure. Now, how are we going with Beryl?"

Toby stared at her a moment longer and then looked down at their client. Wispy, white hair formed a halo around her chalk-like face. The formaldehyde had begun to work its magic and her features already looked more like she was simply asleep. Makeup would add the final touches.

"I've finished draining the body fluids. I was just about to start packing the orifices."

"We need to inject fluid into the body first, remember? To aid in the elimination of odors."

Toby flushed with embarrassment and slapped himself up the side of the head. "That's right! I forgot that step! I'm sorry, Hannah!"

"It's all right, Toby. This is only your second week. You're not expected to have the entire embalming process memorized over night."

He nodded but kept his gaze averted. "It's just that it's a little confusing. We drain all the fluids out and then put more fluid back in."

Hannah smiled in understanding. "You're right, but it's not the *same* fluid. The first process drains all the body fluids away—the disgusting, smelly fluids that accumulate in our tissues and body cavities when we die. The second kind of fluid is injected as a kind of deodorizer. It doesn't work to eradicate every smell, but it does a pretty good job."

He lifted his gaze to hers and smiled. The

cheeky grin and innocent expression on his face nearly took her breath away.

"It's a messy business, this dying thing, isn't it," he stated.

Hannah laughed softly. "Yes, it is." She strode over to the cupboard and retrieved the jar of fluid they usually used at this stage of the procedure and handed it to Toby, along with a syringe.

"Here you go. See how you do."

He took the items from her and went to work on Beryl. Hannah moved back to the storage cabinet and retrieved the cotton wadding that would be required shortly.

"Did you really mean it when you invited Jacob over to celebrate a birthday dinner?"

The question was asked quietly. Hannah turned back to face him, surprised because she wasn't expecting it. Toby continued to work over the body.

"Yes, of course," she replied, hoping she wasn't going to regret it. "Would you like that?"

Toby looked up at her. Hope shone in his eyes. "Yes, I would. I *really* would."

She swallowed the lump of emotion that formed in her throat. She wondered how long it had been since he'd celebrated a birthday with his twin. All of a sudden, she determined to make their day one to remember.

———

Max heard the sound of the front door opening

and stepped out of his office in time to see his nephew stalk past.

"Bobby!" he growled, the anger he'd been sitting on all weekend suddenly springing to life. With exaggerated reluctance, the man came to a halt and slowly turned around.

"What?" he asked belligerently.

Max's jaw clenched with anger. "What the hell were you thinking?"

"What the hell are you talking about?" Bobby shot back.

"Don't give me that nonsense! You know exactly what I'm talking about."

Bobby gave an exaggerated eye roll. "If I knew what you were talking about, I wouldn't have asked."

"I've been more than patient with you, Bobby. I've paid off your gambling debts, given you a job, found you somewhere to live. What more can I do?"

Bobby closed the distance between them and loomed menacingly over his uncle. "I never asked you for any of that, Uncle. You were the one who decided I needed saving, like I was another one of your *projects*."

He spat the word like it gave him a bad taste in his mouth and curled up his lip in disgust. Max's fury burned hotter. *After all he'd done for the ungrateful wretch...*

His fists clenched and his breath came fast. His face burned, along with his eyes.

Bobby sneered. "Go on, Uncle. Do it! Hit me! You know you want to!"

Max stared up at his nephew. The other man stood head and shoulders above him and outweighed him by at least one hundred pounds. His father had been a Pacific Islander. He looked like a footballer wearing all the gear. Max was no match for him. Impotence surged through him and the knowledge of it left him gasping. With a hard look at his nephew, he spun on his heel and left.

Chapter 10

Dear Diary,

Just when I was concerned I might have miscalculated, a solution has fallen into my lap. Like a ripe peach, soft and juicy, and the best thing is, he's oblivious to what I have in store. The plan is brilliant. I am brilliant. I hide behind a bland façade. I am a chameleon. If only he knew...

For the umpteenth time Jacob glanced at the clock on the wall above the nurses' station and cursed under his breath. The day was dragging. It had been a slow morning in the emergency room, with only a smattering of patients and as yet, he hadn't had to deal with any life-threatening injuries or illnesses.

Week days were sometimes like that and occasionally he welcomed the slower pace. It gave him time to de-stress and regroup between patients and sometimes to reconnect with his staff. As the senior emergency resident, his role came with a lot of responsibility, including the supervision of several junior doctors. He was their mentor, their counselor, their sounding board, their boss, their friend and everything else they could think of. These were the roles he enjoyed and it gave him immeasurable pleasure to watch a young doctor grow and flourish, changing from an uncertain, cautious intern to a confident medical professional.

He'd come to medicine reluctantly. When he was younger, the only thing he'd set his heart on was being a police officer, like his dad. Detective Senior Sergeant Warren Black was his hero. Even with the risk, Jacob wanted nothing more than to follow in his father's footsteps. Then the night of November eighteenth had happened and his life and his future had been irrevocably altered. Sometimes, things didn't go to plan.

But that was more than a decade earlier and he'd managed to get his life back on track. He'd found a real passion for healing and though, every now and then, he'd watch and listen to Lane and wonder what it would have been like to walk the beat, for the most part, he couldn't imagine doing anything else. He'd put his rocky past behind him and his future now looked bright. There was talk he might even be promoted before the year was out.

And then there was Hannah, an angel from his past. Knowing he was going over to her place for dinner had his stomach twisted with excitement and nerves. He frowned. He had to get a handle on his emotions before he went quietly insane.

He'd shared a pleasant meal with her and his brother the week before, but she'd given him no overt sign she'd ever think of him as anything other than the man who'd killed her boyfriend. It was a steep hurdle to overcome. Still, he was nothing, if not persistent, and his determination to succeed knew no bounds. He intended to do everything he could to persuade her he was worthy of her attention.

"Doctor Black, you're needed in bay three. We have a ten-year-old who's fallen off a roof. Suspected fracture of his right arm. Possible head injury."

Jacob pushed away from the desk, his mind instantly snapping into gear. With a familiar surge of adrenaline flooding his veins, he followed on the nurse's heels.

———————

For the third time, Hannah rearranged the display of oriental lilies that stood in a crystal vase on her dining room table. Standing back, she surveyed her handiwork and frowned. The flowers still didn't look right. She adjusted a couple of stems and then impatiently shook her head.

For goodness sake! It was dinner with a couple of old school friends. She shouldn't feel so jittery or concerned that things be perfect. Jacob probably wouldn't even notice. Generally, guys weren't good at that. Besides, what did she care how he felt about her condo, or the efforts she'd gone to for the evening?

With a grimace, she touched her hair. The French roll still felt neat and secure, although a couple of shorter pieces had escaped. They hung around her face to annoy her, but she was almost out of time. If Jacob was punctual, he'd be there very soon.

She heard the sound of a door opening and closing from the direction of the bedrooms and a moment later, Toby appeared by her side.

"Something smells delicious," he exclaimed with a smile. "And look at those flowers! They're lovely and they smell so nice!"

Hannah smiled back at him. Jacob might not notice her efforts, but his twin certainly did.

"Thank you," she replied. "I'm not sure I've arranged them just right, but they look okay, I guess."

"Better than okay. What's for dinner?"

"You and your brother's favorite. Beef stroganoff with button mushrooms and fettuccine and there's a triple-chocolate birthday cake for dessert."

Toby beamed. "I can't remember the last time someone made me a birthday cake. Thank you, Hannah. You're the best!"

Not for the first time, his childlike enthusiasm touched her heart. He was the sweetest boy there ever was with a very soft heart to match. She was thankful for whatever stars had aligned to bring him to Max's attention. If it hadn't been for that chance meeting, she'd never have known Toby had fallen on hard times and wouldn't have been given the opportunity to renew their friendship and help him out—like friends did.

"Wait until I tell Jacob about the cake. He *loves* cake!"

At the reminder that Jacob was due to arrive any moment, Hannah's heart skipped a beat. She managed a nervous smile. "Good. I wanted to do something special for both of you. We've known each other a long time."

"Yes," Toby nodded, his expression turning serious. "We used to be good friends."

Hannah's chest tightened. She barely managed a nod. "Of course. We... We still are."

"I'm glad. I really like you, Hannah. Jacob likes you, too," he added. A moment later, his brow furrowed in a frown. "Do you like Jacob? Sometimes it's hard to tell."

"I... I..." Hannah was lost for words. Her feelings for Toby's brother used to be so cut and dried: He'd killed her boyfriend and for years, hatred didn't come close. She'd never forgive him.

But over the last week or so, those feelings had become hazy, more gray than black and white. She was no longer certain how she felt. There were moments when her anger and despair over what had happened nearly overwhelmed her, and other times the face of her beloved Luke was fading to something less than clear.

She didn't want to confess she was totally confused where his brother was concerned. It wasn't fair to offload her baggage on Toby. He was simple and good and kind. He trusted her to do the right thing. But what was the right thing? Could she bring herself to forgive and forget? To leave the past where it belonged? She didn't know, but for the first time in more than a decade, she thought she might want to try.

She looked back at Toby and realized he was still waiting for an answer. She didn't want to remove the hopeful look from his face, but neither did she want to give him false hope. She drew in a deep breath and sighed quietly.

"I'm not sure how I feel about your brother, Toby. After what he did… It's hard for me to forget."

Toby's eyes filled with understanding and he moved a little closer. "Do you still get sad, Hannah?"

She bit her lip against the surge of emotion and nodded. "Yes, Toby, I still get sad."

"I was sad, too," he admitted hesitantly. "I was sad for a long, long time."

Something in his voice caught her attention. "Is that the reason you left home? Began living on the streets?" she asked quietly.

Tears filled his eyes. He nodded slowly.

Her heart clenched at the pain on his face. She remembered how she felt whenever she thought of that time. She could understand how it might have affected Toby. She moved closer and put her arms around him. He hugged her back.

The sound of her doorbell intruded and she dropped her arms and stepped away. With the back of his hand, Toby swiped at the moisture on his cheeks.

I'm sorry," he said with a brave attempt at a smile.

"I'm sorry, too," she said. "We're meant to be having a birthday celebration. It's time to get into the party mood."

With that, she picked up one of the party favors she'd scattered in artful array on the table. Blowing hard through the whistle, she smiled when the colorful paper rolled in and out. To her relief, Toby chuckled and picked up one, too. The doorbell sounded again.

"Coming!" she called and hurried across the room.

———————

Hannah leaned back in her chair, sated. The remains of the stroganoff sat in the pan. The birthday cake had been devoured. To Toby's delight, she'd even produced some candles and they'd all sang happy birthday. It had been a nice evening. It brought back memories of the times when they'd been teenagers and had spent lazy afternoons picnicking in the park or roasting marshmallows by the fire down by the river. Of course, Luke had always been with them, sharing in whatever fun was to be had—often he instigated it.

Jacob pushed away from the table and began collecting the dirty plates. Hannah sighed quietly and brushed aside the memories of those long-ago happy times. She followed him into the kitchen.

"I'll stack them in the dishwasher," she said as he dumped the plates in the sink.

"It's fine. I'm happy to do it." He began rinsing the plates and then placing them in the rack of the dishwasher.

She returned to the table and collected the glassware and condiments. Toby looked up at her.

"Do you need any help?"

She shook her head. "Thanks, but I think your brother has it all under control." She walked back into the kitchen and set the dirty glasses on the counter. In silence, Jacob continued to load the dirty items into the machine.

"Someone has you well trained," she murmured with a smile and was instantly paralyzed at the thought he might be married. He'd just turned twenty-nine. It wasn't beyond belief that he might have a wife. It was just that she'd never considered that he might, before that exact minute. In her mind, he was the Jacob she'd known in high school, forever the teenager who'd been charged with a terrible crime.

Unaware of her tumultuous thoughts, Jacob merely shrugged and replied, "I grew up with three brothers, remember? Mom made sure we all took our turn cleaning up after meals. We even learned to cook. Let's just say, I know my way around a kitchen."

He sent her a crooked grin that made her pulse leap. The wine they'd had at dinner had left her feeling a little lightheaded. Or maybe that was because Jacob had closed the door to the dishwasher and now stood leaning against the counter with his arms crossed, watching her expectantly.

Flustered, she turned away and collected coffee mugs from the cupboard. She switched on the coffee machine and then called out to Toby.

"Would you like some coffee, Toby?"

"No, I'm fine," came his reply. "I think I'll go to bed. I have to be up early for work in the morning."

Hannah grinned and the corners of Jacob's lips tugged up in a smile. Climbing out of bed at seven was early for Toby. He'd been staying with her just over a week, and it hadn't taken her long to work out he wasn't a morning person.

"No problem. I'll see you tomorrow."

"I'll just go and say goodnight," Jacob said and left the kitchen. A few moments later, he returned.

"I'm not sure that I've thanked you properly for all you've done for Toby. The change in him is almost miraculous. When I stumbled across him in the ED that night, I was shocked. I couldn't believe it was him. Now, he's like the same old brother I used to know, years ago, before—"

He stopped abruptly. A tortured expression took possession of his face. Hannah's heart clenched. She'd never stopped to consider how Luke's death had affected Jacob, or anyone else. She hadn't been able to see past her own pain. She bowed her head in shame.

"I'm sorry, Jacob. I treated you horribly. I can't believe how selfish I've been."

He stepped closer, until less than a foot separated them. Her breath caught.

"Don't blame yourself, Hannah," he said gently. "Most people would have reacted that way. Hell, I probably would have, too, if our situations had been reversed."

"Was it terrible inside the prison?" she asked quietly.

He shrugged and his expression hardened. "It was what it was."

"You wanted to become a police officer."

He averted his gaze. "It's hard to apply to the police academy with a criminal record. My chances of being accepted were next to impossible."

Hannah gasped at the bitterness in his eyes. All of a sudden it occurred to her she hadn't been the only one whose future had been stolen that night.

"I'm sorry," she whispered.

"Don't be. It wasn't your fault."

They stared at each other, their breathing loud in the stillness. The air between them grew charged. Jacob leaned closer. Hannah's heart beat double-time. With mere inches between them, she turned her head away.

Jacob immediately stepped back. "I'm sorry, Hannah. I shouldn't have—"

"Max thinks his nephew's caught up in an insurance scam," she blurted in a panic, her only thought to stop Jacob from kissing her once again. She'd enjoyed it far too much the first time. She couldn't let it happen again.

Jacob frowned in confusion. "Who's Max?"

"Max Grace. My boss. The owner of the funeral home."

Comprehension flooded his features. "Oh, *that* Max." He frowned again. "Why would I care that his nephew's caught up in an insurance scam?"

"Because your brother works in the same establishment and... It might be a whole lot worse." In somber tones, she explained about the policy Max had found and what Toby had said the doctor had asked during his physical. After she finished, Jacob shook his head.

"This is unbelievable! I assume your boss has taken his concerns to the police?"

Hannah shrugged. "He said he would."

"I'll make sure of it. I'll call Lane and have him check it out. If what this Max suspects is true, it's possible a murderer's walking the corridors of that funeral home. It sounds dangerous, for you and especially for Toby. There's no good reason why Max's nephew should request a medical on my brother for life insurance purposes. What's the name of your colleague who died?"

"Edward Sutton. He's the one you read about in the paper. But there's more. Remember when you told me about Edward and I thought you were talking about someone else? There was another man by the name of Christopher Lowrey who worked in the funeral home. He was killed a month before Toby started. He was hit by a truck. Apparently, he stumbled out onto the road. The driver didn't even see him."

Jacob looked doubtful. "Two accidental deaths in a short space of time. That sounds a little odd. What was the name of the insurance company?"

"General & Life."

"You're sure?"

"Yes. I saw it on the front page of the policy."

"What's this Bobby Grace like? Does he come off as someone capable of murder?"

Hannah shrugged. "Who knows? He's big and brawny and mean and comes across as being tough, but how would I know? That might just be a front. He likes to intimidate me, but he doesn't really frighten me. His lack of work ethic means he hasn't endeared himself to anyone at the funeral home, but he doesn't come across as truly sinister. I don't know what to think."

"We can't sit on this," Jacob said, a note of urgency in his voice. "It might be nothing, but something tells me it's not. Too much doesn't sit right. We need to make sure Max has alerted the police. Lane will be able to find out. It's outside his jurisdiction, but I'm sure he can do a search on a database and see if a report has been made. He might be able to run a few names through the system, starting with Bobby Grace."

CHAPTER 11

Detective Sergeant Lane Black stared at the computer screen in front of him and yawned. His twelve-month-old twins were suffering from chest infections and it felt like he'd been woken every hour on the hour with their crying. He was thankful Zara had gotten up to attend the boys most of the time, but still, his sleep had been far from restful. Glancing at the clock on the squad room wall, he sighed. It was barely nine in the morning. He still had hours to go.

Dragging his keyboard toward him, he looked down at the names he'd scribbled on the paper after receiving a call from his brother the night before: *Max and Robert aka "Bobby" Grace.* Jacob had raised serious concerns about the people who owned a funeral home in Balmain; the same people who now employed their brother.

Typing in the name Max Grace, Lane waited for the results. Nothing. He tried the name *Maxwell Grace.* Still nothing. *Perhaps the man was clean?*

It was possible. Not everyone had a criminal record, despite what it felt like some days.

Lane cleared the search page and then entered the second name into the field. Almost immediately, the search engine brought up results. Checking the dates of birth, Lane swallowed his surprise. The old man might not have a criminal record, but his nephew was another matter.

Scrolling through the entries, Lane scanned the text. Robert Grace had criminal convictions dating back to his childhood. Break and enters, minor assaults and offensive behavior had escalated to armed robberies. By the time Robert was an adult, he'd spent a number of years in juvenile detention and his incarceration didn't stop there.

Lane skimmed over the entries and his gaze snagged on the dates. He frowned in bemusement. Robert Grace had spent time in the same prison as Jacob and it appeared they'd been in there together for at least part of that time. Lane wondered if Jacob even knew about that; if he was aware one of the persons of interest had actually shared his prison cell. Lane intended to find out.

Jacob smiled down at the little girl who stared up at him with large, blue eyes. Kimberly Kincaid's fat blond braids were splayed across the pillow and fanned out at the ends. He'd just informed her it was necessary for him to retrieve the tiny pink bead she'd stuffed up her nose and fear now shadowed her gaze.

"Will it hurt?" she whispered, her voice edged in panic.

"No, honey," he promised. "I'm going to give you a special medicine that will make everything seem a little funny. You'll still be awake, but you won't be aware of things so much. I'm going to use these tweezers to get hold of that little bead. It will be out before you know it."

The child glanced at her mother who sat beside the bed, holding her daughter's hand.

"Are you sure it won't hurt?" Kimberly asked Jacob again.

He gave her a wink. "I'm sure. Now, I need you to lie really still while we get this done. I'm going to let you hold this little mask. I want you to put it over your nose and mouth and breathe in."

Kimberly did as he asked. A moment later, she wrinkled her nose. "Yuck, this stuff smells gross."

Jacob grinned. "You're right, honey. It does smell a little gross, but it's going to help ease your discomfort when I go in and get this bead out. What's it doing up there, anyway? It's a very strange place to store a bead."

The little girl giggled and glanced across at her mom. "He's funny, Mommy."

Kimberly's mother smiled back and eyed Jacob gratefully. "Yes, he is, honey. Now, lie still and do as the doctor asked."

Kimberly did as her mother said and wriggled

back against the bed. Jacob motioned to the nurse who stood not far away.

"Bridget, if you can remove the mask from our patient and adjust that light so I can see all the way up her nose, that would be great," he said.

The nurse did as he instructed and as carefully and quickly as he could, with a pair of tweezers, he grasped hold of the bead that was lodged in the child's nostril. The bead landed in the stainless steel kidney dish with a little *ping*.

"There, all done!" Jacob announced with another smile.

Kimberly's eyes widened in surprise. "It's out? We're finished already?"

"Yes, we are. Would you like to have a look at it?"

Jacob held the kidney dish where she could see the pink bead lying innocently inside.

The child once again scrunched up her nose. "Yuck."

"You might need to leave the beads in your jewelry box next time, instead of putting them up your nose," Jacob teased.

"Yes, that's for sure," Kimberly's mom wholeheartedly agreed. "Thank you, Doctor Black," she added. "We appreciate all that you've done."

Jacob smiled, accepting her thanks. "No problem, Mrs Kincaid. That's what we're here for. You're free to take Kimberly home."

Kimberly struggled off the bed and then reached for her mother's hand.

"What do you say to the doctor, Kimberly?" her mom asked.

Kimberly turned back to Jacob and gave him a grin. "Thank you, Doctor."

He smiled back at her, ignoring the quiet yearning that surged through him. He wondered if he'd ever have kids of his own. "You take care now, Kimberly," he said.

With a wave, the little girl turned away and headed toward the exit with her mom.

"Good job, Doctor Black. You're going to make a fine daddy one day."

The comment jolted him out of his thoughts. He blinked and stared at Bridget who had remained behind and was now removing the sheet from the bed.

"Thank you," he managed and then blushed. A fortnight earlier, he might have been flattered by the frank interest displayed in the nurse's eyes. He might have even taken her up on her unspoken invitation. But now, Hannah Langdon was back on the scene and back in his life. *No, not back in his life. Just...back* and there was no room for anyone else.

All thoughts of romantic entanglements with anyone else were unceremoniously thrust aside. It was like his heart wanted to think it had a second chance. Or even a first chance... It wasn't like they'd ever dated. He'd been her boyfriend's best mate. That was all. They were friends. The four of them. She and Luke. Him and Toby. And then, Luke was dead and they hadn't even been that.

The vibrating of his cell phone against his chest snagged his attention. He tugged it out and looked at the screen.

Lane.

Jacob's gut tightened in anticipation. His thoughts returned to the conversation he'd had with his older brother the night before and he wondered if Lane had anything important to impart. Pressing the button, he moved away and answered the call.

"Lane, how are things?"

CHAPTER 12

Jacob took a swallow from his bottle of beer and breathed a sigh of relief that his twelve-hour shift was finally over. From his favorite spot on the balcony of his fifth floor apartment, he leaned back against the deck chair and set his feet up on the footstool. The gentle hum of traffic, mostly heading out of the city, lulled him into a relaxed mood.

It had been hours since he'd spoken to Lane, but it was only now that he let himself think about what his brother had said. Robert Grace had done time in prison. The two of them had shared a cell. Jacob had had no idea that the Robert Grace Hannah had spoken of, and The Bobster from prison, were one and the same.

He hadn't had any cause to make the connection. He hadn't even known The Bobster's real name and he hadn't wanted to know. He was there to do his time with the minimum of fuss and keeping to himself was his first priority. One thing he did know was the man had saved his life.

Jacob thought about Hannah's revelations—the death of a work colleague a month earlier; a life insurance policy owned by Robert Grace in the name of a man who'd died in a questionable accident; Bobby requesting a medical on his brother for life insurance purposes. None of these things sat well. On their own, they were less sinister, but taken together, he had a horrible feeling something was dreadfully wrong and Robert Grace appeared to be at the heart of it.

The Bobster was far from an angel. In fact, it was his penchant for stealing that had landed him in prison in the first place, but Jacob found it difficult to believe the same man's behavior had escalated to something almost too awful to contemplate. The Bobster he'd known eight years ago was a drug addict and an honorable thief. Not a murderer.

At least, he hadn't been. The last time Jacob had seen him was the day Jacob's sentence had ended. He'd walked out of prison and hadn't looked back. He'd deliberately refrained from contacting any of the men he'd met inside, including The Bobster, who still had a few years remaining on his sentence. While Jacob would never forget what the man had done for him, he had no intention of remaining connected to or reminded about his prison life—and that included The Bobster.

Taking another sip from the bottle of beer in his hand, Jacob savored the cold, yeasty taste on his tongue and tried not to think about the two long years he'd spent incarcerated. Seven-hundred-

and-thirty days he thought he'd never survive. And yet he had. Thanks to The Bobster.

With another mouthful of beer on board, his thoughts turned to Hannah. He wondered what to tell her. At the least, he could reassure her she had nothing to fear from Robert Grace. The man might be a criminal, but he wasn't dangerous to anyone who hadn't given him cause to hate them, and Jacob couldn't imagine either Hannah or Toby falling into that category. There's no way he killed those two employees. But that begged another question: If not The Bobster, then who?

But what would he say if she asked how he knew with such certainty Robert Grace wasn't a suspect? Would he tell her about their shared history? That they'd met each other in prison? It wasn't exactly the kind of information most people found comforting when they were seeking reassurance about someone's character. Then again, most people at the Sydney Harbour Hospital would have been shocked to discover he'd spent two years of his life in jail.

Thanks in part to The Bobster, Jacob had chosen to use his time while incarcerated, to further his education. With his dream of being a police officer in tatters, he began to think of other ways he might productively engage his mind.

There were always fights in prison and bloodletting was a common occurrence. Quite by chance, Jacob found he had an affinity for healing his fellow inmates and even though he only had basic first aid supplies available, the men began to seek him out. Word soon got around about his interest and aptitude for medicine and the warden paid him a visit. Jacob had expected the warden to forbid him from practicing his skills in the cells, but instead, the man surprised him by suggesting Jacob might want to study to become a doctor.

For a while, Jacob had dismissed the idea as ridiculous. It had never occurred to him when he was younger to seek a career in the medical profession. But that was before the night of November eighteenth; before his life spiraled out of control. Before his youthful dreams of following in his father's footsteps disintegrated into dust.

And now, eight years later, he was a well-respected emergency room doctor at one of Sydney's most illustrious hospitals—still yearning for something he couldn't have...

No, not something. Someone. Beautiful Hannah Langdon. She'd always been beyond his reach. And nothing had changed.

He wasn't kidding himself into believing she'd actually sought out his advice and help. She'd only told him about her concerns in an effort to stop him from kissing her. That was the sad and depressing truth. She'd wanted to distract him from his purpose, so she'd raised the possibility of devious and dangerous deeds. He was glad she had, because her concerns were valid, but it would have been nicer if she'd opened up to him for other reasons and at a slightly more convenient time.

Still, she'd talked to him about it and he now had an excuse to call her. Lane had filled him in on the background checks Lane had run on the

Grace men. Jacob could reassure her she had nothing to fear from either of them.

He tugged out his cell and scrolled through his contacts. He'd saved her number when Toby had called him from her phone. Now, a surge of nervous excitement went through him at the thought of speaking to her again. It didn't seem to matter that his feelings weren't reciprocated. He was happy to have contact with her on whatever terms he could—and that was just plain sad and pathetic.

He'd do better to concentrate his efforts on someone like Bridget Alexander. It was obvious the cute nurse was interested and she'd be a helluva lot easier to date than Hannah Langdon, with all the tumultuous history they shared.

But that was the problem. Bridget was friendly and attractive, yet he wasn't in love with her and could never imagine being so. His heart had been snagged by a blond, blue-eyed teenager who had a smile full of sunshine and warmth. Though it would be kinder if he'd matured out of it, nothing had changed over the intervening decade, not even after a two-year stint in jail.

With a sigh of resignation, Jacob pushed the memories aside and dialed Hannah's number.

———————————

Hannah leaned over the balcony of her eighth floor apartment and stared at the twinkling lights below. The cool night air brought with it the scent of orange blossoms and the occasional gust of exhaust fumes. It had been a busy day at work. Three members of the same family had been killed in a car accident a few days earlier. All three had arrived at the funeral home.

It had been sad, but oddly comforting to prepare them for their final resting places. One of the victims had been a child. Hannah had been a little nervous about how Toby might cope with carrying out the embalming procedure with a young person, but he'd been almost awestruck at the honor of being part of the tragic event.

Hannah was touched by the way he felt. She was always humbled when entrusted with such an important task, but not everyone got it like she did. Toby was special and unique and was fast becoming a valuable member of her team. Not even Christopher or Edward had been as sensitive to the needs of the dead.

Poor Edward. Nobody deserved to die like that, alone in a dark stairwell. She wondered if Lane had found anything unusual during his routine checks. She was sure if anything untoward was happening, Bobby would be the one involved. There was something about him that set her on edge, something she didn't trust.

And then there was his attitude toward his uncle. The disrespect he showed Max just ate at her gut. It wasn't right that Bobby scorned the only person who'd been willing to help him get back on his feet. According to Max, if he hadn't helped his nephew out, the man would have ended up on the street, like Toby, or in jail...like Jacob.

Her phone pealed in the stillness, startling her. She picked it up from the low table where she'd set her drink. Glancing at the screen, her heart skipped a beat.

Jacob.

It was almost as if he had a sixth sense, that he knew she'd been thinking about him. When she answered the call, her voice hitched slightly with nerves.

"H-hello?"

"Hannah, it's Jacob. I hope it's not too late to call?"

Flustered, she glanced at her watch. A little past nine. Late for some people, but not for her. She rarely went to bed before eleven.

"No, of course not. You're fine. What did you find out?"

"Not much, I'm afraid. Lane ran both names through the police database. Max didn't even have a parking ticket. Robert's police record was a little more interesting, but I don't think he's up to anything that should concern you. Certainly not murder."

Hannah frowned at the discovery Bobby had a police record, although she wasn't really surprised. Max had intimated, more than once, his nephew had struggled with a drug addiction.

"Were his arrests drug related?" she asked, curious.

"A few. Not all."

Hannah's frown deepened. "Wow, how many did he have?" she said, half-laughing.

"I'm not sure, exactly. From what Lane said, I

gather Robert Grace is well known to police."

"Did Lane give you any more information? What other kinds of things was Bobby charged with?"

"Some stealing offenses, things of that nature."

"Like stealing a few packets of gum from the local supermarket, or something more serious?"

"What does it matter?"

Hannah frowned again over Jacob's laissez faire attitude. *Why was he downplaying Bobby's crimes? And why the hell should he care what things were on the man's record?* He didn't even know the guy. She drew in a deep breath and continued.

"The thing is, you told me you think Bobby's not up to anything dangerously suspicious and yet you've confirmed he has an extensive record. I'm just curious as to why you think Bobby's innocent of wrongdoing here. Max showed me the insurance policy. From what you've told me, it's obvious Bobby has a contempt for the law. You've admitted he has some convictions for dishonesty. Who's to say he isn't behind some elaborate fraud? Or worse?" She paused and collected her thoughts.

"Last night, you said the whole thing sounded suspicious. Two employees die of accidental deaths within weeks of one another and one of their colleagues just happens to have an insurance policy in their name. Who's to say there wasn't another one in Christopher Lowrey's name, or your brother's? Perhaps Bobby was involved in both of their deaths and Max just hasn't found the proof?"

Hannah's breath was coming fast. She was a little surprised at how quickly her thoughts had carried her away, but what if her suspicions were correct? What if Bobby was involved in something as awful as murder? *And what was with Jacob?* Why was he coming to Bobby's defense? The whole thing had suddenly gotten very weird.

———

Hannah's questions hammered into Jacob's head, coming with relentless speed. *He had to tell her.* He had to give her the reason why he was certain The Bobster couldn't be involved. For all his faults and failings, The Bobster wasn't a murderer. Jacob would bet everything he owned on that.

Drawing in a deep breath, he eased it out between lips that were suddenly dry. He had no way of knowing how Hannah would react to what he was about to say. He wished he could see her face, to gauge her reaction, but it was late and he was at home. He presumed she was, too.

"Talk to me, Jacob. It's not adding up. You know something more. *Tell* me."

The quiet insistence in her voice did him in. "All right," he murmured. "But not over the phone. I'm afraid I've had one beer too many to drive. I could catch a cab and meet you somewhere in the city. Or—"

"I'll come over," Hannah interrupted and then laughed a little nervously.

Jacob could tell she was as surprised by her offer as he was. "Okay," he said. "If you're sure."

"Yes, I'm sure, Toby's in bed. Text me your address details. Toby already told me you live somewhere near the hospital. Give me thirty minutes."

CHAPTER 13

Hannah flicked her hair over her shoulder and swiped her sweaty palms down the legs of her jeans. Traffic was heavier than she'd anticipated and it had taken her over forty-five minutes to get to Jacob's apartment. Now that she'd arrived, she couldn't help but wonder what she was doing there. She'd refused to weigh the pros and cons on the drive over, but now that she was standing in the foyer of his building, the reasons why this wasn't a good idea hit her like a sledgehammer.

She had to be blind and stupid not to see that Jacob liked her. He'd kissed her at the ball and might have kissed her again at her condo the night of his birthday—if she'd let him. The fact was, she'd panicked and blurted her worries about work as a way to get the hell out of the situation before it went too far. But now she'd come to visit him in his home and listen to him reveal some deep, dark secret.

It went beyond being polite and extending the

hand of friendship to an old acquaintance. She was about to knock on his door at nearly ten o'clock at night. Only close friends did that kind of thing and she'd never describe her current relationship with Jacob that way.

Coming to a sudden decision, she turned on her heel and took a step toward the exit. The *ding* of the elevator sounded behind her. A second later, she heard the doors slide apart. She was reaching for the door that led out of the building when Jacob said, "Where are you going? You only just got here."

She pulled up short and cursed silently. She should have known he'd be watching out for her.

"I saw your vehicle pull up. I came down to meet you," he said, stepping off the elevator.

Turning to face him, she offered a tight smile. "How did you know it was me?"

He grinned. "That's easy. It's the same car you drove to the Thai restaurant. A white Mazda3 Hatchback. I also noticed it parked on the curb outside your apartment complex."

She nodded, secretly impressed with his powers of observation. "You've missed your calling," she said and then immediately regretted her words.

Shadows chased themselves across his face. She bit her lip. "I'm sorry, Jacob. I didn't mean to remind you of..." She shrugged, feeling helpless.

"Of everything I've lost?" He grimaced. "Is that what you were going to say?"

Heat infused her cheeks, but she bravely held his gaze. "No. Yes. I mean... You've told me how much it meant to you to become a police officer." Her voice hitched. "You... You would have made a good one."

He smiled, but it didn't reach his eyes. "I guess we'll never know."

She stared at him, hating the hurt and disappointment that clouded the brilliant blue of his eyes. Eyes that were identical in color to his twin's. But that's where the similarity ended.

Where Toby's eyes were clear and bright and most of the time sparkled with a child-like innocence, Jacob's were more often shadowed and troubled, concealing more than they revealed. She was startled to discover she longed for him to tell her his secrets.

"Are you coming up?"

His deep voice broke into her musings. Once again, her gaze found his. He eyed her solemnly. Wariness and hope warred on his face.

"Of course," she heard herself saying and noticed the relief that flooded his face.

"Great," he laughed and punched the button for the elevator.

She lifted an eyebrow in silent query. "What, the brilliant, athletic doctor doesn't take the stairs?"

He sent her a droll look. "I live on the fifth floor. You look fit enough to take the stairs, but I'm going to take the easy way up. It's been a long, hard day."

Hannah laughed softly and a moment later, followed him into the elevator. A nervous silence fell between them and she was glad when they arrived at their destination.

Jacob's apartment was modest, but nicely

furnished with pieces he'd obviously selected with care. The overall color scheme was rich browns and oranges with a splash of red and yellow thrown in. An expensive-looking leather couch sat in front of a large, curved screen TV. She wondered if it was the same one he'd won at the auction. A kitchen and breakfast bar filled the rest of the small space. Several large, framed pictures were aligned neatly on the far wall. She wandered closer for a better look and was surprised to discover they were photographs of bull riders.

"You like the rodeo?" she asked, a small smile tugging at her lips.

Jacob looked a little embarrassed, but smiled back. "Yes, as a matter of fact, I do."

Hannah turned back to the photos. "Who's JB Mauney?" she asked, pointing to the inscription below at least two of the pictures.

Jacob moved closer until he stood beside her. He stared at the photos a moment before responding.

"James Burton Mauney is an American professional bull rider. He's number one in the world. He won the title in 2013 and again in 2015. It's not even halfway through the year yet, but he looks set to win it again—and all before his thirtieth birthday."

He spoke with pride and passion, as if he'd played a personal part in the man's success. Hannah was intrigued. "What got you interested in bull riding?"

Jacob shrugged and looked down at his boots.

"My dad, I guess. I was only three when he died, so I don't really have any memory of him, but Mom used to tell us stories all the time about how Dad used to love bull riding. Apparently, he was quite competitive in his younger days, but his heart was set on being a police officer, so he didn't have the drive required to become a professional."

For a moment, Jacob's face took on a faraway look. "Mom used to tell us how Dad would sit for hours in front of the TV when the tournaments were on. He had a collection of hundreds of videos of various professional American bullriding championships, filmed over the course of more than a decade. Back then, his favorite rider was Lane Frost."

Hannah smiled in surprise. "I remember that name. There was a movie made about his life. He died from injuries sustained while in the bullring, didn't he?"

"Yes," Jacob replied softly. "Dad named my brother Lane after him."

A moment of silence fell between them. Hannah broke it quietly. "Do any of you ride?"

Jacob shook his head. "No. There was never enough money for extra things like bullriding lessons, or even going to the shows, but I like to go to the rodeo whenever it's in town. It kind of helps me feel connected to the Dad I never knew."

His gaze slid to a couple of smaller framed photos that stood on a bookshelf a little further along the wall. Hannah followed his gaze. The photos showed a man standing with his hands on his narrow hips in the bullring, a cheeky grin on his lips. On his head, sat a tall, black Stetson. He looked enough like Jacob to be his father.

"Your dad?" she asked gently.

"Yes. Warren Black. Mom said he was about nineteen in this picture." Jacob picked it up and looked at it. The ghost of a smile drifted across his face. "Mom gave me Dad's hat."

He lifted his head and Hannah followed his gaze. Above the low bookcase was a black hat on a peg affixed to the wall. It looked identical to the one in the photo. Hannah wondered why it hadn't been given to Lane. After all, he was the oldest son and the one named after the bull rider.

"Mom gave it to me the day I was taken to prison," Jacob said softly, as if reading her mind. "She thought it would help me get through it, to know that Dad was close. I was lucky that the warden let me keep it."

At the reminder of their shared history, Hannah took a step back. She'd spent a decade hating this man and everything that he'd done. She didn't want to feel empathy for him, she didn't want to let her anger go. She didn't want to like him...and yet, she did.

With a sudden surge of irritation, she turned away from the pictures and strode over to the breakfast bar. It was late and she hadn't come over for this. She didn't want to know any more about him than she did already. It was past time to remember that.

"You were going to explain why you're so certain Bobby Grace isn't a threat to anyone at work."

Jacob's eyebrows rose at her abrupt change in topic, but he nodded and replied. "Yes."

Hannah looked at him expectantly, waiting for him to continue. When he didn't, she prompted him. "So?"

With a heavy sigh, he headed over to a small bar, partially hidden behind a large potted plant. "This discussion calls for another drink. Would you like one?"

"A beer would be great, thanks," she replied.

He pulled open the door of a bar fridge and came out with two bottles of beer. Twisting the top off one, he handed it to her, before heading over to the couch. Taking a healthy swallow, he leaned his head back against the soft cushion and sighed again.

Nerves edged their way along Hannah's spine. It was obvious whatever Jacob was about to say wasn't going to be easy. All of a sudden, she wondered if she was ready to hear it. Then she thought about Max and Bobby and Toby and knew she had to know why Jacob had dismissed Bobby as a threat. She didn't want to wait for another colleague to go missing or wind up dead. Her first thoughts might not be right, but something was going on at the funeral home and she needed to find out what.

"Take a seat," Jacob offered quietly and then added, "I promise, I won't bite."

Heat crept up Hannah's neck and spread across her cheeks. It wasn't that she didn't want to sit next to him. It was just that...

She wasn't quite sure what it was that held her

back. She inched toward the couch and perched at one end.

Jacob flashed her a knowing grin, but she didn't smile back. Let him think what he liked. It didn't matter to her. She was there to get answers. If it wasn't Bobby behind the awful deaths, she needed to dig deeper. As if sensing her impatience, Jacob began to speak.

"I went to jail for driving in a manner dangerous and causing death, less than six months after I turned eighteen. I was a high school graduate with the world at my feet. And then that night in November happened and my life was turned upside down. In the eyes of the law, I was an adult. I was taken to an adult jail."

He drew in a breath and then continued. "The first night I spent in jail, I cried myself to sleep. My throat was parched, my gut was tight and totally knotted up with fear. I didn't eat the meal they offered. I could barely respond to their questions. All I could think about was how the hell I was going to spend the next two years inside."

Hannah's heart clenched in sympathy, but she forced her expression to remain neutral. He was well aware she knew he'd done time in jail. For years—maybe even still—she'd been convinced two years hadn't been enough.

"My cellmate was another teen who went by the name of The Bobster. He towered over me and outweighed me by nearly fifty pounds and I was no lightweight. He told me once his grandfather had been a Maori warrior and though inmates told lies about themselves all the time, it was easy to believe his story was true. Everyone on D Block was afraid of him, even the older men.

"I don't know why he befriended me. He never asked for anything in return. We just kind of clicked, even though we had nothing in common, apart from a shared cell. The Bobster had done it tough over the years he'd been growing up. His father had abandoned both him and his mother before The Bobster was born. His mother struggled to make ends meet. There was never enough to go round. He learned from an early age to supplement what they had."

"By stealing," Hannah guessed.

Jacob nodded. "Yes, by stealing. At first it was food and shoes and clothing, but it soon escalated to much more expensive things. By the time he was thirteen, he had a lengthy criminal record. At sixteen, he stole a motor vehicle and drove to the next town. He broke into an electrical goods store and filled the trunk with DVD players, boom boxes and TVs. He put them up on eBay and made a tidy profit."

"What did he do with the money?" Hannah asked, hoping he'd used it to help support his mother.

"Somewhere along the line, he'd been introduced to drugs. By the time he was sixteen, he was a full-blown addict. Methamphetamines, mostly. It was cheaper than some of the other stuff and readily available."

Hannah sighed, disheartened. She should have known.

"Eventually, the police caught up with him. It

was only a matter of time. His criminal behavior had escalated to feed his drug habit. It's a vicious cycle and unfortunately, it happens all the time. I see enough of it in the emergency department—crack heads, ice addicts, people hooked on heroin. They're sad and desperate and many of them know they're cutting their lives short, but they can't stop."

"They don't call it an addiction for nothing," Hannah commented quietly.

She felt sorry for the kind of people Jacob described and was grateful her parents had steered her through those dangerous times when she was a teenager and far more easily influenced by her peers.

"You're right and I understand too well their need to fight, to steal, to do whatever it takes to get their next fix. The Bobster told me about it. Before his last jail sentence, he was exactly like that."

"So, he got clean in prison?"

"Kind of. It was more or less forced upon him. Though drugs are easy to come by in prison, they come with a hefty price. The Bobster didn't have any money and no one to bring it in. By that time, his mother was living in a hostel, barely able to look after herself. The only thing he could bargain with was his brawn."

Hannah tensed, not at all sure she liked the direction the story was heading. She wanted to tell Jacob to stop, but she couldn't. She had no choice. She needed to listen to the end.

"Inmates would pay him to take their beatings

in lieu of them taking the beatings themselves. It was a barbaric system, but it worked. Weaker inmates weren't beaten senseless and The Bobster got access to cash. It was never enough to buy drugs in the quantities he was used to, but it was something—enough for him to get by."

"What about the punishment he took? Was he ever seriously hurt?"

"Absolutely. More times than not. Notwithstanding his enormous size, The Bobster had a soft heart. He wasn't violent or aggressive, despite what people thought. He'd take the beating without flinching or fighting back because that's the way he was. He figured if his opponent finished the fight feeling justified and pleased with the outcome, it would bring an end to it. At least, between those particular combatants. What he hadn't figured on was more and more inmates coming to his door, wanting him to stand in their place."

Hannah shuddered. "It sounds brutal."

Jacob nodded. "It was, especially for The Bobster. There were many times when I patched up his wounds and bought pain medication and other first aid equipment on the prison black market."

Hannah shook her head in confusion. "What about the prison infirmary? Surely he was taken there when necessary?"

Jacob shook his head. "Not always. Sometimes they were already full and other times, The Bobster just didn't want to go. He was so sore and hurt, he just wanted to stay on his bed and let his wounds heal with time. He was usually bruised from head to toe. The screws got good at looking the other way."

"Is that how you became interested in medicine?"

"Yes. My criminal record meant entering the police service was no longer an option. The Bobster encouraged me to look at other things. It was the least of the things he did for me."

Hannah's gaze flew to his. There was something in his quiet, somber tone that caught her attention and filled her stomach with dread. She barely dared to voice the question.

"Did he… Did he ever take a beating for you?"

He closed his eyes and his shoulders slumped. A moment later, he looked at her and slowly nodded. "Yes."

"W-what happened?"

Jacob laughed without humor. "It usually didn't take much for someone to take offense in the big house and demand retribution. I got distracted in the dining hall one evening and collided with an inmate by the name of Mean Joe. His mashed potato went flying halfway across the room. He wore most of his plate of stew.

"The room erupted into laughter. Mean Joe screamed and came at me like a wounded bull. He got two or three punches in before the screws pulled him off me, but I knew it wasn't over. Nobody humiliated Mean Joe like that and got away with it, even if it was accidental."

"So, you went to your cellmate," Hannah guessed.

Jacob shook his head. "No. I'd lain awake far too many nights, listening to The Bobster's labored breathing after he'd been beaten by someone or other, and I'd patched up enough of his wounds. I didn't want him hurting more over me. It was *my* fight. I should have been more careful, watched where I was going." He paused and then added quietly, "The Bobster didn't see it that way.

"He told me about Mean Joe and how the man had a reputation for fighting dirty. The last time he'd been in a fight, he'd beaten someone nearly to death. It was only that the screws intervened just in time to save the poor bastard's life, but the guy he beat up will spend the rest of his life in a wheelchair, drinking his meals through a straw."

Jacob sighed. "The Bobster told me this and insisted I couldn't fight Mean Joe. He was convinced I wouldn't get out of it alive. Mean Joe was bigger and heavier and his heart was as black as the night.

"I didn't want The Bobster to take the beating in my place. I was worried he'd be killed, like he was worried for me. But it didn't matter what I said to him, he refused to change his mind. The fight was arranged without my knowledge. The first thing I knew about it was when I was told The Bobster was in the infirmary."

Jacob's voice cracked and his eyes filled with pain. Hannah's stomach clenched with dread and emotion burned behind her eyes. Her fingers tightened around her bottle of beer. As much as she didn't want to feel sorry for the men who were forced to live that way, she couldn't help but feel their pain way down deep inside.

"What happened?" she asked softly, barely daring to breathe.

Jacob leaned forward and rested his elbows on his thighs. His head drooped. "Mean Joe came armed with a weapon. It wasn't just fists that time. He took to The Bobster with a knife that had been made from a toothbrush. My cellmate was carved up."

"Oh, my goodness," Hannah gasped, once again covering her face. She forced herself to ask the question. "Did he... Did he survive?"

"Yes, but barely. He was never quite the same after that. The inmates left him alone. He'd fought enough of their fights."

"What about you? I can't even imagine how you must have felt."

"No. You can't."

He sat back against the couch, but kept his face averted. Hannah could only guess what memories were tracking their way through his head. A long while later, she broke the silence.

"I'm so grateful that you've shared this with me, but I'm still not sure what it has to do with work."

Jacob turned his head to face her, his expression solemn. "The Bobster is Bobby Grace."

Hannah gasped in shock. Her hand flew to cover her mouth. "You shared a cell with *Bobby Grace?*"

"Yes. Although I didn't know that was his name until Lane told me this afternoon."

Hannah squeezed her eyes shut for a moment,

trying to take it all in. The man she'd disliked almost on sight was Jacob's hero, the man who'd saved his life. She could hardly reconcile that with her knowledge of Max's nephew. She could only assume Bobby's life outside of prison had once again spiraled down into drugs.

From what Max had told her, Bobby was a full-on addict when he came across him in a shelter. It was only because Max had kept tabs on his younger sister—Bobby's mother—that he even knew where Bobby was. It was then that he'd offered his nephew a job and a place to stay. In return, Bobby had promised to get clean and remain that way. Hannah wasn't certain Bobby had kept his part of the bargain.

"So," Jacob said quietly, "now you know why I don't think Bobby Grace is behind the wrongful deaths—if they *are* wrongful deaths. As far as we know, both deaths were ruled accidental."

"Yes, you're right," Hannah replied. "From what you've told me, I can't imagine Bobby being the one to murder Christopher and Edward for insurance money. It seems so cold and calculating and totally without heart. It doesn't sound anything like the Bobby you described. He's far from perfect, but somewhere beneath his imperfections, I realize now he has a lovely soul."

Jacob stared at her, his eyes shadowed with emotion. "That's a nice way of saying it and it sums up The Bobster well. He didn't go out of his way to harm people, even though he had the wherewithal to do it."

Hannah sighed. "So, where does that leave us?

If he wasn't involved, why would Bobby own an insurance policy on Edward's life?"

"I'm not sure. I guess I could ask Lane to dig a little more and see what he can find. He has access to a whole lot more databases than we do and given what we know, I think we need to find out who's at the bottom of this."

Hannah nodded grimly. "I agree. I can't help feeling like something's not quite right and until I'm completely satisfied my colleagues' deaths were accidental, I'm afraid I'm not going to sleep very well at night."

"Are you worried about your safety?" Jacob asked quietly.

She shrugged. "Not so much mine. It's your brother I'm more concerned about. He fits the profile of the others. Max found Christopher and Edward living on the streets. He befriended them and offered them a job. Both of them loved working at the funeral home. They were nice guys, down on their luck. They were my friends. Just like Toby. And Toby mentioned an insurance policy... I want to make sure nothing happens to him."

Jacob moved closer on the couch. She could see the dark flecks in his blue eyes.

"You're the one with the lovely soul, Hannah Langdon," he whispered.

She stared at him and her heart kicked up a gear. He was close enough that if she reached out the tiniest distance, she could touch the sleeve of his shirt. He leaned forward until his lips were inches from hers...and then he was kissing her.

Warm and pliant, his lips moved over hers, slowly, hesitantly, as if feeling their way. The dark stubble that shadowed his cheek scratched her face, but she barely noticed. He tasted of warm male and yeasty beer. And then his hand came up to cradle the back of her head and even through the pleasure, panic settled in. With a gasp, she wrenched away.

"Stop! Please, don't kiss me. I don't want you to kiss me."

Jacob stared at her, his eyes tumultuous with confusion and need. "That's not what it felt like."

Hannah sprang up from the couch and put some distance between them. She crossed her arms over her chest.

"I'm sorry, I... I know I probably gave you the wrong idea. I shouldn't have ever let it go that far. The thing is, I've spent so long hating you, blaming you... I... I can't just let it go."

"Why not?"

The question was asked softly and it was like he'd stabbed her through the heart. *How could she explain to him what had happened to her the night he'd stolen her boyfriend's life?* Luke had been her one and only true love. From the moment they'd met, she knew she'd love him until the end of time.

Okay, Jacob had suffered too, and she hadn't thought about that over the years. It killed her to listen to his stories, but he was the drunk who'd climbed behind the wheel. *Surely he understood how she felt?*

"Something inside me died the night Luke was

killed," she said quietly. "He was my first love, my true love. He was my present, my future, my everything. And he loved me just the same. He was the captain of the rowing team, he could have had any girl he chose. And he chose me. He chose *me*.

"And it wasn't for sex, like some of my girlfriends insisted. They were sure he was only after one thing. They'd heard stories about how guys would pretend to be in love and as soon as the girl slept with them, he wouldn't give them the time of day."

She paused and took a couple of breaths, slowing down her heart rate. Jacob stared at her, his expression unreadable.

"But it wasn't like that with Luke and me," she continued. "We were still kids, but our love was real. It wasn't all about sex. Of course, we both wanted to, but we'd promised to remain pure until we were old enough to marry. It would be our gift to each other. It was one of the reasons we couldn't wait to get married. And then that night in November happened and the nightmare began..."

Jacob stared down at his feet, his face set in hard lines. A pang of sympathy went through her, but she stood her ground.

"I'm not trying to dredge up the past and all that followed, but nothing can change the facts. The truth is, you were drunk when you ran off the road and slammed into a tree, killing Luke instantly. There's no forgetting that. You ask too much of me to expect that I can."

He lifted his head, desolation stark on his face. She stood stiff and silent, helpless to alleviate his suffering. She was suffering, too. She couldn't help him. She just couldn't take that on.

"I'm sorry, Jacob..." Turning on her heel, she strode to the breakfast bar and collected her handbag where she'd left it and then headed toward the door. He half-stood, but she held up a hand.

"No, please. Don't say anything. Don't do anything. I need to go. I just...need to go."

CHAPTER 14

The squad room buzzed with the usual morning activity. Lane ended the call to his brother and dropped his phone back in his shirt pocket. Dragging his keyboard closer, he was filled with a surge of anticipation. Jacob had called him to ask if he could dig a little deeper into the people who worked at the Max Grace Funeral Home and Lane was glad his brother had reconsidered.

Despite Jacob's insistence that it wasn't Robert Grace who was behind the strange happenings at the funeral home, Lane wasn't so quick to dismiss the man. He'd taken a closer look at Robert Grace's criminal record. The entries dated back to when he was only a kid. At nine and ten years of age, he was being arrested regularly for petty theft and occasionally an assault. The victims were mostly other kids. Other than the list of charges and punishments handed out, there were no specific details of any of the crimes.

The offenses grew in frequency and severity

until Robert Grace was often spending a month or two in juvenile detention. Many of the later charges were drug related. Eventually, he turned eighteen and found himself in adult prisons where he would have come into contact with much more hardened criminals. Lane knew all too well that instead of steering inmates in the right direction, incarceration often had the opposite effect.

In Lane's experience, a criminal with the kind of lengthy record like Robert Grace didn't just stop committing crimes when they were released. There was ample evidence over the course of Robert's life that even in between his stints in jail, he'd continued to break the law.

There was no indication that anything had broken the depressing pattern that had repeated itself over and over during the course of Robert's life. Recidivism had always been a problem for people who'd spent substantial time in jail. It was almost as if incarceration spurred them on to greater heights—resulting in much worse deeds. Looking at Robert Grace's record, it was clear he supported that sad statistic.

Of course, it wasn't always like that. Jacob was a prime example. He'd studied hard in prison and had turned his life around. He'd risen above the pack. But Jacob was an exception and he hadn't come to prison from a life of crime. A stupid decision on a night out with his friends had set the wheels in motion and could have been enough to ruin his life. Lane had nothing but admiration for his younger brother and the way he'd conducted himself since. As a police officer, he knew better than most that it hadn't been easy.

The first name he entered into the search field of the police database was Edward Sutton's. Lane scanned the police report that had been made on the man's death. Preliminary autopsy findings were also attached. The coroner had come to the conclusion that Sutton died from a subarachnoid hemorrhage that had occurred as a result of a direct impact to his skull. The police report concluded that Sutton had been drunk and fallen down the stairs and hit his head on the concrete landing.

It sounded reasonable enough. Lane flicked back to the autopsy report and checked the blood results. Sutton's blood alcohol concentration at the time of death was 0.25. Lane frowned. The reading was extraordinarily high. In fact, he couldn't help but wonder how on earth Sutton had been able to stand, let alone climb up a set of stairs... Could he have had assistance? *Had someone else been there that night?*

Opening another screen, Lane typed in Christopher Lowrey's name and clicked on the file. Once again, the autopsy report indicated high alcohol levels in Lowrey's blood, despite the fact the death was also ruled accidental.

According to Jacob, the men had been "rescued" by the owner of the funeral home and had apparently turned their lives around. This wasn't reflected in the fact they were both found dead in the early hours of the morning, so drunk they should have died from alcohol poisoning before they fell. Lane wondered why the coroner hadn't flagged the anomaly.

Dragging the phone on his desk toward him, Lane dialed the number of the Glebe Morgue. With a bit of luck, Samantha Coleridge might be in.

"Glebe Morgue."

"It's Detective Senior Sergeant Lane Black of the State Crime Command. I was wondering if I could speak with Doctor Coleridge?"

"Hold the line, please."

A moment later, the phone was answered by Samantha. "Lane, what a surprise. I hope you had a good night at the ball."

"Yes," he replied. "It was nice catching up with you and Rohan again. How are you doing? Feeling better?"

"Great. Still suffering from morning sickness for most of the day and night, but I keep telling myself the end result will be worth it."

She chuckled and Lane laughed with her, thinking of Zara and their twins. "You're right," he said. "It's definitely all worthwhile."

"Easy for you to say," Samantha replied good-naturedly.

"Absolutely," Lane readily agreed. "Hang in there. That's all I can say."

"What can I do for you?" Samantha asked, changing the subject.

Lane sobered. "I'm wondering if I can speak to you about a couple of post mortem reports. One was carried out on a guy by the name of Christopher Lowrey. The other guy's name was Edward Sutton."

"Sure. I assume they were done here?"

"Yes. Lowrey fell into the path of a truck about six weeks ago. Sutton was found dead in a stairwell three weeks later."

"Who did the PMs?"

Lane scrolled the cursor back through the report. "Doctor Charles Venutti."

"I see."

Samantha's measured response piqued Lane's interest. "What's that supposed to mean?"

"Nothing. What do you need to know?"

"Sutton's autopsy listed the official cause of death as being from a brain hemorrhage. His blood alcohol reading was well off the charts. He apparently fell down the stairs and hit his head. Lowrey had similar pathology. I'm wondering if the pathologist ever considered the affect the alcohol would have had on the ability of these men to walk, let alone anything else."

"Give me a minute and I'll pull up the report. Do you have full names and dates of birth?"

Lane gave her the information. He heard the clicking sound of keys on a keyboard. A few moments later, Samantha sighed.

"You're right. These guys should have been passed out on a sidewalk, not crossing streets and climbing stairs. That should have been noted in the report as an abnormality."

Lane frowned. "Why do you think it wasn't?"

Samantha sighed again. "I shouldn't be telling you this, but the thing is, Charles has been struggling through some personal issues the last couple of months. I'm not sure that his head or his heart is focused on the job. The boss has suggested he take some personal leave, but Charles has insisted his family troubles aren't having an impact on his work." She paused and then added, "It looks like that's not the case. I wonder how many more there are. We're going to have to review all his cases..."

Her voice drifted off. Lane could only imagine the additional workload such a thing would cause her and the other forensic pathologists who worked at the Glebe Morgue. Still, she'd managed to give credence to his theory that Edward Sutton might not have climbed the steps alone. It wasn't too much of a stretch to consider he might have also received assistance on the way down.

Such a possibility wouldn't have seemed worthy of so much consideration if there wasn't a life insurance policy floating around. Five-hundred-thousand dollars was a lot of money. A lot of reasons to do away with someone. Especially if you were confident you could get away with it. *What better victim to target than a man who was homeless and presumably without a supportive family network?*

A sudden thought occurred to him. "Who took delivery of the body?" he asked.

"Give me a minute and I'll check."

Lane heard more keys clacking and then Samantha spoke again. "He's still here."

Lane frowned. "What do you mean?"

"I mean, he's still in the fridge."

Lane started in surprise. "Really? Isn't that unusual?"

"A little," Samantha admitted, "but if the deceased has no next of kin or other family to claim the body, it remains here much longer. Sutton only came in three weeks ago. If he has no one around to retrieve his body from the morgue, we'll keep him here until someone comes forward."

"For how long?" Lane asked, intrigued.

"It can be as long as six months. The police look at his personal records, for example, bank accounts, tax records and the like, to establish if there is any next of kin."

"What happens then, if no one comes forward?"

"He becomes what we call a destitute case. The state pays for a burial or a cremation. It's organized by the police. The body's removed by the contracted funeral director."

"I hate to ask this of you, Samantha, but is it possible you could redo the autopsy? I'm curious about Sutton's wounds. Along with the fractured skull, Venutti's report referenced several other broken bones and contusions. I'm curious about what you might make of them."

"Are you suspecting foul play, Detective?"

Lane considered her question and then answered honestly. "At this stage, I'm not sure, but someone took out a life insurance policy on at least one of our guys. If nothing else, it provides *that someone* with motive."

"But wouldn't that someone come forward and claim the body?" Samantha asked. "To claim on the life insurance policy they'll need a death certificate and in order to get one of those, they'll have to provide evidence that they're related to the deceased, or somehow otherwise entitled to it, if they're not. Not everybody has the right to apply. Having proof that they claimed the body for burial would aid their application if the person processing it was less than diligent and took the information at face value. Do you know if a claim's been made on the policy?"

"Not yet. I haven't gone that far with my enquires. I wanted to talk to you first about the autopsy report and whether my suspicions might be justified. If the death continues to be ruled accidental, then the investigation comes to an end."

Samantha sighed. "Okay, okay. I hear you. I'll reschedule the PM as soon as I can."

Lane was filled with gratitude and relief. "Thank you, Samantha. I really appreciate it. If your conclusion concurs with Venutti's, I'll have wasted your time and for that, I'll be sorry."

"You're just being thorough, Detective and I respect that. If there's a chance this poor guy could have been murdered, homeless or not, he deserves for us to know the truth."

Once again, Lane was filled with gratitude. "Thank you for your understanding, Samantha. It makes things a little easier knowing we're both on the same side."

"You're just doing your job, Lane. Too bad everyone isn't as devoted to the cause."

She said it lightly, but Lane was certain she was referring to her colleague and the additional work he'd now generated. While Lane sympathized, he was relieved she'd agreed to do the post mortem again.

A sudden thought occurred to him. "Can a funeral director apply for a death certificate on behalf of the family?"

"Yes, of course. It often happens that way. The funeral director does it as part of his service to the family. It's done for compassionate reasons, so that the family doesn't have to fill in the blanks on the form. Naturally, there's an additional fee involved."

"What happens to the certificate once it's been received by the funeral home?"

"It's handed over to the family or, in the case where a lawyer has been engaged to administer the estate, it would be delivered to the legal counsel."

Lane absorbed her information and nodded to himself. After thanking her again and asking her to pass on his best wishes to Rohan, he ended the call. Leaning back, he blew out his breath. A moment later, he pushed back his chair and strode down the short corridor to his boss' office. Detective Superintendent Bruce Mitchell looked up as Lane entered.

"Lane, you're looking a little disheveled. Another bad night with the twins?"

The question was asked matter-of-factly and Lane knew Mitchell wasn't looking for a response. The superintendent was a damned good cop, but he had little time or interest in chit chat.

"What can I do for you?" he added.

"I had a call from my brother. He's a doctor at the Sydney Harbour Hospital."

Mitchell shot him a look and Lane got to the point. "My brother has some concerns about the deaths of two employees of a funeral home in Balmain. In particular, the most recent death of Edward Sutton, which occurred about three weeks ago."

Mitchell frowned. "People die all the time. What's so special about these two?"

Lane held his gaze. "For a start, the deaths occurred only three weeks apart and both of them were ruled accidental."

"How did they die?"

"One stepped off a road into the path of a semi. The other one fell down the stairs. I've pulled up the files and looked at the autopsy reports. I've found enough discrepancies to raise a few questions, including the existence of a life insurance policy on one of the men. The policy was owned by the nephew of the owner of the funeral home where the men worked."

Lane drew in a breath and continued. "I've spoken to Samantha Coleridge at the morgue. She concurred the initial findings for both men might not be accurate." Lane grimaced. "They're having a few staffing problems of their own, if you get my drift. Fortunately for us, Edward Sutton is still at the morgue. She's agreed to redo the post mortem."

"What about the other one?"

"He was buried six weeks ago. It will take a court order to have his body exhumed."

"And a lot more evidence of foul play," Mitchell said dryly.

"Yes, sir. If Samantha's findings contradict Edward Sutton's earlier autopsy report and she indicates the death wasn't accidental, together with the life insurance policy, it should be enough to commence a formal investigation into both of the deaths. Christopher Lowery was the first employee to die. I haven't yet made any enquires about the existence of an insurance policy connected to him, but if Samantha finds Sutton was murdered, it will be the first thing on my list."

Mitchell nodded thoughtfully. "Where did these deaths occur?" Mitchell asked.

"Darlinghurst," Lane replied, mentioning the inner-city suburb.

Mitchell shook his head. "Not our jurisdiction. Get the boys in the city on it. I'm sure they have nothing better to do," he added with a wry smile.

"Boss, I'd rather look into this myself, if I could. My younger brother works for the funeral home. He's a little naïve as far as people go and trusts way too easily. He told a colleague that during a standard medical arranged by his boss, the examining doctor mentioned the reason for the visit was for insurance purposes. On top of what we know, it seems a little strange. I want to make sure nothing untoward is going on."

Mitchell frowned. "I thought you said your brother was a doctor?"

"That's another one. I have three of them."

Mitchell smiled briefly. The action took years off

his face. "Three brothers," he murmured a little wistfully. "That must have been boisterous."

Unused to his boss making personal comments, Lane didn't reply. A moment later, Mitchell heaved a sigh. "What is it you want from me, Lane?"

Lane drew in a deep breath and plunged in. "I understand this isn't the kind of case we usually devote our time to, but we're pretty quiet in the office at the moment. I promise, if something comes in, I'll put this aside right away. I just want to dig a little deeper, ask a few more questions. Something about this whole thing doesn't sit right. Two deaths in less than a month, both of them strangely similar and both ruled accidental. Both men were drifters, with no family or fixed abode. Then there's the question of life insurance. Besides, the city boys are always run off their feet. They might not get to this for weeks."

Mitchell stared at him a moment longer and then gave a brisk nod. "All right, Lane. Why you care whether a couple of homeless drunks fell or were pushed is beyond me, but have it your way. It sounds like these deaths might need further investigation. Just don't let it interfere with your real work."

Lane grinned. "Thanks, boss. I appreciate your support. I'll keep you informed."

"Yeah, yeah, yeah," Mitchell grumbled. "Don't go out of your way. I have plenty more serious issues to concern myself with."

Lane headed back to his desk, filled with anticipation. Until he received Samantha's autopsy report, there was no proof anything illegal had occurred, but his cop senses were humming. He was sure the report would indicate foul play. Added to his innate desire to see justice served and remove a possible murderer off the street, there was the added urgency to this: His brother now worked at the funeral home. Lane needed to find out what was going on.

He hadn't been lying to his boss when he told him Toby trusted way too easily. He had the mental capacity of a ten-year-old. He relied on other people—and his family, in particular, to look out for him and Lane intended to put every effort into discovering what had gone down the night Edward Sutton died at the bottom of the stairs. If the evidence went the way his gut was telling him it would, Christopher Lowrey's death would receive his full attention.

CHAPTER 15

Hannah removed the trocar and tubing from the man who lay pale and still on the table and carried it, along with the suction pump, back to the sink.

"Are you ready for this?" Toby asked, holding up a jar of embalming fluid from the other side of the room.

"Yes, thanks. Can you bring it over to the table and make a start? I really need to use the bathroom."

Toby nodded, smiling brightly. It had been nearly a month since he'd started and his enthusiasm for the job hadn't waned. As he'd become more and more confident, Hannah gave him additional responsibilities. Soon, he'd be competent enough to attend to the embalming from start to finish on his own. Her job as mentor would be done.

She let herself out of the embalming room and headed down the short corridor to the staff restroom, her thoughts still on Toby. He was an easy student. Quick to learn and eager to please. He asked questions when he didn't understand something and never presumed he knew more than he did. It was a refreshing change from most of the assistants she'd had in the past.

Even Christopher and Edward had suffered from misplaced confidence. She remembered the time Edward had injected the wrong chemical into a body, mistaking it for formaldehyde. Though there was no harm done and Hannah was able to overcome the error, it was fortunate their clients weren't relying on her assistants to save their lives.

But Toby wasn't like that. He listened and observed and only attempted tasks once he was sure he knew what he was doing. He showed genuine care and respect for the people they labored over and for Hannah that was the most important thing.

With a flush of the toilet and a wash of her hands, she returned to the embalming room and stood by and watched while Toby injected liquid into the body cavities. Quietly and competently, he went about the task until it was finished. Setting the jar of liquid aside, he stared with fondness down at the man laid out before them.

"He sure had a decent head of hair," he commented with a rueful smile.

Hannah smiled back at him. Kevin Lamb was a man in his eighties who still sported a mass of tangled, white curls. The formaldehyde had begun to work its magic and had brought a little fullness to his cheeks. Tastefully applied makeup would have him looking as good as if he were asleep.

It would be a balm to the spirit of his loved ones, to see him looking so at peace. It was the kind of outcome she strove for every time she pulled on her gloves and it warmed her through and through to know that she'd found a kindred spirit in Jacob's twin.

At the thought of Jacob, her thoughts sobered. It had been two weeks since the evening at his apartment when he'd filled her in about prison and Bobby, and she hadn't heard from him. Not that she expected to. After making it clear she could never forgive and forget, she didn't presume to hear from him again. Though she'd given Toby a prepaid cell phone for his birthday and assumed he continued to speak with his twin, the communication between her and his brother had come to an abrupt halt.

It annoyed her to realize she accepted the reality of the situation with mixed emotions. On one level, she was relieved not to have to face Jacob again and deal with the hurt and anger and disappointment his presence seemed to bring. Then again, there had been something so lovely about being with him and knowing that he cared. It had been more than a decade since she'd felt cared for by a man.

"Why are you frowning, Hannah? Have I done something wrong?"

Toby's question snapped her back to the present. She blinked and noticed his concerned expression and hurried to reassure him.

"No, of course not. You're doing great. Kevin is lucky to have you attend to him today. You're doing him and his family proud."

Toby looked relieved. "Thank you, Hannah. You say the nicest things, but why are you frowning if I'm doing everything right?"

Hannah's shoulders slumped on a sigh. *What could she say to him?* Her dark thoughts were about his twin. The two brothers might have been estranged for a long time, but it had been obvious to Hannah each time she saw them together how much they cared about each other.

"N-nothing," she stammered, choosing to remain silent.

"Jake told me you paid him a visit a couple of weeks ago and you had an argument," Toby said, surprising her. "Why don't you like him?"

Her mouth fell open in shock. She couldn't believe Jacob had discussed her with his twin. Then again, they were twins. Now that they'd found each other again, they probably told each other everything.

"Who... Who says I don't like him?" she replied, buying time.

"No one, but when I asked Jake if he'd come around for dinner again, he told me about the argument. He said you found it hard to be his friend."

Toby glanced up at her and then quickly averted his gaze. "It's because of what happened in high school, isn't it?" he asked quietly.

Hannah was stricken with panic. *What was she going to say?* She couldn't very well explain her anger with Jacob to his twin. It wouldn't be fair. It wasn't Toby's fault that his twin had made a stupid, fatal decision that ended another man's life. She wouldn't burden him with such guilt or even assume he'd understand.

"N-no, of course not," she stammered and then flushed with shame. He was an innocent, a friend. He deserved better. He looked at her again, his expression uncertain and confused, adding to her guilt.

"Are you sure? Because Jake said—"

"Let's hurry up and get finished," she interrupted, all of a sudden feeling panicked at the thought of hearing what else Jacob might have said. "We have another two clients waiting in the fridge."

Toby immediately lowered his gaze and crimson flooded his cheeks. Hannah felt awful at her rudeness, but she wasn't prepared to talk about it a minute longer. She didn't want to soften her attitude toward Toby's brother. At the same time, her heart ached at what Jacob had endured during his incarceration. She was sure there were many more occasions when he'd been attacked or subjected to other forms of violence. Everything she'd seen and heard and read about prison pointed to the institution being a violent and dangerous place. Nobody came out of that kind of environment without enduring scars—physical and emotional.

It was a testament to Jacob's strength, courage and determination that he'd gone on to become a doctor—and not just any doctor, but a well-respected emergency room doctor in Sydney's most prestigious hospital. Hannah could only assume the hospital hierarchy were aware of Jacob's criminal history. Such record checks were now mandatory across most of Australia. Despite the fact that he was a convicted criminal, the powers that be had seen something in him that caused them to overlook his past and focus on his future. His success was certainly an achievement that most people couldn't help but admire.

Was she one of those people? The truth was, she didn't know and right here and now, she wasn't brave enough to find out. Turning abruptly, she headed out of the room and stumbled blindly back into the staff restroom. With her breath coming fast, she splashed water on her face and forced herself to calm down.

Toby would be confused about her abrupt departure. No doubt he was wondering right now what had happened. One moment they'd been having a conversation about his brother and the next she'd disappeared out the door. She needed to get back into the embalming room and finish the work she'd started. Pack Kevin Lamb's orifices, wash him down, dress him, make him up; comb his tangle of curls and get him ready for viewing. And then do it all over again with the other two clients who waited in the fridge.

With a sigh, she patted dry her damp cheeks and reapplied her bright red lipstick. Slipping the tube of gloss back into her pocket, she glanced at her reflection and was satisfied with what she saw. Her long hair was still contained in its neat ponytail, tucked up inside her surgical cap. The expression in her eyes was a little wilder than usual, but she'd get a handle on her emotions if it killed her. She'd force thoughts of Jacob Black and their shared history to the furthest recesses of her mind and use all the skill she possessed to keep them there.

Bobby shifted his weight from one foot to the other and glanced over his shoulder. The alley was dark and smelled like rotten garbage. A trash bin, overflowing with food scraps and other detritus discarded by the Chinese restaurant on the ground floor of the old apartment building, stood nearby. The sound of scurrying and scratching snagged his attention and he shifted his weight again. He hated rats. They'd almost overrun some of the older prisons he'd spent time in over the years. He'd had enough of rats for a lifetime.

He should have had enough of prisons, too and he had—but no matter how he tried, he couldn't shake his drug habit. He was barely thirty and yet he looked a decade older and he had nobody to blame but himself.

Plenty would point to his disadvantaged childhood as an excuse for what had happened, as a way to explain the inch-thick criminal history. They'd murmur and shake their head and offer him sympathy, but the whole thing didn't mean shit.

The only person responsible for the fuck-up of

his life was Robert Grace: not his father or his mother or even his sad excuse for an uncle. It was Bobby's fault, fair and square, and that's why he found himself hiding in a dark alley, waiting for the arrival of his dealer and shaking with anticipation for the relief he'd shortly feel.

He'd stolen the money from a drawer of his uncle's desk. He'd been overjoyed to spy the wad of bills hidden beneath a pile of papers. His uncle was always leaving cash lying around. It was like he had so much of it that he couldn't keep track. It made Bobby sick.

He'd spent a couple of seconds wondering why his uncle hadn't bothered to lock the drawer, but those thoughts were quickly swept away by the knowledge he suddenly had the money, not only to pay back his dealer, but to purchase enough ice to get him through the next few weeks. The waiting was killing him.

His thoughts drifted back to his uncle and his lip curled up in a sneer. *Who the fuck did the man think he was?* Max Grace pretended to be the guardian angel, swooping in and saving Bobby and others like him from themselves, when all the time he was doing nothing but lining his own purse.

Bobby knew all about it. He'd overheard the old man extolling the virtues of the ten thousand dollar coffin to his clients when the five thousand dollar version would do perfectly well. He took advantage of people when they were at their lowest—grieving for a dead relative or friend. It wasn't right and Max had no place judging Bobby and finding him lacking.

He thought of the latest addition to the Grace funeral home and shook his head. He was good with faces and he was sure he'd seen Toby Black somewhere before. It niggled on the edge of his memory, as if any moment he'd make the connection between the name and the face, but the years of self-inflicted abuse interfered with his brain processes and the memory had faded. He cursed beneath his breath.

Still, what his uncle did with his time was of no concern to him. As long as the old man didn't come across all high and mighty with him again. Now that he knew what his uncle was up to, there was no way he was taking any of his shit. Max was no better than Bobby: a common thief.

"Hey, dick face! You'd better have my fucking money or I'll slit your fucking throat."

The words erupted out of the darkness and a moment later, the mean face of Bobby's dealer appeared. With shaking hands, Bobby offered the pock-faced, weasel-eyed asshole the wad of cash.

"Here's what I owe, plus another two hundred. What have you got?"

Rat chuckled and the sound of it grated on Bobby's nerves. He glanced around him, quickly counting the number of bodyguards the dealer had brought with him. There were six of them this time, all broad shouldered and hunched over, their faces concealed beneath dark hoodies. Bobby was no lightweight and had honed his fighting skills in jail, but still, he'd come without a weapon and couldn't bear the thought of engaging in another meaningless battle. He was through with that kind of shit.

He raised his hands in a sign of surrender. "I'm not looking for any trouble," he said, hearing the weariness in his voice. "Take the money and give me the shit and we'll all go back to where we came from. How does that sound?"

The dealer stepped closer and shoved his ugly face in Bobby's space. Fetid breath filled the air and it was all Bobby could do not to choke.

"Don't go givin' me fuckin' orders, you fuckwit," Rat growled low in his throat. "I'm the only one who gives orders and don't you forget it."

The man snatched the wad of bills out of Bobby's hand. After counting it, he shoved it straight into the pocket of his filthy jeans. Spinning on his heel, he stomped away.

"Hey!" Bobby protested and then clamped his mouth shut. He hadn't spent most of his life in prison without knowing when to keep his mouth shut.

Rat's hired thugs stared at him hard, their uncompromising expressions leaving him in no doubt that another protest at their boss' behavior wouldn't be tolerated. Taking a step backward, Bobby's shoulders slumped. The bodyguards smirked.

"That's it, big fella. Get the fuck outta here," one of them snarled.

"But—" The protest burst from Bobby's throat.

A vicious punch to his gut sent the air whooshing from his lungs. Bent over, he gasped for breath. The sound of the thugs departing amidst chuckles and guffaws brought tears to Bobby's eyes, along with a feeling of desperation that he wouldn't find the relief he sought that night.

Jacob finished up the notes he was writing on the chart of the patient he'd just discharged, and sighed. It had been a busy day in the ED and he was looking forward to calling it a night. The sun had set an hour ago and night had settled in.

The automatic doors that led into the emergency room opened and closed with regular monotony, bringing with them a swish of cold air. It wasn't a time of year that he relished. Winter brought with it too many bad memories of jail cells with thin, government-issue blankets and cold concrete walls.

The phone inside his shirt pocket vibrated against his chest. He tugged it out and glanced at the screen.

Lane.

A surge of anticipation went through him. It had been a fortnight since he'd spoken to his brother. He wondered if Lane had discovered anything about the death of Edward Sutton.

"Lane, how are you doing?"

"Great, bro. For the first time in months, I slept through the whole night. Didn't get up once for the kids. Not once, do you hear? It's got to be some kind of record."

Jacob smiled, silently sympathizing with his brother's plight. Living with young children wasn't for the faint of heart. Though he didn't have any personal experience, he knew enough about babies and toddlers to know the first few years could be tough—on everyone.

"Anyway, enough about that," Lane continued. "I wanted to call and fill you in on what I've found out."

Jacob's heart skipped a beat. He wasn't sure what he was hoping or even expecting to hear, but all of a sudden, he was tense.

"Is there any cause for worry?" he asked.

"I'm not sure," Lane replied, "but there's definitely something weird going on. Christopher Lowrey was buried shortly after his death, but Samantha Coleridge was able to do a second autopsy on Edward Sutton. In her opinion, the trajectory of the leg fractures suffered by Sutton indicate he was pushed from behind with some force. She's reversed the earlier decision."

Jacob's heart thumped and his mouth went dry. "You mean, it wasn't an accident?"

Lane's voice turned grim. "That's exactly what I'm saying. And there's more. I made some enquires with the General & Life insurance company. They confirmed they have policies in the name of Christopher Lowrey and Edward Sutton owned by the same person and very recently, this person took out another policy—on our brother."

Jacob's head spun. It was too much for him to take in. With a ragged breath, he gathered his courage and asked the final question. "Who owns the policies?"

It was a long moment before Lane responded. "Robert Grace."

Chapter 16

Dear Diary,

Damn! Damn! Damn! How could I be so stupid? How could I have forgotten to get rid of the body? It's so easy for me to collect it. I work in a funeral home. I collect bodies every day and nobody thinks anything of it. Stupid! Stupid! Stupid! Now it's been drawn to someone's attention, someone who's curious about a man who used to work for the Max Grace Funeral Home.

I can't afford to attract the attention of anyone, least of all the police. Dear God, please, not the police. For years I've been patient. I've waited and watched and prayed. And finally my time came and everything fell into place. Now it's all unraveling and I can't figure out what to do.

―――――――――

Hannah swiped at the faint sheen of perspiration that had formed across her forehead and bent to collect her bag from the floor of the university gym she liked to frequent as often as time allowed. She usually made a Zumba class at least two or three times a week. It kept her fit and flexible and helped her clear her mind. It was a welcome escape from the daily grind. Today was no different.

The muffled ringing of her cell phone snagged her attention. Digging through her bag, she found it buried under her towel. She pulled it out and checked the screen.

Jacob.

Her heart skipped a beat. It had been so long since she'd seen him, she'd given up on hearing from him again. The thought had brought her more than a measure of relief. But now he was calling her and she was curious to know why. Knowing she shouldn't, but unable to help herself, she answered the call.

"Jacob, what can I do for you?"

There was a moment of hesitation before he answered. "Hannah, I'm afraid I have some bad news."

Her stomach clenched with nerves. *What kind of bad news?* He wasn't in contact with her parents and as far as she was aware, he barely knew most of her friends. She was conjuring up all kinds of situations when he spoke again.

"It's about Robert—Bobby—Grace. I... I'm afraid I've led you astray."

Hannah frowned in confusion. "What do you

mean?" she asked as she slung her gym bag across her shoulder and made her way out of the building.

"I vouched for The Bobster's good character and it appears I've made a mistake."

Her frown deepened. Nerves once again danced in her stomach. "How so?" she asked through lips that were suddenly dry.

"Lane spoke to your friend, Samantha, and she agreed to do a second autopsy on Edward Sutton. Fortunately, his body was still at the morgue. Samantha came to the conclusion his death was no accident."

Hannah gasped. "You mean, he didn't fall down the stairs?"

"Yes, that's exactly what I mean. Samantha's of the opinion he was too intoxicated to climb any stairs and his injuries indicate he was pushed. It appears Edward Sutton was murdered."

Hannah barely had time to digest the news when Jacob spoke again.

"That's not all. Lane did a little more digging. He discovered General & Life has three life insurance policies owned by Robert Grace."

Surprise shot through her. "Three?" she asked.

"Yes," Jacob responded, his voice grim. "You already know of the one connected to Edward Sutton, but they also had one out on Christopher Lowrey."

He paused and Hannah waited impatiently for him to continue. When he didn't, she said, "And the third?"

"It's Toby. The bastard's taken out a life insurance policy on my brother."

Hannah went icy cold; then fire raged through her veins. Right from the start, there had been something about Bobby Grace she neither liked nor trusted and her instincts had proven correct. It made her ill to think he could be responsible for the deaths of two of her colleagues and to think he might even have Toby in his sights. It was too awful to contemplate.

"What are the police doing? Have they arrested him?" she asked, oblivious to the crowds of pedestrians and the noise of the traffic streaming past her as she walked to the parking station to pick up her car.

"No, they don't have any evidence he was with Edward or Christopher the nights either of them died. The police need to find a witness or something else tying him to the crimes. According to Lane, the existence of the insurance policies isn't enough."

"But, *three* benefiting the same person? And what about Christopher? Doesn't Lane think it strange Bobby has a policy on another former employee who also died suspiciously? Surely the police can't believe it's a coincidence. And why would Bobby have life insurance on your brother, other than to cash in on it at some point? None of it makes sense unless he's up to no good."

"You and I might suspect that Lowrey's death also appears suspicious in light of what we know, but you have to remember, his death was ruled an accident by the coroner's office and as far as I know, the guy's long buried."

Hannah suddenly recalled the day Max had

asked if she'd embalm Christopher and prepare him for burial. It appeared he had no one else to see to the funeral. Max said he'd cover the cost and Hannah had agreed to deal with the body. Her shoulders slumped on a sigh.

"You're right. Max asked Bobby to collect Christopher's body from the morgue and bring him to the funeral home. Apparently he had no family to speak of. We were the ones who buried him." Another thought occurred to her. "Did Samantha carry out the autopsy on Christopher?"

"No, they were both done by another pathologist by the name of Charles Venutti."

Hannah frowned. Sam had often complained about that work colleague and the decided lack of focus and discipline he brought to his job. "Is that why she agreed to do a second autopsy on Edward?" she asked.

"I'm not sure. Lane didn't say, but there must be some reason it was done again."

"Too bad we buried Christopher. I'd like to have Sam's opinion on the way he died."

"Yeah, well, all might not be lost. Lane's going to keep investigating. He told me a claim for the insurance money over Lowrey's life has already been submitted, presumably by Robert Grace. Lane's going to confirm this with the insurer and then use it as evidence to petition the court to exhume Lowrey's body."

"Just as well Max doesn't own a crematorium," she added dryly. "Any evidence of wrongdoing would have gone up in smoke."

"Unlucky for The Bobster that he doesn't."

"I'm sorry, I know he was your...friend."

"Don't be sorry. We all make our own choices in life."

Hannah arrived at her Mazda and unlocked it with the remote. Climbing behind the wheel, she started the ignition and let the car kit pick up her phone.

"Are you still there?" Jacob asked.

"Yes, sorry, I just started my car. The call switched over to Bluetooth."

"Where are you?" Jacob asked.

"I'm just leaving the gym."

"Where's Toby?"

"He wanted to go into the city. We left work together. I dropped him off at the bus station. He's going to meet me at home."

Jacob's voice lowered. "Keep an eye on him for me, Hannah. He's so trusting and naïve. It's easy for people to take advantage of him. I bet he doesn't have a clue about the extent of evil that might be lurking around the funeral home. We've been apart for too many years. I'd never forgive myself if anything happened to him now that we've found each other again. He... He means a great deal to me."

Jacob's voice hitched and Hannah swallowed a lump in her throat. "You're lucky to have each other," she murmured, her voice husky with emotion. "I'm an only child."

"That's right, I remember now. You wouldn't believe it, but sometimes I used to envy you back in high school. I couldn't imagine how cool it would be to have your own room and never have to fight over the best spot on the couch or who was in charge of the remote."

Hannah chuckled without humor. "It isn't all it's cracked up to be. I would have given anything for a sister or brother. It's probably why I fell so hard and fast for Luke. I was searching desperately for a soul mate, someone who could help ease the loneliness."

"Yes... Well..." Jacob cleared his throat.

Hannah sighed quietly. Jacob wasn't comfortable talking about her boyfriend and her feelings of loss. She could understand why. The last time they'd spoken about Luke, she'd told Jacob she could never forgive him and though she still ached with loss every time she thought about Luke and the future that had been taken away so suddenly, the pain was easing. For the first time, she couldn't help but wonder if one day, it might not be there at all.

"I'm taking Toby to the rodeo out in Picton tomorrow night. I was wondering... That is, Toby was wondering if you...if you might like to come along."

Butterflies took flight in Hannah's stomach and she searched desperately for something to say. A part of her wanted to leap at the invitation, but the rest of her urged caution. Was it fair to either of them to resume a friendship? To take back up where they'd left off all those years ago? Could she put Luke's tragic death behind them and truly move forward?

And what about Toby? Was it fair to him to encourage a closeness and togetherness that might not last more than a few outings? Working side by side in the funeral home, they'd reignited their friendship. Though it was ten years or more in the past, in a lot of ways, the connection between them was as if it had never been broken.

"He's really fond of you, Hannah," Jacob continued, interrupting her tortured thoughts. "You're all he talks about when we're together. Please, say you'll come."

Hannah was wracked with indecision. She wanted to say yes, but the more sensible side of her wondered if it was the wisest thing to do. It was true that she enjoyed Toby's company and it was getting harder and harder to maintain her distance from Jacob, but did that mean she should just forget about the past decade by throwing caution to the wind?

"Please, Hannah. Just a few hours. I'll drive us all out there and back. It would mean so much to Toby...and to me."

Hannah recalled him telling her about his father and the rodeos. She thought of the black cowboy hat and felt herself weakening.

"All right, I'll come," she said and immediately wondered if she'd done the right thing. When Jacob responded, she could hear the smile in his voice.

"Really? That's great. Wait until I tell Toby. Thank you for the phone, by the way. I offered to get him one the night we came across each other in the hospital, but he refused my offers for help. I guess he's in a better place now, or maybe he just feels more comfortable accepting help from you. I don't know, I was jealous for a bit, but now I'm grateful for whatever it is."

A warm glow spread inside Hannah's belly. She smiled softly. "Jealous? You have no need. He loves you; there's no question. Besides, I'm more than happy to do it. Toby's like the little brother I never had. I know we're the same age—but...you know..."

"What I know is that you have a beautiful heart, Hannah Langdon," Jacob replied.

His deep voice glided over her and all of a sudden, she felt tongue-tied and flustered. "I-I guess I'll see you tomorrow night," she managed.

"Great. I'll drop by and pick you both up around six."

Max pushed back a hank of white hair that had fallen across his eyes. His pen moved with quiet efficiency across the pages on his desk. The business of dying was thriving and grieving relatives would often pay a hefty price to see their loved ones farewelled in style. Max kept a range of coffins, but made certain the ones with all the gold trimmings were more visible than the rest. It seemed to work. He sold the top-of-the-line coffin to his customers more often than not. Nobody wanted to be seen pinching pennies at a time like that. If he weren't so impatient, he could die an extremely wealthy man.

The problem was, he wanted the money *now*. There were things he wanted to do with his life.

He'd taken in his nephew with the hope the man would learn the business and take over from him when he retired, but it wasn't working out like that.

Bobby was next to useless. He should have known that, before he picked the man up off the streets. The fellow's mother had been weak and stupid, her head turned by the first man who gave her a smile. The asshole waited around just long enough to get Mary-Jane pregnant and then he'd taken off running. Max ought to have known a boy who'd grown up without ever knowing his father would turn out to be no good.

Still, he'd wanted to leave the business to someone and family meant more to him than most, even family as useless as his nephew. So, he'd done his best to encourage the boy, but his efforts had come to nought. Recently he'd come up with another plan, one that would make good use of the boy's dubious reputation and skills.

Now, everything was going as it should be and retirement was almost within his grasp. All he needed to do was stay calm and wait out the skirmish that appeared likely to happen just around the bend.

With a flourish, he added his signature to the bottom of the page. The invoice totaled fifteen thousand dollars. Not bad for a couple days' work. So much more than what it cost him in wages to see the job done.

Yes, if only he was a little more patient, there'd be no need for Plan B.

The problem was, patience had never been one of his virtues and that's just the way it was.

CHAPTER 17

The upbeat country music reached them clear across the car park and sent a tingle of excitement running down Hannah's spine. People poured out from everywhere, all heading toward the rodeo ring that was lit up like a football stadium at night. She'd never been to a live rodeo and she was genuinely looking forward to it. Over the last few days, she'd begun to realize that spending time with Jacob was something else she was looking forward to, although it was difficult to admit.

Ever since she'd agreed to his invitation, she'd been thinking about what letting go of the past might mean. Her memories of Luke and the night he died were so ingrained in her psyche, she didn't know if she *could* let it go, even if she wanted to.

But somewhere in the early hours of the morning, after tossing and turning most of the night, she'd come to the decision that she wanted to try. She'd woken, tired and with gritty eyes, but ready to face what needed to be done.

The day had dragged by and even with Toby to distract her, it had felt like a lifetime before five o'clock swung by. With a quick farewell to Max, who sat in his office, busy sorting the usual invoices, customer orders and doing all the other administrative tasks he attended to every day, she and Toby climbed into her Mazda and headed for home.

They were caught in a traffic jam on Cleveland Street, so they barely had enough time to shower and change before Jacob knocked on her door. She watched Toby greeting his brother with an enthusiastic hug, excited to be attending the rodeo. Earlier, he'd confided he was even more excited that she and his brother were getting along.

Hannah's greeting was much more subdued and at the sight of Jacob dressed casually in Levis and a chambray shirt and with his father's black cowboy hat in hand, she was immediately beset with nerves. Even so, she managed a smile and was sincere when she told him she was very much looking forward to attending her first rodeo.

"Come on, we don't want to be late," Toby said, urging them toward the front door.

Hannah stifled a grin. It was good to see Toby so animated. Though he often assured her how much he enjoyed his work at the funeral parlor, the somber tone of the place didn't give rise to much frivolity and laughter. Over the weeks, ingrained dirt and the effects of years of hard living had slowly disappeared and he was almost the Toby of old. The more he returned to the boy she remembered from her childhood, the more he looked like his twin.

"Are you ready?"

As Jacob's deep voice slid over her, a shiver of awareness coursed down her spine. She'd never allowed herself to think of him as a potential boyfriend and had refused to dwell on his sinfully dark good looks.

His short hair was so dark it was almost black and his olive complexion reflected his European heritage. She knew his mother's family originated from France and his father had emigrated from Spain. It was a deadly combination of steamy dark Latino looks, teamed with an air of sad vulnerability. It did strange things to her equilibrium.

Collecting a fringed leather jacket from the coat tree in the corner of the entryway, Hannah stood back and allowed Jacob to open the door. With his arm, he indicated that she should precede him. His old-fashioned manners surprised her once again and she nodded her thanks with a smile. It was nice to be treated like a lady, if only for a night.

Toby bounced out behind her and Hannah laughed at his exuberance. "You really like the rodeo, don't you?" She chuckled.

Toby gave her a wide grin. "Yes, I really do. My dad was a rodeo rider, did you know that? Before I was born. Mom showed me all the pictures. He was really cool and he wore a real cowboy hat. The same one Jacob's got. Did you see it?"

Hannah glanced at Jacob, who followed

closely behind, and then returned her attention to his twin. "Yes, I saw it. It suits him. Was your dad as handsome as he is?"

The words fell out of her mouth and she couldn't drag them back. Heat crept up her cheeks. She didn't dare look back to Jacob. To her relief, Toby laughed.

"Jacob! Handsome! Ha! Hannah, you say the funniest things. If you think he's handsome, then I guess that means I am too, right?"

His laughter was contagious and Hannah grinned and shook her head. She couldn't believe how oblivious Toby was to his good looks. It was almost as if he'd never noticed. Then she thought about it a moment and realized it wasn't inconceivable at all. He looked at the world through eyes that were as innocent as a child's and physical appeal didn't rate a mention.

Thankfully, Jacob didn't offer any additional comment other than to direct her to his twin cab truck, which was parked on the street opposite her apartment block. A silver Ford Lariat stood under the street lights, looking very shiny and clean. Toby let out a *whoop* of glee.

"You brought the truck, Jake! Cool! Can I sit in the front? Can I?"

Jacob smiled with fondness at his brother, but slowly shook his head. "I don't think so, buddy. I was hoping you might let Hannah ride up front. She's a lady, and ladies first, remember. She's probably never been in a twin cab truck." He turned to face her, the smile still on his lips. "Am I right?"

The teasing light in his eyes stole her breath. "You're right," she managed and then added, "but I'm more than happy to sit in the back."

"Sit up front, Hannah! Sit up front!" Toby insisted, taking her hand and pulling her toward the front passenger side door. "It's way more fun than being in the back."

She laughed and went along with him, having no other choice. Toby pulled open the door. Even with Hannah's generous height, the step up from the running board into the cab was a challenge. She laughed again when Toby did his best to help her into the seat.

"There!" he sighed, looking more than pleased. "How's the view, Hannah? Isn't it great?"

Jacob slid behind the wheel and waited for Toby to get settled in the back before he started the engine. It growled with power and authority beneath Hannah's feet. Like its owner, the truck was all male.

They'd made good time out of the eastern suburbs and before too long, found themselves on the motorway heading west. Toby kept up a monologue, cataloguing the seemingly endless virtues of the Lariat.

"I think Toby's a little in love with your truck," she murmured, sneaking a peek at the man who steered the large vehicle in and out of the traffic with expert precision.

He shot her a deadpan look. "You think?"

She chuckled. "I didn't realize the two of you had been spending so much time together. I thought Toby was coming home on public transport. I've offered to drive him home nearly every day since he started working, but most of the time he declines and asks me to drop him off at the nearest station."

Jacob continued to stare at the road in front of him. "I've been collecting him from the station," he admitted quietly. We've been going out for a drink, or a coffee. Sometimes we just go for a drive. We lost so much time together. It's almost as if we're trying to get some of it back."

She nodded and wondered why Toby hadn't told her his brother was giving him a ride home after work. As if reading her mind, Jacob spoke again.

"I asked him not to tell you. I wasn't sure you'd want to see me and I could hardly turn up at your place of work to collect him without you knowing about it and perhaps having to go to the trouble of avoiding me. I didn't want to make things awkward for you. The last couple times we saw each other, we didn't exactly leave on friendly terms."

Hannah blushed, remembering how she'd left early from the ball and her outburst the night she came over to his apartment. Both seemed like a lifetime ago.

"I'm sorry," she said softly. "I shouldn't have said those things."

"It's all right. You were only speaking the truth."

She glanced at him, but he continued to look straight ahead. She sighed quietly until they pulled into the fairgrounds and he pulled the car to a stop. Before she had time to open the door,

Jacob had come around the front of the truck and opened it with a flourish. She had to grab his hand to climb down and stumbled a bit on impact, falling into his hard wall of a chest. She quickly stepped back, but not before she'd breathed in the musky smell of him. Eye contact wasn't something she wanted as they waited for Toby to join them.

"Oh, I almost forgot," Jacob said and opened the rear door. He pulled out two cream-colored cowboy hats and gave one to her and Toby.

"Gee, thanks, Jake! This is so cool! Does it look good?" Toby laughed, happiness shining in his eyes.

Hannah smiled and nodded her thanks and set the hat upon her head. With a soft look, Jacob keyed the lock and as the truck beeped behind them, they set out.

The sounds and smells of the rodeo loomed closer and a fresh wave of excitement surged through Hannah's veins. She calmed the erratic beating of her heart and slowed her breathing, then looked around. Almost everyone was wearing a cowboy hat, mostly white or black or tan. Her gaze drifted to Jacob where he walked beside her and she silently agreed with her earlier assessment: He looked good in a cowboy hat. Better than good.

"Let's get some hotdogs and soda before we go up into the stands. I got paid today! My treat," Toby said, loping along beside them, his eyes gleaming with excitement.

"Sounds like a good plan, buddy," Jacob

replied and gave his brother a smile. "Just stay close, all right. I don't want to lose you in the crowd."

Hannah's heart clenched at the tenderness in Jacob's eyes. It was obvious he loved his twin more than anything and she was sure he'd protect him with his life. That was the reason he felt such concern that Bobby was still on the loose—and not only on the loose, but frequently in close proximity to his brother.

Jacob had asked her to look out for Toby, and Hannah had taken her responsibilities seriously. From the moment Jacob informed her of Lane's discoveries, she'd kept Toby well out of the way of Max's nephew. But she'd worried when Toby wanted to be dropped at the bus station because she tried to know where he was at all times. Whether Bobby had devious intentions toward Max's newest employee, or not, she wasn't going to allow anything to happen to him on her watch.

She'd always felt protective of Toby, even when they were teens. She guessed it had something to with the fact that Toby's trustworthy nature meant that less honorable people often took advantage of him. Though Jacob was a fierce protector of his brother, Hannah also felt that way. Between the two of them, they'd kept him safe.

Luke hadn't understood her need to look out for and champion Toby's cause. It was the only thing they'd argued about. Hannah suspected Luke had been jealous of Toby and she'd gone to pains to reassure her boyfriend that there was nobody for her, but him.

And then he was dead and there was no longer any need to discuss or even think about her relationship with Toby Black. He was the brother of the man who'd killed her boyfriend. She'd cut all ties with both of them.

The sad thoughts dampened her mood. Jacob turned and stared down at her, an indefinable expression in his eyes.

"What is it?" he asked softly, his gaze probing hers.

She shook her head in dismissal. Only the night before, she'd vowed to put the past behind her, to let go of the hurt and pain. And she was about to enjoy her first rodeo. Now wasn't the time to belabor things that couldn't be changed.

"It's nothing," she said and managed a half-convincing smile. "Tell me who's who in the world of rodeo."

———————

It was way past midnight when Jacob pulled up the Lariat outside Hannah's apartment block. His brother was already asleep in the back seat. They'd enjoyed a night of fun and laughter, of the highs and lows that went with being part of the audience at a professional bull riding event.

He'd been thrilled when Hannah had screamed and grabbed hold of his hand every time it looked like the cowboy was going to be trampled by the bull and again when she shouted in triumph each time a competitor made it through. The eight-second count had seemed to last a lifetime.

He thought of his father and wondered if Warren Black had missed the feel of the powerful beast between his thighs and the thrill of the high stakes that came with being brave enough to climb on the back of a bucking bull. From what Jacob could tell, the riders were addicted to the adrenaline rush, like a junkie was to their next hit. Instead of pursuing that high-stakes career, his dad had taken on the more responsible role of police officer. Sure, it came with its moments of tension and high drama, but Jacob guessed police work had nothing on riding a wild bull.

And then sadly that so-called "safer career choice" had cost him his life. It was sad, when Jacob thought about it. He couldn't help but wonder if his father had regretted his decision to give up his dream and climb off the bucking bulls. It reminded him of his own decision to pursue medicine.

At the time, it had been more of a reaction to needing something to do now that his dream of being a police officer was shattered. Luckily, over the years, he found he really enjoyed being a doctor and he was good at it. There was nothing like the buzz that came with the knowledge he'd saved someone's life.

With a soft sigh, Jacob switched off the ignition and turned to face the woman who sat beside him. Her long blond hair had been plaited over her shoulder and hung across one breast. His gaze strayed to the cleavage that peeked out from her pink-and-white, checked cowboy shirt. He didn't know where she'd gotten it, but he hazarded a guess that until recently, it hadn't been part of her wardrobe.

The street light softly illuminated the curves and planes of her face. Even in the dimness, her beauty stole his breath.

"I hope you had a good time tonight," he murmured, breaking the silence.

She turned in her seat to face him and offered him a gentle smile. "Yes, thank you, it was great. The most fun I've had for a long time. I can't believe those men can fall like that and get stomped on and still get up again. Most of them walk away with barely a limp."

"Yes, if they're lucky. It was a good show tonight. Everybody got to go home. It isn't always like that."

She shuddered. "I'm glad I didn't have to witness one of the riders getting seriously injured, or worse." She paused and then added, "Thank you for inviting me. It was exciting, and I had a really good time."

Her gaze remained on his. Long seconds passed. Jacob's heart thumped. Desire coursed through him, hot and urgent, and centered in his cock. Because of her reaction so many times since they'd reconnected, he'd hardly dared to think about Hannah in any way other than as the girlfriend of a friend who'd been killed. But right here, right now, with her seated a foot away, it was beyond him not to wonder how it would feel to take her in his arms and pull her to him and kiss her until both of them were breathless and wild with need.

And then he didn't want to wonder a second longer. He leaned slowly toward her. She didn't move away. His lips found hers and he sighed quietly in relief. A moment later, it registered in his brain that she was kissing him back.

It was like a dam had released, like a switch was flicked. He groaned deep in his throat and dragged her as near as the gear shift would allow. He kissed her with increasing pressure, trying hard to control himself, but almost frantic with need. Heat traveled along his veins and exploded in his groin. He kissed her again and again. He couldn't get enough.

Instinctively, his hand reached out and cupped her breast through the soft fabric of her shirt. It filled his palm to overflowing. He stroked her nipple and it pebbled instantly beneath his thumb. He groaned against her mouth. His cock was rock-hard and throbbing. He was desperate for her touch. Releasing her breast, he took her hand and gently pressed it against his erection.

She gasped and her eyes flew open, dazed and wide with shock. "Jacob! I... I'm sorry. I-I think I ought to go in."

He blinked and shook his head to clear it, staring at her in confusion. "What the...?"

"I'm really sorry. Do you mind waking your brother and bringing him in?"

Somehow, he managed to nod and then

climbed down out of the truck. Making his way around to her side of the truck, he opened her door.

"Thank you again for the lovely evening," she said in a rush and then stood on tiptoe and pressed a kiss against his cheek. Moments later, she disappeared along the path that led inside her apartment building.

———————

Hannah stared down at the pages of the scrapbook that were spread open across her bed. She'd heard Toby close the door to his room and had listened to the sound of Jacob's truck rumbling away. Silent tears made tracks down her damp cheeks.

She'd done it to him again: Let him think there could be something between them and then push him away. It wasn't fair. She owed him much more than that. She owed him honesty and maturity. She owed the same things to herself.

She turned over a page in the scrapbook and was assailed with memories. Pictures of three wedding dresses in different styles covered the surface. She remembered poring over bridal magazines for months during her senior year, choosing one dress after another and carefully cutting them out. It had been like a fairytale, an endless golden dream. Her knight in shining armor was waiting to claim her for his bride.

And then the fairytale was over, shattered

beyond belief and all she was left with was a scrapbook of broken dreams.

But that was more than a decade ago and she now realized the prince might not have been all that he seemed. It was funny how utterly perfect Luke had been back when they were both eighteen. Looking back, she wondered if he'd been as devoted to her as she'd been to him. They'd promised to save themselves for marriage, but even before his death, she'd had niggling doubts about his sincerity.

It wasn't like she'd caught him in an outright lie. It was more the subtle things like the time she found a note from a girl in his locker and he swore he knew nothing about it. The note hinted at a level of intimacy with him that even Hannah hadn't reached and even though she believed him, her heart hadn't been quite convinced.

Still, thanks to Jacob Black, they'd never been given the opportunity to know whether their love would go the distance.

Jacob.

She wanted to keep hating him, but she couldn't. He was so much more than the man who'd caused the loss of her boyfriend's life. He was a man who'd suffered for his crimes and had paid the price in ways she'd never imagined. The man who loved his family. The man who made her heart race. The man she wanted to touch and be touched by. The man she could fall in love with, if she let herself.

Turning another page, Hannah smiled sadly at the names she'd written there. Brandon, Emily and

Jack. They were the names of the children she'd dreamed of having; children who would look exactly like their dad. Only, she could hardly remember what Luke had looked like, apart from the fact his hair was brown. Oh, and he had brown eyes, too. Or perhaps they'd been hazel? It saddened her that she couldn't remember.

Was it a sign that she'd finally let it go and put the past where it belonged? Was it because of Jacob? Was that the reason Luke's image was no longer clear?

Swiping at her tears with the back of her hand, she sniffed and brought her knees up to her chest. Wrapping her arms around her legs, she rested her head on her knees. A long sigh escaped her and with it, the pain of the past. Luke was her yesterday. It was time to look to the future and make new memories, new dreams. Alone or with Jacob, only time would tell.

Chapter 18

Lane Black stared at the middle-aged claims officer of the General & Life Insurance Company and frowned. "I'm sorry," he said, "could you repeat that?"

The woman, whose name badge identified her as Diandra Robinson, rolled her eyes and shook her head, sending her double chins wobbling.

"It's really very simple, Detective. Like I said, the claim has been paid out. That file was closed last week."

"That seems awfully fast," Lane replied, scribbling in his notepad. "Christopher Lowrey only died a couple of months ago. The way I've heard it, these kind of things can drag on for years."

"Yes, in some cases that's true, Detective, but this one was straightforward. The policy owner furnished us with a death certificate which indicated there were no suspicious circumstances and we paid the claim. We pride ourselves on our efficiency. As far as we're concerned, the matter has been dealt with. Truly, I'm at a loss as to why you're here."

Lane struggled to hold onto his patience. "There have been some new developments. They might relate to this case."

The woman frowned and scratched at her gray curls. "What kind of new developments?"

"Let's just say there's another case with similarities too striking to ignore and we're looking into it. Edward Sutton's life was also insured by your company. The latest autopsy report seems to indicate the man's death was likely not accidental. We're wondering if the same might be true for Christopher Lowery."

The claims officer paled. "Are you talking suicide, or something else?" Her voice took on a note of panic. "Please don't tell me it was suicide. Our policy expressly excludes suicide! We've already paid out the claim." She gripped the sides of her head. "What am I going to do?"

Lane offered what little reassurance he could. "We haven't yet confirmed any anomalies in Mr Lowery's death. Another autopsy will require exhumation of the body. We're gathering further information before we decide if we have enough to take it to a judge."

His assurances did little to ease the panic from her face. She continued to wring her hands. Lane tried again.

"If it helps you any, the forensic pathologist ruled out suicide in the most recent death. The blood alcohol levels in that deceased were too high for him to be making any kind of conscious decisions. It was a wonder he could even stand. We're investigating it as a homicide."

The relief on the woman's face was palpable. She put a fleshy hand to her chest.

"Oh, thank goodness! You don't know how relieved that makes me feel. Homicide is fine. Death by homicide is covered under the policy... Provided the beneficiary wasn't the one who did the killing." Once again, her expression was filled with concern. "You said the deceased was insured by General & Life. Do you have a suspect? It's not the owner of the policy, is it?"

Lane compressed his lips. "It's early days into the investigation. At this stage, we don't know who's responsible." He leaned forward in his chair. "Do you mind telling me if there's been a claim made on the life of Edward Sutton? I understand the policy is also owned by Robert Grace."

Diandra shrugged. "Of course. A client is usually allocated the same claims officer, even for different claims, but every now and then they are allocated to someone else. For example, if I was away on leave when the subsequent claim came in or something like that, it would be handed to another officer in our building to deal with." She tapped on the keys and scanned the computer screen.

"Robert Grace. Yes, here he is. He's listed as owning life insurance policies over Christopher Lowrey—which is the file I just closed—Edward Sutton—the man you just mentioned—and another man by the name of Toby Black."

She peered up at him. "Is that what you were after?"

Lane clenched his jaw in an effort not to snap at the woman. "I was already in possession of that information, Ms Robinson. What I'd like to know is if Mr Grace has made a claim on the Sutton policy. Mr Sutton died a little over a month ago."

Once again, the woman tapped away at her keyboard. A moment later, she nodded. "Yes, it's as I suspected. The claim was filed last week. I'm afraid I've been away sick. It must have come in while I was indisposed. It was allocated to one of our other claims officers. I guess that's why I wasn't aware of it."

Lane tensed. "So, a claim *has* been filed? Is that what you're saying?"

"Yes… No." She looked uncomfortable. "What I mean is, a claim's been made, but we're still waiting for the death certificate. Naturally, we never pay out a claim without proof the insured's life has come to an end."

"So Robert Grace has claimed on both policies, all in the space of less than two months. Hasn't anyone in this office decided that might be a little strange?"

Diandra's discomfort deepened. She stared at her keyboard. "I've only just become aware Mr Grace has two claims in the system. I can only assume Andrew Bloomberg—that's the claim officer dealing with the later claim—isn't aware of the claim I dealt with earlier. It's no one's fault, Detective, if that's what you're implying."

Her voice had taken on a defensive tone. Lane was quick to reassure her because he needed more information from her. "Tell me, the claim you managed—the claim over Christopher Lowrey… Was it paid out by way of check or bank deposit?"

"Company policy is for all claims to be paid by way of direct bank deposit."

"I'd appreciate it if you could provide me with the details of Robert Grace's bank account."

The woman frowned. "I'm not sure—"

Lane shot her his most charming smile. "Ms Robinson, you and I are on the same side. We get up each day and go to work. We try hard to do what's right. We take satisfaction from knowing we've done an honest day's work and helped someone out along the way. Now, I don't know where this investigation is going or what will be important and what won't, but any information you have on the claim could help me, and possibly prevent another crime."

She lowered her gaze and her lip wobbled, her earlier bravado gone. A moment later, Lane spied two fat tears in her eyes. "You... You still think Robert Grace might have defrauded the company, don't you? Or worse?"

Lane held her gaze and gave her the truth. "Yes."

"Oh, my goodness! What if the company blames me for not seeing it? What if I lose my job?"

Lane remained silent, unable to offer her any reassurance. With a sniff, the claims officer swiped at her eyes and opened the file on her desk. Flipping over a few pages, she ran a finger down a type-written form.

"Robert Grace provided us with details related to an account held with the National Bank. In accordance with our usual procedure, and at our client's request, five-hundred thousand dollars, less fees, was deposited into that account."

Lane absorbed the information. While it didn't come as a surprise, it supported his growing conviction that Robert Grace was, in some way, tied to the death of at least one of his brother's coworkers. Lane felt a sense of foreboding when he thought about Toby. His extremely vulnerable brother could be in danger. The thought sent a shiver of apprehension down his spine. He had to call Jacob and bring him up to date. He had to impress upon him the need to keep a close eye on his twin.

Explaining the situation to Toby, wasn't an option. If they tried to tell him one of his work colleagues might be trying to do away with him, he'd more than likely find the idea hysterically funny and think it was a joke. It would never occur to him that such a thing could happen—had probably already happened.

Lane's jaw tightened with determination. Getting to the bottom of what was happening to the employees of the Max Grace Funeral Home had suddenly become a priority. He'd go to his boss, bring him up to speed and then get authorization to follow up on his hunch to prove that Robert Grace was an evil man who needed to be removed from the streets and the funeral home where he worked, much too closely with his brother.

Jacob tried to concentrate on the cheerful banter that filled the tearoom housed just off to the side from the emergency department's ward. Memories of the rodeo kept distracting him: the magical kiss he and Hannah shared in the cab of his truck, the fire and passion that had consumed them...

Though she'd ended things rather abruptly and hadn't responded to his early-morning text, it had been a less abrupt departure than the previous time and he wouldn't believe her if she told him she hadn't enjoyed it as much as he had. He wasn't sure what upset her this time, but he wasn't going to sit back and let things slide.

He'd had a crush on her as a kid. From as far back as he could remember, she'd set his heart on fire: a casual smile, a shared joke... Sometimes it had been no more than a friendly look. It hadn't seemed to matter. The only reason he hadn't told her how he felt back then was because she'd been in love with his best mate.

He respected and supported their relationship and the fact that Hannah, at least, was in love. And then the fateful night in November had happened and everything had been turned on its head...

"Doctor Black, your phone's ringing."

The gentle prompt interrupted his dark thoughts. He glanced up at the nurse who'd spoken to him. "Thanks, Polly."

He reached down and picked up his phone off the table. A sudden surge of hope flooded through him at the thought it might be Hannah and then he glanced at the screen and his heart plummeted.

Lane.

Pushing back his chair, he stood and moved out of earshot, unwilling to have his conversation overheard by his colleagues. He assumed Lane was calling with an update regarding Bobby Grace and the insurance claim. "Lane, how are you doing?"

"Good. Are you at work?"

"Yeah, but I'm on a break. What did you find out?"

"I spoke to the claims officer at General & Life. She confirmed two claims have been made by your old cellmate on the policies held in the names of Christopher Lowery and Edward Sutton. They already paid out the first one."

Jacob's heart pounded. "Let me guess, it was paid to The Bobster."

"Good guess, bro. Deposited right into his account."

Jacob tried to slow down his breathing. He felt like tearing The Bobster limb by limb. He couldn't believe the man he'd trusted with his life and considered a loyal friend, at least while he'd been a prison inmate, would murder innocent people for money—and that he might have Jacob's brother in his sights. It just didn't fit with the man he'd known.

But that was a nearly a decade ago...

The thought fell into his mind and stuck there. It was true. The Bobster was only nineteen when Jacob met him. Two years later, Jacob had served his time and was released. He hadn't seen his cellmate since. A lot could happen to a man in ten years—for the better, or for the worse. How did he know the young man hadn't changed—grown harder, angrier, more aggressive?

What Lane told him had to be true. There couldn't be any other explanation. Perhaps it was the drugs that had done it? The Bobster had always had a weakness for ice. It was common knowledge the drug made many people violent and unpredictable. Good people became monsters. They became something no one ever dreamed they could be. Some became dangerous. He vowed silently to track down his former cellmate and demand a few answers.

"You need to stay close to Toby," Lane was saying, snapping Jacob out of his reverie. "This Robert guy is up to no good. I'm sure of it. He had life insurance policies on two of his work colleagues and now they've both turned up dead. We know he has a policy on Toby, too. I'm going to talk to my boss and try to get a court application to exhume the body of Christopher Lowrey. We need to find out if foul play could have been involved in his death. In the meantime, I have some more checking to do—but we need to protect Toby."

"Of course, I'm happy to stick to him like glue. He's been staying with Hannah. I'll call him and see if he's ready to move in with me."

"I'd offer to have him at our place, but we've recently moved the twins into the spare room. All I could offer him is the couch. We're full to bursting."

Jacob chuckled. "Don't stress it, bro. I'm sure we can work something out. I have plenty of room. It's just a matter of convincing Toby it's in his best interest to move to my place."

"Get Hannah on side. Lay it all out for her and don't sugarcoat it," Lane urged. "This Grace fellow's dangerous, but until we have something more than circumstantial evidence linking him to a crime, there's nothing we can do. In the meantime, he's on the streets and remains a threat. I'm sure she'll understand."

"What if Toby refuses?" Jacob asked.

Lane sighed on the other end of the phone. His voice turned grim. "Then, I guess you'll have to convince Hannah to let you move in with the pair of them until this is resolved. With all due respect to Hannah, I'm not leaving Toby without any protection other than that offered by a woman."

Jacob instinctively opened his mouth and offered a protest. "I don't think that's fair. Hannah—"

"Is very capable of defending herself, I'm sure," Lane interrupted, "but from what I've seen of Robert Grace in the police files, she's no match for the likes of him. I'd feel a lot better if you were close by, for both of them."

"So would I," Jacob agreed, his protective instincts for both Hannah and his brother coming to the fore. After all, Toby was the target. Hannah was putting herself at risk by sheltering him on her own. Determination surged through him. "Don't worry, Lane. Either Toby agrees to move over to my place pronto, or I'll move in with them. That's a promise."

Chapter 19

Dear Diary,

They're exhuming Christopher's body. I saw it on the news. They don't know what they're looking for, but the fact is, they're looking. I can't rely on the possibility the next forensic pathologist might be as incompetent as the last.

It's time to make plans for my glorious exit, to put final preparations in place. It was fun while it lasted and I wish it had lasted longer, but there's no sense in putting greed over sensibility. No, the best thing to do is fade into the shadows. Go quietly, stealthily before I am missed.

Before it's too late...

As soon as he was able, Jacob left the hospital and climbed into his truck. Burning some rubber as he left the car park, he headed the relatively short distance to the Max

Grace Funeral Home. The afternoon traffic was building, even though peak hour had yet to hit. Jacob hoped to speak to Hannah and his brother, get them to agree to the plan, and then return to work until his shift ended at midnight. It would be a long day.

Finding a parking place across from the funeral parlor, he switched off the ignition and climbed out. He spied Hannah's Mazda on the other side of the street and swallowed a sigh of relief. At least she was there.

He hadn't wanted to phone ahead because they'd ask why he was coming over in the middle of the afternoon and that would give either or both of them a chance to argue. He'd wanted to speak to them in person and try and convince them what he had to say was the only way. He would impress upon them the importance of staying safe and that meant having him nearby.

He might not have the brawn of The Bobster, but he could handle himself in a fight and he'd do whatever was necessary to protect the people he loved.

Loved. Yes, he loved them. Had never stopped loving them. Even when he didn't have a clue about Toby's whereabouts, he still yearned for his twin's company and to know that he was safe. As for Hannah, no boyfriend, no conviction with time spent in jail, and no anger and hurt could stop him from feeling the way he did.

Having her so resistant to his attentions would prove a challenge—and he knew she had good reason. Even so, he was sure, with patience and time, he could overcome that. She wasn't as immune to him as she liked to say she was. The passion in her kisses spoke volumes. She was a mass of contradictions.

For a fleeting moment, he considered telling her the truth about what happened that fateful night and then, just as quickly, he dismissed it. *What good would it do to dredge up that awful time all over again?* No, it was better if they pushed it aside, back to the dark recesses of their minds. They needed to focus instead on starting fresh, looking to the future. And right now, that future meant convincing both Hannah and Toby it was best for both of them that they share a house with him.

Jogging up the short flight of stairs that led to the front door of the funeral home, he pressed the buzzer and waited for it to be answered. Thinking about the last time he'd seen Hannah, he was filled with a sudden wave of nervousness.

Just like she had the very first day, Hannah met him at the door. Her mouth parted slightly in surprise and almost immediately, a wariness shadowed her eyes. He could tell she was recalling the night of the rodeo, when he'd kissed her.

"Jacob, what are you doing here?"

"I'm looking for Toby. I need to talk to him. To both of you, actually."

She frowned. "Here? Can't it wait until later? We're at work."

"I understand; but no, this can't wait. Is Toby here?"

"Yes, he's in the back, but—"

Jacob pushed past her. She opened her mouth to protest, but he ignored it, intent on reaching his brother.

"I'm sorry, Hannah, but this is important," he threw over his shoulder. "I've been speaking to Lane. There've been some new developments."

She closed her mouth, bringing an end to any further arguments. In silence, she overtook him and led the way down a corridor, past a waiting room and an office. She continued to the far end of the hall, opened the door and waited for him to catch up.

"Toby's in here. We're in the middle of an embalming. Are you sure you're up for this?"

He raised an eyebrow. "I'm a doctor, Hannah. I've seen more than my fair share of blood. I think I can handle it."

A tiny smile tugged at the corners of her lips. "Oh, there's no blood involved, Doctor. The blood's long since been drained away."

She turned on her heel and by doing so, her ponytail escaped from her cap. The scent of her shampoo wafted toward him. Strawberries and cream and vanilla—it was the same scent that had driven him wild with need when he'd held her in his arms the Friday night before. With an impatient sound in the back of his throat, he pushed the distracting thoughts aside and followed her through the doorway, into a large room.

The embalming room looked more like an operating theater, with its whitewashed walls and gleaming instruments. Two stainless steel gurneys dominated the room. Only one was occupied. Toby was bent over the cadaver. He looked up as they entered and smiled widely with pleasure and surprise.

"Jake! What are you doing here?"

Jacob walked over and slapped his brother on the shoulder in a friendly greeting. "Good to see you hard at work, Tobes. So, this is where you spend all your time."

Toby's grin got wider. A flush of pleasure crept across his cheeks. Jacob's heart clenched. The man before him was so different to the one he'd found in the emergency room. *Had it only been six weeks ago?* It seemed like a lifetime had passed.

"Jacob's here to talk to us about something important, Toby," Hannah said quietly.

She put on her latex gloves, ready to get back to work, but leaned up against a counter that was lined with equipment and other supplies. Her arms were folded across her chest. Now that the moment was upon him, Jacob wasn't quite sure where to start.

He cleared his throat. "It's about Robert Grace."

Toby looked at him in confusion and his gaze flicked to Hannah. "Who's Robert Grace?"

"It's Bobby, Max's nephew," Hannah supplied.

Toby's expression sobered and fear flickered in his eyes. "Oh, him. I don't like him. He says he knows me from somewhere and he keeps looking at me kind of weird, but I've never set eyes on him until I came here. I'm sure of it."

"It's all right, Tobes," Jacob hastened to reassure him. "It's not you Bobby thinks he's seen before. He's mistaking you for me."

Toby frowned again. "How would he have seen you? You don't work here. You've only been here once and that was my first day."

Jacob glanced around him and then looked at Hannah. "Is Bobby here now?"

Hannah shook her head. "I don't think so. I haven't seen him all day."

Jacob released his breath and looked back at his brother. "The thing is, Tobes, I met Bobby in jail."

The color left Toby's face. He stared at his brother in shock. "What? Bobby's been to *jail?* But...but... I don't understand."

"It's all right, Tobes. I know it's not what you expected. The thing is, Bobby's been in and out of trouble with the police for a long time. I met him when he was nineteen and it wasn't the first time he'd been to prison."

Toby's eyes narrowed. "I knew there was a reason I didn't like him. He's been to *jail!*"

As if only just becoming aware of what he'd said, Toby gasped and his eyes went wide. He looked at Jacob, blinking furiously. "I'm sorry, Jake. I didn't mean... I mean... Going to jail doesn't mean you're a nasty person. I just—"

Jacob's heart went out to his brother. "It's okay, Tobes, I understand. And the fact is, Bobby *is* a nasty person."

Toby looked on the verge of tears. "Was he nasty to you in jail?"

"No, buddy; in fact, he was my friend. But that

was a long time ago and a lot has happened since then. Lane's been looking into a few happenings here at the funeral home—as a police officer."

Toby's brow furrowed. "Lane? Why would Lane be worried about this place?"

"We had a couple of other guys working here before you started," Hannah explained. "They both died from accidents. The last one died not long before you arrived."

Toby shook his head. "Wow, that's kind of weird."

"Yes," Jacob agreed, "and that's why Lane's been doing a bit of investigating. He just found out that at least one of the deaths wasn't an accident and he thinks Bobby might be involved."

Toby's eyes went wide. "You mean, Lane thinks Bobby *killed* them?"

"Lane's not sure of anything at the moment," Jacob hurried to clarify, "but he's concerned about you working here. We both are."

Toby smiled. "Just because I work here doesn't mean Bobby's going to kill me, right Hannah?"

Hannah gazed back at him, her expression solemn. "I'm not sure what it means, Toby, but your brothers are right. Until we know what Bobby's involvement is, you need to stay out of his way."

A look of panic filled Toby's face as the implications became clear. "I'm not leaving here, Hannah! I'm not giving up my job. Not for Jake, not for anyone! I'm not scared of Bobby. He wouldn't dare hurt me. He has you and me to stand up to him. Doesn't he?"

His voice had turned almost pleading. It tore at Jacob's heart. He loved seeing his brother passionate about his work, but not to the point he would risk his life. He cleared his throat and delivered the bad news.

"Until we get to the bottom of this, it's not safe for you to be here, Tobes. I want you to think about taking some time off and just keeping low for a while."

Toby shook his head frantically, his gaze jumping from one to the other. "No! I'm not leaving. Hannah can keep me safe! Can't you, Hannah? Bobby won't try anything on me. I'll... I'll knock him flat if he does. I know how to fight, Jake. You're not the only one who's done it tough."

Jacob drew in a deep breath and eased it out between his lips. "I know, buddy and I'm sure you know how to handle yourself, but what if he takes you by surprise? What if he has a weapon? Maybe even a gun?"

"Did he use a gun on the other guys?" Toby asked.

"No, not as far as I know. One fell in front of a car and the other guy was pushed down a flight of stairs."

"See, he doesn't have a gun or he'd use it, wouldn't he?" Toby stated, a triumphant gleam in his eyes.

Jacob swallowed a groan. "The thing is, Tobes, it's not safe for you around here until Bobby's either cleared of any wrongdoing or arrested and tossed into jail. I don't want to have to worry about what might or might not be happening to you whenever I'm not around. And that's another thing. I want you to move in with me."

"No!" Toby's objection was loud and immediate. "I live with Hannah. I love living with Hannah." He threw a look tinged with desperation in Hannah's direction. "I even pay a little rent... We have a great time, don't we, Hannah? We talk all the time and sometimes we play cards. You tell him. There's nothing to be afraid of at home."

Jacob turned to stare at Hannah. "Does Bobby know where you live?" he asked quietly.

Her shoulders slumped. Slowly, she lifted her gaze to his and nodded. "Probably. It's listed on all of my employment papers. It wouldn't be hard to find out."

"But nobody knows I live with her!" Toby protested again.

Hannah's expression froze. Jacob rounded on her. "What is it, Hannah?"

She flushed and averted her gaze. "I... I think I mentioned to Max that Toby was sharing my house. I don't know if he mentioned it to Bobby. There wouldn't have been a reason to, but..."

Jacob stared at her, feeling grim. "We can't take that risk."

He turned back to his twin. "Toby, you're to stop working here until we know for sure what's going on with Bobby Grace and what kind of threat he poses and you're going to move out of Hannah's and come home with me. I have plenty of room and I promise I won't cramp your style." He tried for a grin, but it fell flat.

His twin looked furious. Toby's eyes flared and twin spots of color reddened his cheeks. "No, Jake! No! You can't tell me what to do! I'm not a child! I'm perfectly safe here with Hannah and we're perfectly safe at home. You have to work and so you won't be there all the time. Bobby's not going to hurt me. He barely knows me."

Jacob's patience snapped. "For fuck's sake, Toby! Wake up and open your eyes. The man has a life insurance policy with your name on it. Do you even know what that means?"

Toby's face filled with shock. "Life insurance?" He turned to Hannah, his expression dazed. "Is that the same thing that doctor talked about?"

Hannah nodded. "Yes, Toby, it is. You told me the doctor said you were there for a medical check-up for life insurance purposes."

Toby continued to stare at her. "What does it mean?"

"Bobby Grace took out a life insurance policy with you as the insured," Jacob explained brusquely. "It means that if you die, he'll receive money. A lot of money. It was the same with the other guys," he added.

Toby's face paled again. "You mean, Bobby took out insurance on them and then killed them for the money?"

Jacob nodded grimly. "It looks that way."

Toby turned away, his shoulders slumped in defeat. Jacob felt bad for him, but he was doing this for his twin. Toby needed someone to look out for him and Jacob was in the best position to do it.

Jacob turned his attention to Hannah. "I'd like

for *both* of you to come and stay with me for a while, just until this is all sorted, one way or the other. It's the only way I'll know for sure the two of you are safe."

Hannah opened her mouth. He could see she was about to protest. Before he could speak again, Toby spun on his heel and faced her.

"Yes! Please, Hannah! Say yes! And don't worry about Pepper. Jacob loves cats, too! If I have to go, so should you. You already said Bobby knows where you live. What if he comes after *you?* I'd *die* if anything happened to you!"

Hannah's gaze flew from Jacob's to Toby's and back again. "Toby, I don't think... I mean, what Jacob's saying is right. You need to stay somewhere safe, somewhere that Bobby doesn't know about, just in case, but it doesn't mean I'm at risk. I'm happy to stay where I am. I don't need to—"

"If you're not going, then I'm not going. Besides, he could take insurance on you, too," Toby declared, folding his arms across his chest. His mouth set in a stubborn line.

Jacob gritted his teeth. "Tobes, be reasonable, buddy. I need to know you're safe. I'm more than happy for Hannah to come with us and Pepper, too, but it's you who appears to be in Bobby's sights. You're the one named in the insurance documents. You're the one who has a price on his head."

Toby continued to stare at him stubbornly. "I'm only going, if Hannah goes with me. I won't leave any other way."

Jacob sighed and looked over at Hannah. She shuffled her feet and recrossed her arms and wouldn't meet his gaze. He could only imagine she was remembering the last time they were together. *Was every detail seared into her mind, as it was in his?*

He'd be thrilled if she accepted his invitation. Spending more time with her was something he was eager to do, but he wouldn't force her into it. Convincing Toby to move in with him would be easier if she threw her support behind the idea, but he understood her reluctance to uproot her life with very little discussion and no firm idea how long the arrangement would last. But Toby was right, Hannah could be in danger too.

"Hannah?" He posed the question softly, without inflection. This had to be her decision.

The seconds of silence dragged out until he almost couldn't stand it. She was going to turn him down; she didn't want to be in close confines with him or take the risk that something else might happen—that they might continue, or even finish, what they started in his truck. And then she looked at him. Her eyes were huge and somber in her face.

"Okay, I'll do it," she said and his heart took off in flight.

With an effort, he reined in his jubilation. "Are you sure?"

She nodded, looking a little more convinced. "Yes. If it means keeping Toby safe from Bobby, I'll do it. And I trust you."

Jacob allowed himself a small smile of relief.

She trusted him? "Great. I guess that's settled then. I'm working late tonight, but I have the next couple of days off. I can help move a few of your things over then, if that suits."

She nodded hesitantly, still clearly far from certain that she'd made the right decision.

"I guess so," she responded slowly. "I could pack up some stuff tonight and come over tomorrow, but I don't think I'll need any help. I'll throw some clothes and a few other things into a suitcase and drive us both over. Are you sure you're okay if I bring Pepper?"

He nodded. "Of course. Like Toby said, I'm fine with cats."

"Great," she replied. "What time suits you?"

Jacob shrugged, forcing himself to remain nonchalant. "I'm usually an early riser. Does nine sound all right?"

"Sure, I guess." Hannah looked at Toby. "Are you okay with that?"

The grin on Toby's face split him from ear to ear. "I'll be ready whenever you are, Hannah! I can't believe it! The three of us are going to live together! Whoopee!"

Heat crept up Jacob's cheeks. He risked a glance in Hannah's direction and was perturbed to discover she'd compressed her lips. Toby's suggestion that they were all one happy family hadn't gone down well. Jacob vowed silently to make her see he was worthy of her attention and that he was so much more than the irresponsible teenager who'd caused the death of her boyfriend.

"What about work?" asked Toby, breaking into Jacob's musings. "I'm not going to give up my job. I love working here. You can't make me give it up."

Impatience once again surged through Jacob. He clenched his jaw tight in an effort to stem it. "Bobby works here, too, Tobes. It's not safe for you to be here with him."

"I've been thinking about that," Hannah said. "I'll still be working. I think he's probably safer here, where I can keep an eye on him. It isn't feasible for either of us to take an extended leave of absence from work and if we leave Toby at home, we won't know where he is during the day. At least if he's here, I can watch out for him, make sure he doesn't cross Bobby's path. I could also speak to Max," she added. "He told me he was going to report the matter to the police. I'll find out whether he did so and who he spoke to."

"That would be good. I already mentioned this to Lane. He was going to look into it, too. If you find anything out, let me know and I'll pass the information on to Lane. Whoever your boss spoke to might be able confer with Lane, share resources. Get this asshole behind bars that much faster."

The door behind Jacob swung open and a mountain of a man filled the narrow space. "Who's calling who an asshole?"

Jacob stared at The Bobster. The man had aged drastically since he'd last seen him. They were close in age, but the passage of time had been far from kind to Bobby. Even more scars crisscrossed his face and arms.

His eyes were bloodshot and weepy. It looked like he hadn't shaved for more than a week and his hair hung long and lank. The rank smell of body odor wafted across the room and Jacob breathed through his mouth. The Bobster looked almost as bad as Toby had the first time Jacob had spotted him in the ED. If the half million dollars had indeed gone into The Bobster's bank account, it was clear he hadn't spent any on himself.

The Bobster's gaze scanned the room and finally landed on Jacob. It took a few moments, but Jacob knew the instant his former cellmate recognized him. Bobby Grace's eyes widened and his mouth gaped.

"Jacob Black? Is it you? Where the fuck did you come from?" Bobby looked from Jacob to Toby and back again. His brow creased into a frown. "What the fuck? You're *twins?*" He narrowed his eyes on Toby. "I *knew* I'd seen you somewhere before."

Toby moved closer to Hannah, who still stood against the counter. Jacob clenched his fists and stepped forward. He'd had enough of Bobby frightening his brother—or anyone else. He moved even closer, until he crowded The Bobster's personal space. Bobby held his ground, but Jacob refused to feel intimidated.

"Stay the hell away from my brother," he growled low in his throat.

Bobby moved back slightly, eyeing Jacob uncertainly. "What the fuck are you talking about?"

Jacob's anger stirred. "Don't give me that bullshit. You know exactly what I'm talking about. The life insurance policies? I'll tell you again, friend or no friend, when it comes to my brother, I'll do whatever it takes to protect him. You were good to me in jail, when I really needed a friend, but you touch my brother and you'll regret it for as long as you live."

Bobby stepped back and raised his hands in surrender, still looking confused. "You've got me mixed up with someone else, buddy. Either that, or you're not right in the head. I thought I was the only one who got knocked around like that, but I'm beginning to wonder if you didn't take a few that I didn't hear about. I don't know anything about insurance policies. What the fuck would I want with something like that?"

CHAPTER 20

Lane spied Samantha Coleridge striding toward him and nodded a greeting. The noise of the excavator that was in the process of exhuming the coffin containing the remains of Christopher Lowrey precluded conversation. The fact that the body had only been in the ground for a couple of months was in their favor. Samantha had a better chance of discovering evidence of foul play when the decomposition wasn't so advanced.

Still, it wouldn't be pretty. Even with the cooler temperatures and the fact the wooden coffin was almost airtight, Lane was glad he didn't have the job of carrying out the autopsy.

"How are we today, on this bright, sunny morning, Detective? Can you think of anywhere else you'd rather be?" she asked, smiling.

Lane chuckled, appreciating Samantha's humor. If Lane hadn't been bowled over by his wife, Zara, and if Samantha were single, he'd have given her more than a passing glance. Like

Zara, Samantha had dark coloring, with midnight hair and golden skin. And she was as smart as she was beautiful. Another thing she had in common with his wife.

"I'm glad it's you doing this and not me," he admitted, eliciting a wry grin.

"I live for these moments, Detective. At least it's given me something else to think about other than the last time I had my head over a toilet bowl."

Lane glanced down at the gently protruding belly that was outlined against her black slacks and chuckled. Next to Zara, his twins were the best thing that had ever happened to him.

"What else do you know about this guy?" Samantha asked, focusing on the cheap pine coffin that was now exposed to the air.

"His body was claimed by the Max Grace Funeral Home. Robert Grace signed the paperwork and collected it from the morgue. In itself, that fact isn't necessarily sinister. After all, Lowrey was a destitute case. The police couldn't track down any next of kin. As his employer, Max Grace came forward to claim the body. And I understand he covered the funeral, including the cost of the plot."

"It would have been cheaper to cremate him," Samantha murmured.

"Yes, but the funeral home doesn't accommodate cremations. It's strictly burials."

"I guess that explains it," Samantha said.

Lane compressed his lips. "The problem is, and the reason we're here, is because Robert Grace took out a life insurance policy on Christopher

Lowrey. He pocketed a cool half million last week when the life insurance company paid up."

Samantha's dark eyebrows rose in surprise. "That's a fair incentive to hasten a colleague's death."

Lane nodded grimly. "Exactly. Let's hope you have enough to determine whether our guy fell over drunk and went under the wheels of that truck, or whether someone gave him a helping hand."

———————

Max took a sip from his coffee mug and surveyed the mess of papers scattered across his desk. A sense of anticipation surged through him. It was only Tuesday. The week still had so many possibilities... He smiled at the thought. A knock on his door interrupted his musings and he looked up and spied Hannah standing in the open doorway.

"Good morning, Hannah. What can I do for you?" he asked.

"Can I come in?"

"Of course. I always have time for you," he replied and waved her in with a smile. "What's happening? Are you staying out of trouble?"

Hannah cleared a space off the only available chair and perched on the edge. "Not much. After all, I spend most of my waking hours here. How much trouble can I get in to?"

She smiled. Max smiled back. He knew her well enough to know that she was teasing. She loved her job and he'd always treated her well. He was sure she had no complaints about her employer.

"Is there something you wanted to speak with me about?" he asked in an effort to prompt her.

She regarded him nervously, as if unsure where to start. He frowned at her strange behavior and a faint stirring of unease made itself known in his gut. "Hannah, is there something wrong?"

"No. Yes. I mean… It has to do with your nephew. I'm not sure how to say it, but I recently became aware Bobby's spent time in jail and has a considerable criminal record. He's been convicted of a number of violent offenses."

She blushed with embarrassment and Max could tell she was uncomfortable revealing such things to him. He wondered how she'd come upon her information. Not that it mattered. After all, it was the truth. He schooled his features into an appropriately repentant expression.

"I'm sorry, Hannah. I should have told you. I'm well aware of the boy's violent past. I was hoping… I thought if I gave him a job and helped him find a place to stay, he'd try harder to keep out of trouble. I wanted to give him a chance to start again." He shrugged sadly. "I guess it didn't work."

Hannah's expression filled with remorse. "I'm sorry, Max. I wish I didn't have to say anything. I can't imagine how awful you must feel. After all you've done for him… It's just that, I've always felt uncomfortable around him and now, knowing his history and the police suspicions, I'm even more afraid of him and what he might be capable of."

"I'm not sure that he's dangerous," Max stated, deliberately sounding unsure, to convince her of the opposite. He had to conceal a smile when she responded in the way he hoped.

She frowned. "But what about the insurance policy? The one you found in the bottom of his desk drawer?"

Max forced his expression into one of thoughtful concern. "Yes, you're right. That *is* rather strange. There doesn't seem to be any reasonable explanation for that."

Hannah frowned. "Did you go to the police, like you said you would?"

Max nodded and lied straight to her face. "Of course I did. I have the detective's card right here." He hunted around through the papers on his desk, pretending to search for it.

Hannah looked relieved. "Oh, thank goodness! I'm so glad! Toby's brother, Lane, is a police officer. He's been looking into the matter for us. He might be able to confer with whoever you spoke to and pool resources."

A police officer? That explained where she'd gotten the information about Bobby's criminal record... He nodded in response to her suggestion, keeping up the pretense of support. "Yes, that sounds like a good idea. If only I could find that card. It must be here somewhere..."

"The truth is, I've moved in with some friends because I feel safer than living on my own," Hannah confided. "At least, until this thing with Bobby's resolved one way or the other. I'm not saying he's guilty," she added hurriedly and flushed.

Max hastened to reassure her. "Of course not." He needed her to keep thinking they were both on the same side. "We both know Bobby's not an angel and the evidence against him is far from weak. I've been wracking my brain to come up with a reasonable explanation about why he'd own an insurance policy with Christopher Lowrey as the insured, but I can't."

"It isn't only Christopher," Hannah said softly. "Lane Black discovered Bobby also owns a policy in Edward's name and there's one for Toby, too—all with the same company." She paused and then added, "I don't have to tell you how things worked out for Christopher and Edward. I have fears for Toby. I don't want him to be next."

Surprise and concern surged through Max when he heard the police had discovered all three policies, but he forced his face into a neutral expression and responded in the manner expected.

"I'm sorry, Hannah. I had no idea it was that bad. It's even worse than I thought. I'll have to ring the detective right away. If I can just find his card..." Once again, he made a show of looking for it.

"Did you talk to him about it?" Hannah asked, curiosity frank on her face.

Max frowned. "Who? The detective?" he asked, deliberately misunderstanding her.

"No, Bobby."

"Oh. Bobby. Yes, of course. He denied knowing anything about it." Max shrugged. "I'm no closer to the truth. It's the reason I decided to report it to the police. They know how to get to the bottom of these things much better than I."

He drew in a breath and regarded her somberly. "I might be a silly old man, but my gut's telling me something isn't right. Bobby's my nephew, but I'm not prepared to sit by and ignore what's right before my eyes. I'm more and more afraid he murdered those boys for the insurance money and the knowledge breaks my heart."

Hannah stared at him, shock flooding her face. Max suppressed a smile of satisfaction. No doubt she hadn't expected him to put all the pieces together, yet alone offer such a candid disclosure.

"Now you can see why I'm so frightened for Toby," she said. "I wanted to ask you if you could possibly keep Bobby away from here—just until the police have enough evidence to arrest him."

Max was quick to assure her. "That shouldn't be a problem, my dear. He's hardly ever here, anyway. He's been such a disappointment and to think he's my only heir. I don't know what I'm going to do with this place now, when I'm gone."

Hannah waved her hand dismissively. "Don't talk like that, Max. You have plenty of good years ahead of you, yet."

Max sighed and ran a hand through this thick, white crop. "I'll be seventy-six next birthday, Hannah. Not exactly a spring chicken. My Eileen's been dead nearly fifty years. She died on my twenty-sixth birthday. I'll never forget it..."

His voice drifted off. This time, he didn't have to fake his reaction. Eileen had been his whole world. Her death had hit him hard. In fact, if he were being honest, he'd admit he'd never gotten over her untimely death. It was one of the reasons why he'd recently given up living a clean and honorable life and had turned to the dark side. He was through with doing good. It didn't get him anywhere worth anything.

"What happened?" Hannah asked softly.

"Cancer," he replied. "I buried her next to our son."

Hannah blinked in surprise and he understood her reaction. She'd worked for him for six years. Apart from Bobby, she knew nothing of his family.

"How old was your son when he died?" she asked gently.

"Three. He was three years old."

Hannah's face reflected her sadness. "Oh, Max! What happened?"

Max remained silent, remembering that awful time. Finally, he let out a heavy sigh. "He drowned. In the swimming pool. We were both there—Eileen and I. We were both watching him, but somehow, neither of us noticed he'd pulled off his floaties and had climbed back in the pool. It all happened so fast. One moment, he was splashing and playing and laughing in the water and the next he was lying on the bottom. We tried to resuscitate him, but it was no use. He was dead."

Hannah shook her head slowly back and forth, her eyes glinting with tears. Max's throat constricted at the sight. She was such a beautiful girl, inside and out. She reminded him of his wife.

"Is that why you reach out to so many people who are down on their luck?" she asked softly.

"Christopher? Edward? Even Toby. They aren't the usual type of people a stranger would choose to help."

Max looked up at her and conjured up some tears. "I guess so. I see someone like Christopher or Edward or Toby and I just want to help them out. I think about my own son and I wonder what might have become of him if he'd been given the chance to grow up.

"Would he have followed me into the business? Would he even now be tallying up the bills? Or would he have followed a different path entirely? I like to think, if he'd fallen on hard times, someone else might have offered him the hand of friendship, like I do. I guess that's what drives me to do it, over and over again."

Hannah swiped at the moisture that had gathered in her eyes. "You're a good man, Max Grace and don't let anyone else tell you differently."

Max looked down at his desk, feigning embarrassment. "It's very nice of you to say so, Hannah. You're not so bad yourself."

———————

Bobby heated the ice crystals with a cigarette lighter and then filled the needle with the clear liquid gold. With the belt tourniquet tight around his upper arm, he skilfully found a vein. It was wrong, so wrong and he knew better than to let his life spiral once again out of control, but he wasn't strong where it counted and couldn't seem to help himself.

Everywhere he looked he was a fuck-up. In jail, he'd become a punching bag for other people's battles. He'd only done it to make friends. It was too bad it hadn't worked out like that. The only true friend he'd had was Jacob and that had only lasted the two years they'd shared a cell. Jacob had been released and never looked back. Not once had he gotten in contact.

And then, out of the blue, he appeared in Bobby's workplace—the funeral home, no less. It was unbelievable enough to be called a miracle, and yet Jacob had come across almost aggressive and definitely unfriendly.

Bobby couldn't understand his former friend's animosity. *What the fuck was he going on about— life insurance policies?* Bobby barely knew what a life insurance policy was, let alone owned one. And yet, Jacob had accused him of owning more than one and one of them had involved Jacob's brother. It didn't make sense. None of it did. Then again, nothing much over the course of his entire life ever had.

CHAPTER 21

Dear Diary,

I look back over my life and it doesn't take me long to pinpoint where it all went wrong. I was raised a good Christian and I tried so hard to live my life that way. But then, Emory was drowned in the swimming pool and a few years later, Eileen was taken from me, too.

I railed against God, against anyone who would listen and yet, for a long time, I managed to keep my life on track. I built up a successful business. I enjoyed my work, I went to church, I prayed regularly for all the lost souls.

And now I'm just another one of them—another lost and lonely soul.

I tried so hard to live a good life, to be considerate of my fellow man, but over the years, I've just plain worn out fighting another part of myself, kept hidden for so long. One day, that part of me came up with a plan. It was time to forget about being good. It was time to get even with God. I was through with playing Christian. The Devil had scored a new soul.

And so, I sold myself to the Devil and I made a tidy

sum. Enough for me to sail away and retire in some distant land where the sun shines warm on my face and the sand is crystal white. I'll leave behind my wife and son in their cold, dark graves and I'll focus on happier things for the rest of my lonely days...

Lane adjusted the surgical mask over his nose and mouth and did his best not to breathe in too deeply. Samantha was similarly attired, but seemed not to notice the putrid smell. The winter had brought cooler temperatures, but a couple of months had passed since Christopher Lowrey had been interred. It was plenty long enough for decomposition to have made headway and with it, the accompanying smell. It filled the small autopsy suite.

"What do you think, Sam?" he asked, his voice slightly muffled behind the mask.

Samantha leaned over what remained of Christopher and frowned. "Charles x-rayed the body the first time it arrived in the morgue, but from the notes in the file, I don't think he paid much attention to the results. The x-rays showed several leg fractures which were consistent with the way Christopher died—falling into the path of a truck would do that, but what I'm interested in seeing is whether there are any wounds that might indicate earlier trauma."

"And are there?" Lane asked, forcing himself to move a little closer to the gurney.

Samantha straightened and sighed. "Unfortunately, the decomposition's far too advanced to tell, but I took the time to examine the leg fractures more closely. I've done a few calculations and applied a little physics."

She stared at Lane. His heart skipped a beat at the intensity in her gaze. "What is it? What did you find?"

"It's my considered opinion that the direction and trajectory of the fractures indicates Christopher Lowrey was pushed from behind with considerable force, straight into the path of the oncoming vehicle."

Lane stared back at her. His pulse picked up speed. "You're saying it's possible he was murdered, like Edward Sutton?"

Samantha held his gaze, steadily. "Yes."

"No chance it could have been suicide?"

Samantha nodded. "The injuries could also be consistent with suicide—throwing himself in front of the truck would result in similar fractures—but a check of his blood alcohol levels discounts this. Like Sutton, Lowrey had way too much alcohol in his system. So much, that it would have prevented him from standing there and carrying out such an action. He wouldn't have been able to walk without assistance, let alone throw himself in front of a truck."

A sense of urgency poured through Lane's veins. It was midday. Toby was more than likely at work. At the funeral parlor. The same funeral parlor that had employed two men who'd both been murdered in similar circumstances for insurance money and the man who was more than likely responsible was still working there. He had to call Jacob.

Offering Samantha his thanks and a brief good-bye, Lane moved into the adjoining room and pulled off his protective clothing. Tossing them into the trash can, he headed for the exit, tugging his phone out as he went. He dialed his brother's number, praying that he'd pick up and was relieved when he did.

"Jacob, I've just come from the morgue. Samantha Coleridge has done a second autopsy on Christopher Lowery."

As efficiently as he could, Lane filled his brother in on the results. "It was the perfect crime," Lane continued. "It happened about four in the morning. The truck driver didn't see a thing. He didn't even realize he'd run over the poor bastard."

"Jesus," Jacob muttered.

Lane silently agreed. "Where's Toby?" he asked.

"He's with Hannah. They're at work. We thought it was safer to leave him there, around other people."

"Call him," Lane urged. "Tell him to stick close to Hannah and call her, too. Impress upon her the importance of keeping Robert Grace away from our brother."

"I will," Jacob promised. "Hannah spoke to her boss. Max assured her he'd already reported the matter to the police. They might already have someone else working on this."

Lane frowned. It was possible an officer stationed elsewhere had already started an investigation based upon Max Grace's report, but he would have thought he'd have received some kind of notice that a file in the same name had been opened on their system.

"Do you know the name of the officer he reported it to?" he asked.

"No."

"What about the station?"

"No, I don't know that, either, but I can find out. I'll ask Hannah when I speak to her."

"Don't stress about it. I'm headed back to the office. Robert Grace's bank account details checked out. I'm going to bring the boss up to speed and then get authorization to attend upon the funeral home with an arrest warrant. Robert Grace will very soon be removed from the streets of Sydney."

Jacob sighed in relief. "How long will it take?"

Lane checked his mirror before pulling out into the traffic. "An hour or so," he replied. "I'll have to get an arrest team together and set up a plan. We'll hit the funeral parlor first and if we don't find him there, we'll search any other known place of abode. He has enough entries in our system that we should be able to track him down at one of his listed addresses. I'll let you know when we have him behind bars."

"Thanks, Lane. I appreciate it. That moment can't come soon enough."

"You're telling me," Lane replied grimly and stepped on the gas.

———————

Once again, Jacob rang the bell outside the Max Grace Funeral Home and waited for someone to answer it. Neither Hannah nor Toby had answered their phones, so he'd decided to drive over and warn them that Lane and his men were on their way. He also wanted to check for himself that Toby was okay. He trusted Hannah to look out for his brother, but it was unreasonable to expect she could watch him all the time, or protect Toby and herself if things turned sour.

The front door remained closed. Jacob frowned and rang the bell again. This time, he heard the sound of footsteps and a moment later, an elderly man with a thick head of white hair and rosy cheeks opened the door. The man's eyes widened in surprise at the sight of Jacob.

"You must be Toby's twin."

"Yes, I'm Jacob Black. You must be Max Grace." Jacob stuck out his hand and Max shook it in greeting.

"Nice to meet you. I can see why my nephew was confused. You're like peas in a pod, until you look a little more closely."

"Bobby told you about me." Jacob guessed.

"Yes. He had no idea you had an identical twin. It bugged the life out of him for weeks after he first met your brother. He was sure he'd met him somewhere before. Of course, Toby denied ever knowing him. Bobby was a little more irritable than normal with that. He thought your brother was lying to him and if it's one thing Bobby can't tolerate, it's dishonesty and deceit."

Jacob stared in disbelief at the man who

looked like the sweetest, kindest grandfather a person could ever meet. *How could he be so oblivious to his nephew's failings?* It seemed beyond belief. Hannah had told him her boss was a kind and generous man who went out of his way to help the less fortunate. *Was that the reason he didn't see what was right in front of his nose?* Jacob wished he could be so non-judgmental and trusting.

"Is Bobby here?" he asked.

"Yes, I think so. I heard him moving about in his office a while ago. Why? Are you here to see him?"

"No, no. Not Bobby. I... I'm here to see Hannah and my brother."

Max nodded. "They should be in the embalming room. It's my guess they're elbow-deep in body fluids. No doubt that's the reason they didn't answer the door."

Jacob tried not to grimace at the picture Max's words conjured up and followed the man through the doorway and down the hall. With a flourish, Max opened the door to the embalming room and waved Jacob inside.

He spied Hannah and his brother immediately. As Max had guessed, they were both bent over a body, their gloves shiny with liquid.

"Jake!" Toby exclaimed after looking up. "What are you doing here?"

Hannah also looked bemused. Jacob had left for work before Hannah and his brother were awake. With a string of twelve-hour shifts, including two night shifts, they'd barely seen each other. It wasn't quite like Jacob had envisaged when he'd invited Hannah to move in and he was determined that on his next days off, he'd do all he could to persuade her to spend some time with him. But for now, Toby's safety was paramount.

Jacob glanced at Max before speaking and then decided to deliver his news anyway. Lane and his men were on their way. It wouldn't be long before everybody in the funeral parlor became aware of what was going down.

"Hannah, Toby. There's something I need to tell you."

Hannah glanced up at him and then returned to her work. It looked like she was suctioning fluid out of the woman who lay stiff and pale gray on the stainless steel gurney.

"It's about Bobby."

Something in Jacob's voice must have snagged Hannah's attention, or maybe it was the reference to her colleague. She set down her tools and turned to him. "What about Bobby?"

Once again, Jacob glanced at Max who had inched his way into the room. Turning back to Hannah and Toby, he told them.

"Lane's on his way over to arrest Bobby."

Toby let out a shout of glee.

Hannah gaped in surprise. "Lane's on his way over, now?"

Jacob nodded. "The second autopsy, carried out on Christopher Lowrey, proved he was pushed into the path of the oncoming vehicle, like Edward Sutton was pushed down the stairs. Robert Grace owned life insurance policies in the names of both men and he's named as the sole beneficiary. He'll be arrested on suspicion of murder and insurance fraud."

Max made a noise of distress behind him and Jacob turned to face him again. "I'm sorry, Max. This must be awful for you. From what I've heard, you did everything you could for The Bobster when he got out of jail and he's thrown it back in your face. To repay your kindness and generosity by murdering two of your employees... It's beyond evil."

Max compressed his lips and Jacob could see he was making an effort to hold back the tears that glinted in his eyes. To Jacob, he suddenly seemed older, frailer, weaker; as if the spark had somehow disappeared. Jacob hardly knew the man and yet, he felt saddened by the sight.

"I never imagined my own flesh and blood could turn on me like that," Max said, his voice trembling. "I did everything I could for that boy. He didn't ever know his father. His mother never learned to fend for herself, or her son. He was in and out of jail for years. I offered him a job, a place to stay, a *life*. And this is how he repays me..."

Jacob shifted his gaze to stare at the floor, helpless against the man's distress. From the corner of his eye, he saw Hannah step toward her boss, her face full of compassion.

"Is Bobby here?" Hannah asked Max quietly.

"I think so, but I'm not really sure. I saw him earlier, but who knows? He comes and goes as he pleases with little respect for his job."

Hannah nodded, her lips compressed. The sound of the front doorbell made all of them jump.

"Police! Open up!"

Jacob's head came up and he stared across to where Max and Hannah stood. "It's Lane."

"He's here to arrest Bobby," Hannah murmured and Max's face lost a little more of its color.

Despite his distress, Max squared his shoulders and nodded. "We might as well get it over with."

With his head held high, Max strode through the doorway of the embalming room. He continued down the short corridor to the entryway and then flung open the front door without pause.

Jacob and Hannah followed him, with Toby not far behind. Lane stared at them in surprise.

"Hi, guys," he said. "I wasn't expecting to see all of you. Jacob, what are you doing here?"

Before Jacob could form a reply, Lane turned to Max. "Never mind. Are you Maxwell Grace, the owner of these premises?"

Max nodded, his expression somber. "I am."

"I'm Detective Senior Sergeant Lane Black with the State Crime Command. We're here to arrest your nephew, Robert Grace. Is he here?"

Max shrugged. "I'm not sure. He was here earlier. You're welcome to look around."

As if unsure whether to trust Max's congeniality, Lane's eyes narrowed, but without another word, he pushed past Max and the others and started searching the funeral parlor, calling out to his men to accompany him.

The search was over almost as quickly as it

began. Lane arrived back in the entryway where Jacob and the rest of them had remained.

"He's not here," Lane growled, to no one in particular, and then got up close and personal in Max's space. "Your nephew's wanted by the police. The next time you see him, I suggest you call me."

And with a final glare, he left.

CHAPTER 22

Hannah stacked the last of the plates into the dishwasher and rinsed her hands in the sink. They'd enjoyed an early dinner and were now in the process of cleaning up. Moving past Jacob, she dried her hands on the small towel hanging from a peg near the pantry.

"Thank you for dinner," she murmured.

Jacob shot her a brief smile. "It's a nice change to be home in time to share it with you both."

Hannah nodded, her mind on the fact that now Bobby's arrest was imminent, there was no need for Jacob to watch over her and his brother. As soon as Bobby was locked behind bars, the threat would be over. She and Pepper would move out of Jacob's apartment and her life would go back to the way it was before. Work, an occasional social get together with her friends, and then back to work again.

It wasn't until she began sharing her home with Toby and then later, moving in with the two brothers, that she realized how lonely it was living on her own. It wasn't like she had a job where she interacted with any number of people during the day. Apart from her conversations with Max and whatever assistant happened to be around, she worked most of the time in solitude. Just herself and the deceased.

It wasn't a job for everyone, but it was one that she loved. It was just that it hadn't felt quite so lonely until recently, after the Black brothers had barged their way back into her life. One Black brother in particular was keeping her awake at night. Knowing he was only a few yards down the hall had wrought havoc on her equilibrium.

"Would you like a coffee, Hannah? Or something stronger?"

The man who had haunted her dreams murmured the question, his eyes warm and curious on her face. Her gaze drifted over his broad shoulders and studied his impressive physique. She remembered how it felt to kiss him and press herself against his strength. Even when they'd kissed in the confines of his pickup, she'd wanted more. And then, she'd come to her senses and realized this was *Jacob Black*, her nemesis, and that she was luxuriating in the feel of being in his arms.

"Hannah?" he asked again.

Her gaze snapped back to his and she blushed, hoping desperately that he couldn't read the path of her thoughts.

"Um... I... I think I'll have a glass of Merlot, if it's all right with you. I bought a bottle on my way home tonight. After the day's events, I thought the three of us could do with a drink." She tried on a smile, but it came out shaky. Thankfully, Jacob didn't appear to notice. He turned and retrieved two wine glasses from a shelf above her head.

"Only two? What about Toby?"

"He went to bed while you were in the bathroom. He said he needed an early night. I think the stress of the last little while's catching up on him. I'll be pleased when The Bobster's back in jail. Lane promised to call me as soon as they track him down. He's confident it won't take too long."

Hannah nodded. "I'm glad. As much as I feel sorry for Max and the way his nephew's turned out, I'll be relieved when we don't have to worry about Toby and what plans Bobby might have for him."

She drew in a breath and then forced herself to add, "I... I guess I should move back home. Toby seems happy here, and now that he's had time to get used to the idea, I'm sure he'll be keen to stay. You don't need me here."

Jacob stared at her. "I might not need you here, but... I like having you around. I... I want you to stay."

His gaze held hers. She couldn't look away. Her heart took off at a gallop and nerves danced like wildfire through her veins. She opened her mouth to speak, but no sound came out. Clearing her throat, she licked her dry lips and tried again.

"I'm not sure that's a good idea, Jacob. We have a lot of history—not all of it good. It might be best if we leave the past where it is and move forward as...friends."

His eyes darkened with emotion. *"Friends?* Is that what you want?"

Seconds passed. Every breath sounded loud in the silence. Once again, Hannah made an effort to speak. "How can we be more than that, Jacob? Almost every time I look at you, that awful night comes back to me. It must be the same for you. What kind of relationship could we have when we feel that way?"

"Is it the same when I kiss you? Are you thinking of that night even then?" he asked, his voice hoarse.

"Yes!" she lied, feeling desperate. How could she even think about setting Luke aside for Jacob, the man who'd caused his death?

Jacob's expression turned stormy and he shot her a steely glare. "Liar. You were wild and warm and passionate. You wanted those kisses as much as I did and we both know you wanted a whole lot more. Don't tell me you were thinking of Luke the whole time. I won't believe you."

His words stabbed through her heart like daggers, each one dipped in poison. She was bleeding from a thousand cuts and there was nothing she could do about it. Luke's beloved face had faded until she could barely remember what he looked like. For the past six weeks, it had been nothing and no one but Jacob.

Jacob was in her thoughts constantly and the questions ran over and over inside her head. His image everywhere, including in the face of his twin. While Toby was all sweetness and light and had an endearing, heartfelt innocence, Jacob was darker, moodier, more complex and harder to read. But that was one of the things she'd come to love about him—the challenge in his eyes. He was an enigma and she was more than a little intrigued.

The things he'd suffered in jail—and she was certain she'd barely heard any of it—made her want to comfort him and hold him close. It was madness. He was the man responsible for killing her boyfriend. And yet, she knew it hadn't been intentional. Jacob had lost his best friend that night. Somehow, perhaps because they'd both loved Luke, she felt deeply connected to him and there was nothing she could do about it. The knowledge irritated her. She took a step back, needing to put some distance between them.

His gaze narrowed. "Admit it, Hannah; you like me. You like me a helluva lot. If this thing with Luke wasn't between us, we'd be together already. There's something between us I can't explain, but for me, it's been there for years. I loved you when you were a teenager and time hasn't changed a thing."

Surprise shot through her. She stared at him, aghast. She'd been so immersed in Luke, she'd had no idea his best friend felt that way.

"But... But I was with Luke. How...?"

He cursed under his breath and looked away. "I don't know how. Love doesn't give a reason. It can't be easily explained. Love is love. It is what it is. How did you love Luke?"

She frowned at the question. She loved Luke because he was good and kind and they had similar outlooks. They both wanted to save themselves for marriage. While many teenagers were having sex on the back seat of someone's car or in a cheap motel, she and Luke contented themselves with stolen kisses and hand holding.

While she'd longed to take things further and she knew Luke felt the same, it was important for both of them to remain pure. Only, Luke had died before they could marry and consummate their love. It was just another thing Jacob had stolen from her.

"What? You can't remember?" Jacob uttered, a scornful look in his eyes.

Hannah blinked hard and focused on him. "Of course I can remember! Our love was good and pure and real. We respected each other too much to sully that love with the tawdriness of premarital sex. We were going to get married right after high school! We had our whole lives planned out! You took that from us, Jacob, and it wasn't fair!"

He frowned. "I can't believe you're still angry at me. I repaid my debt for that mistake!" His voice rose. "I spent two years of my life in prison! It was hell every second of the day! What else do you want from me?"

All of a sudden, the anger she'd held inside her for more than a decade ignited and found its voice. Her face went hot.

"Two years!" she scoffed. "Big deal. What's two years when you've taken a man's life? It was only because you were the son of Warren Black that you were let off so lightly and everyone knew it.

Your father was a legend in our town. A man who gave his life in the line of duty; a hero to all around."

Jacob's eyes widened in shock. "You think the sentence was *inadequate?*" he shouted in disbelief. "Do you mean to tell me you think the judge treated me lightly because of who my father was?"

Hannah put her hands on her hips and narrowed her eyes. "Of *course* it was inadequate! I wasn't the only one who thought so. If Warren Black hadn't been your father, we all know you would have done a lot more time. You climbed drunk behind the wheel of a car and killed someone. How long do you think you should have gotten?" she shouted, tears now blurring her vision.

"My sentence was fair and reflected the circumstances. If you'd bothered to show up at the sentencing, you would have heard the judge's reasons for finding as he did. But no, you couldn't be bothered. My life and what happened to it was of no concern to you. You were too busy mourning your saintly boyfriend who apparently could do no wrong. That just goes to show you didn't know him well at all," Jacob sneered, his breath coming fast.

Hannah's heart skipped a beat and then a fresh wave of fury gushed through her veins. "What the hell's *that* supposed to mean?" she yelled.

Jacob turned away from her and began to pace the small confines of the kitchen. "Your perfect Luke Parker? The boy who could do no wrong." Jacob came to a sudden halt. In three long strides, he was beside her, crowding her against the breakfast bar.

"Let me tell you about Luke Parker. I'd known him since we were in diapers. He was good at being the kind of person people wanted him to be. He spent his whole life pretending."

Hannah stared at Jacob in horror and began to shake her head. Even though she'd had suspicions of her own, she couldn't bear to hear them voiced by someone else.

"No, no, you're wrong!" she cried. "Luke wasn't like that. Luke was good and kind and true. We loved each other and what we had was real! You were *jealous!* That's why you're saying these things. You're trying to justify your actions and hide behind the fact your stupidity got him killed!"

"He was having sex with half the cheerleaders, Hannah! For fuck's sake, wake up and see him for what he was!"

Shock and pain rendered her momentarily speechless and then she found her tongue. "How *dare* you! How dare you sully his name! You're despicable! He was worth ten of you! You aren't—"

"Stop it! Stop it! Stop it! I can't stand it anymore!"

Hannah and Jacob turned as one and stared at Toby who stood in the doorway that led down the hall. He had his hands over his ears and swung his head from side to side. Tears streamed down his cheeks. At the sight of his distress, Hannah's heart clenched with pain.

Dragging in deep breaths, she fought to regain control. This wasn't Toby's fault. It had nothing to do with him. It wasn't fair for him to be a witness to the anger that had been boiling over between her and his brother for more than a decade.

"I'm sorry, Tobes. We didn't mean to wake you. Please, go back to bed," Jacob implored.

Hannah repeated Jacob's urgings, but Toby continued to shake his head. "I can't stand it anymore! I can't stand nobody knowing the truth! It's been eating me up inside. I have to let it out!" he wailed.

Jacob strode across the room and halted beside his brother. "Tobes, it's all right. Calm down and stop shouting. I promise I won't yell at Hannah again and she won't yell at me, right Hannah?"

He turned slightly and threw a glance in her direction. She nodded, happy to do whatever it took to pacify the distressed man.

"Of course, Toby," she hurried to reassure him. "I'm sorry, too. I lost my temper, but I'm okay now. In fact, I think it's time for me to leave."

"No! You can't leave!" Toby begged her. "Not until you know the truth."

"Toby—" Jacob's voice was thick with warning. Hannah frowned.

Toby stared at his brother, his expression full of resolve. "No, Jake. You've protected me for long enough. You love Hannah and I think she likes you, but she's never going to love you until she knows what really happened that night."

Hannah's stomach plummeted and icy dread formed a hard lump in the bottom of her belly. The room around her receded until all she could see was Toby. His lips were moving and she strained to hear. A sense of foreboding filled her. She was certain she didn't want to know what he was about to disclose.

Instead, she wanted to turn and run and forget she'd ever met the Black brothers. Her life was fine until they'd pushed their way back into it. But her feet were rooted to the spot. She couldn't move. Toby turned to her, his eyes filled with sadness and remorse.

"Jake wasn't the one driving that night," he said quietly.

Hannah reeled back in shock. He could have told her he'd grown wings and could fly to the moon and she wouldn't have been more surprised.

"What... What do you mean?" she stammered, trying to take it in. "Are you saying *Luke* was behind the wheel?"

Once again, Jacob tried to intervene, his voice filled with desperate warning. "Toby..."

Toby turned on his twin, anger and determination glinting in his eyes. "No, Jake. It's time Hannah knew the truth. It's time I owned up to what I did."

Hannah blinked, sure she'd misheard. "What are you talking about? What do you mean—what *you* did?"

"I was the designated driver that night. Both Jake and Luke were drunk. We'd been out celebrating the end of our high school education. I'd agreed to take everyone home. It was late and I was tired, but that's not what caused the accident."

He paused and Hannah barely dared to breathe. Dread had morphed into terror. She didn't want to listen to another word.

"Luke was sitting up front, with me. He started bragging about a girl he'd chatted up in the bar. It had happened earlier in the night. Both Jake and I had noticed, but we ignored it. Luke was always flirting with the girls.

"When he disappeared for a while, we didn't think too much of it, but as I was driving us home, he told us all the details about the girl he'd been with and what they'd done together."

Hannah stared from Toby to Jacob, aghast. She couldn't believe what she was hearing; didn't *want* to believe it. If it was anyone but Toby recounting it, she would have told them they were telling lies.

Luke wasn't a womanizer, despite her occasional disquiet. He barely *looked* at other girls and never when they were together. It was one of the things she loved about him. She wasn't ready to accept it might all have been an act.

"It wasn't the fact he'd slept with another girl that made me angry," Toby continued softly. "I'd seen and heard that kind of thing more than once from Luke before. It was when he started scoffing at you and your wish to stay pure that I got angry."

Hannah gasped with pain. It felt like a hot sabre had pierced her heart. The desolation on Toby's face said it all. There was no way he was lying.

"What... What did he say?" she whispered, not wanting to ask the question, but knowing she had to face the truth.

Toby shrugged and looked uncomfortable. "I don't know exactly, but it wasn't nice. He was laughing at you for not wanting to have sex with him. He scoffed at the knowledge that you thought he was saving himself for marriage. He called you nasty names."

Jacob stood as still as a stone, with his fists clenched by his side. His face was expressionless. Tears filled Toby's eyes and slid down his cheeks.

"I couldn't listen to him talking about you like that, Hannah," he sobbed. "It wasn't right. You were so good and kind and beautiful. I loved you as much as I loved Jake and Lane and Rusty and my mom. You were the sister I never had, the angel who looked out for me. You always had time for me, no matter who was around. It didn't matter to you that I'm... I'm not good at things. You never once made me feel bad. I couldn't let Luke say those things about you and laugh at you like that."

Tears burned behind Hannah's eyes. Her chest was so tight, she could barely breathe, but she forced the words out.

"What did you do, Toby?"

"I yelled at Luke. I told him to stop. To stop saying those awful things. He just laughed at me and called me stupid. I...I tried to punch him with one hand. I just wanted to get him to stop. He reached for the steering wheel and I hit him again. I took my hand off the wheel and looked away, just for an instant...but it was long enough.

"I didn't even see the gum tree. The first thing I knew was the sound of the car as it hit the trunk and then I heard the screaming..."

Toby was sobbing in earnest and Hannah was crying, too. She wanted to go and comfort him, but she had to hear it right to the end.

"Please, tell me the rest. I want to know what happened."

Toby drew in a deep breath and sighed. "Jake and I were both wearing seatbelts. Luke wasn't. The car hit the tree on the passenger side. The side Luke was on. He was killed instantly. Jake and I fared better. We had nothing but a few scratches. We climbed out of the car. When the police arrived, Jake told them he'd been behind the wheel."

Hannah gasped and her gaze flew to Jacob's. His face looked like it had been carved from stone. She shook her head in confusion. "*Why?*"

"Why do you think?" Jacob replied, almost spitting the words. "Toby was hysterical. He was in no position to take the blame. It was bad. It was very bad. Luke was dead. I knew we were in big trouble. I couldn't stand by and see my brother sent to jail."

He shrugged, as if his announcement was nothing special. "I did what anyone would have done," he added and stared at her, as if challenging her to disagree.

She held his gaze, meeting his challenge head on. "No, not everyone," she said.

Toby's sobs came harder. "He did it for *me*,

Hannah! He went to jail for *me*! It should have been me in that prison, getting beaten up, bullied and bashed. Why do you think I ran away? I couldn't face the pain. Jake was in hell and I was the one who'd put him there! So, I... I found my own hell."

Hannah took a step toward him, but he spun on his heel and turned away. Running toward the front door, he fumbled with the lock.

"Toby!" Jacob called out. "Mate, don't be silly. Stay here. We can work things out."

Ignoring his brother, Toby finally got the door open and slipped through. A moment later, he was gone.

CHAPTER 23

Hannah looked at Jacob, feeling wrung out and exhausted. She was still coming to terms with the truth about what had happened all those years ago.

"Should we go after him?" she asked uncertainly.

Jacob shook his head wearily. "No, he'll be fine. He won't go far. He's always been afraid of the dark. He'll probably hole up in the garden. I'll give him some time to himself and then I'll go and talk to him."

She kept looking at him. "Why didn't you tell me?" she asked quietly. "Why did you let me hate you all these years?"

He held her gaze. "I didn't have any choice; I did it for Toby. You would have done the same."

The tears that burned behind her eyes spilled over and her chest tightened on a surge of emotion. "You're a very special man, Jacob Black. A rare and exceptional find."

He moved closer, his expression unreadable. "If

I'd been behind the wheel when Luke started slinging off at you, I would have done the same thing. I would have tried to beat the crap out of that piece of shit. You deserved so much better than that. As it was, I made sure he knew, in no uncertain terms how angry I was at the way he'd treated you.

"So, it could just as easily have been me that caused the accident that ended Luke's life. Fate stepped in that night and it was Toby behind the wheel, but it didn't matter. It was my job to protect him. I'd done it all my life. He'd never have survived in jail. I knew I could get through it.

"When the police arrived, I told Toby to stay quiet and I'd do all the talking. They didn't question my story. There was no need to. I kept to the truth for the most part. It was only when it came to who was driving that the story deviated. I was arrested and charged and pleaded guilty. I wanted it to be over as quickly as possible. I could see how it was affecting Toby. I couldn't add to his pain any more than was necessary. And I grieved for my friend, too. We'd been together since we were kids."

Hannah's heart swelled with emotion. For too long, she'd been blinded to Jacob's goodness and she'd had no idea about the selfless act he'd done for his brother. She moved closer until she could see the flecks in his eyes. Reaching out, she cupped his cheek. She heard his sharp intake of breath just before her lips connected with his.

Like fireworks on the Fourth of July, heat and passion exploded. They kissed blindly, madly, frantically, their lips and tongues tangling like flamenco dancers. Hannah's fingers buried themselves in his thick hair and she held his head in place. She kissed him on his lips, his nose, his cheeks, his chin, and all the while her heart was racing.

He pulled her close against him, until her breasts were crushed against his chest. She reveled in the hard planes of his muscles, the warmth of his skin. His breath came fast, almost as fast as hers, and sounded harsh in the stillness. At last, Jacob eased himself away. He stared down at her.

"I want to make love to you, Hannah." His voice was low and guttural and sent a wave of excitement surging through her veins.

She stared back at him and slowly nodded. This was how it was supposed to be. Making love with someone she deeply cared about. After Luke's death, she'd been angry and bitter at his sudden departure from her life. She'd railed internally about the unfairness of it. As a teen, she'd kept herself pure as a sign of her devotion and love and now the intended recipient of that gift was dead. After his death she realized her purity had become useless, a thing to be laughed at and pitied. She was furious at how highly she'd prized it.

Within months of his passing, she was frequenting bars on the seedier side of town. It hadn't taken her long to divest herself of her virginity. It had happened in the back of someone's truck. She couldn't even remember his name.

The whole episode had been so awful, she refused to think about it. She thought she'd be relieved to no longer be a virgin, but the night it happened, and for many nights after, she cried herself to sleep. She vowed never to treat herself with such disrespect again. The next man she slept with would deserve her.

Jacob's eyes darkened with emotion. "Are you sure? I remember you mentioning once before you believed in saving yourself for marriage."

She nodded again. "Yes, and I still believe in that, but after Luke died... I made some stupid decisions. I regret them now, but back then, my judgment was too clouded by my pain. Let's just say, I'm not a virgin now and leave it at that."

"I don't care about any of that, Hannah. I love you for who you are. It pains me to hear you say you did things you might not have otherwise done if Luke had still been alive, but I'm in no position to judge you and I don't want to. To me, you have always been beautiful, inside and out. That will never change."

Something that felt very much like love swelled up from inside her heart. Tears sprung to her eyes and she hurriedly blinked them back. His words filled her with happiness and she knew the joy of truly being loved. She couldn't help but wonder if Luke's feelings for her had only been a sham.

How could he have loved her like he'd said and yet sleep with other girls? How could he talk about her like Toby said, and still love her?

It would take a long time for her to reconcile her memories with the likelihood he probably didn't love her at all. His premature death had brought their relationship to a sudden halt, but maybe it wouldn't have lasted, regardless? The fact was, she'd never know.

With loving hands, she framed Jacob's face and pressed her lips against his in a soft and tender kiss. He was a wonderful man with a beautiful soul and she couldn't believe he loved her. On some level, she felt unworthy, but she vowed to strive harder to become a better person, to set aside her anger and hurt and love him as he deserved.

Taking her hand, Jacob led her down the hall and into his darkened bedroom. He switched on a lamp that stood on the nightstand and bathed the room in a soft glow and then moved to close the door.

"What about Toby?" she murmured.

"He'll be fine. The front door's unlocked. He'll come in when he's ready. I'll talk to him in the morning. I think the fact that we've managed to work things out will go a long way to helping him through his pain. It was killing him knowing how I felt about you and how you felt about me. He felt responsible for the fact the woman I loved, despised me."

"I'm not sure I des—"

Jacob pressed a finger against her lips, silencing her protest. "*Shh*," he murmured. "No more talk. Tonight's all about feeling."

And with that, he took her in his arms once again and kissed her. This time, his lips moved leisurely over her mouth and then trailed down her neck. He nibbled at the soft skin of her earlobes, while his hand cupped one of her breasts. He squeezed the soft flesh and stroked her nipple and she gasped at the surge of desire that arced its way down to her core.

"Do you like that?" he growled, his voice husky with need.

"Yes."

He reached down and undid the buttons on her blouse, slowly inching the fabric open. His fingers were gentle and cool on her heated skin.

"You're so beautiful," he whispered, his eyes taking her in.

Standing exposed to his gaze, she went to cover herself, but he stopped her.

"Please, don't be shy. Let me look at you."

The tenderness in his voice did her in. She stood still while he ran the back of his hand over the soft curve of her breast and down over her flat belly, then he pushed the blouse off her shoulders and eased her bra straps down. Slowly, he reached around behind her and undid the clasp. The white lace released its hold on her and without removing his gaze, Jacob tossed it away.

His hands returned to her naked breasts and he cupped one in each hand. A look of wonder crossed his face.

"You don't know how many times I've dreamed of doing this," he whispered huskily. "How many times I yearned to be the one to love you."

He bent his head and pressed a kiss against the soft skin of her chest. Gently, she eased him away and then reached up to his shirt.

"My turn," she murmured and set about releasing the buttons. He'd discarded his tie before dinner and within moments, his shirt was on the floor. He stood before her, bronzed and smooth. His pectorals were beautifully defined, glowing golden in the soft light. There was only a hint of dark chest hair.

She ran her hand over the warmth of his chest, loving the feel of his taut muscles. Her fingers skimmed over his nipples and he captured her hand and pressed it against his heart.

In silence, his hands came around her and released the button on her skirt. The slide of her zipper quickly followed and a moment later, the garment pooled at her feet. She was wearing matching underwear and a sensible pair of black stockings. He stared at her in wonder and once again, she fought against the urge to cover herself.

She'd never before stood naked in front of a man and it was a little unsettling. She wasn't embarrassed about her body. She was just...embarrassed. And shy.

With gentle fingers, Jacob tilted her chin upwards until she was looking at him.

"Don't be embarrassed," he murmured, as if reading her mind.

She blushed. "I'm not," she replied, hoping he believed her.

He chuckled and gave her a knowing smile, but said nothing. Instead, he undid the button and zipper on his suit pants and stepped out of them. His underwear and socks quickly followed. Before she could draw breath, he stood, tall and proud and naked before her.

Somehow, it made things easier. She stared at him, ogling the firm musculature, the long thighs, the broad chest, the erection that stood to attention. He reached out and drew her close, until she was pressed up against all that naked, hard flesh and she shivered with delight and need.

Her arms came up around his neck and she drew his head down. They kissed with mindless passion, gasping for breath. Jacob walked her backwards. Her legs came up against his bed and she sat. He followed her down and gently pushed her onto her back. With their lips still fused, they kissed again and again, while their hands explored each other's bodies.

Jacob's fingers tweaked her nipples and then stole lower, across her abdomen, and down to her nest of curls. His fingers stroked the soft flesh of her womanhood and she tensed.

"It's all right, honey. I won't hurt you. I promise. I just want to love you. Please, let me love you."

His gentle words of reassurance worked their magic and gradually, she relaxed. His fingers delved deeper into her slick warmth. And then one finger...two, were inside her, stroking in and out. She moaned and moved beneath him. A sweet pressure began to build.

Gaining confidence, she pulled his head back down to hers and kissed him with all the love and desire that filled her heart. His erection pressed against her belly, hard and huge. He pulled away from her and reached across the bed. Opening the nightstand drawer, he removed a condom and sheathed himself.

Kissing her again, he moved lower down her body, his lips trailing fire across her breasts, over her abdomen and lower, until he buried his face against her curls. When he breathed in deeply of her scent, it was the most erotic thing she'd ever experienced. Moving again, he nudged open her thighs with his knee and positioned himself between her legs.

"I want to love you for hours, honey, but I'm not gonna last much longer. I need to be inside you. I need to feel your warmth."

The husky words sent another surge of desire rushing through her and centered deep in her core. Heat flooded her.

Holding onto her hips, Jacob eased his cock inside her. Inch by inch, he filled her and stretched her wide. She gasped in wonder at the magic feel of it.

Slowly, he began to move and she tightened her hold on his shoulders. The delicious feeling of anticipation began to build. Over and over, he thrust inside her until she was tense and expectant, clinging to the edge. Her fingernails dug into his skin. Her breath came in desperate pants.

"That's it, Hannah. Go with it. Relax and let yourself come."

His gentle words sent her over the edge and she cried out as she climaxed. Her muscles clenched in beautiful rhythm and he stilled, as if to savor the magical sensation. A moment later, she collapsed on the mattress.

"Good?" Jacob asked, giving her a tender smile.

"Amazing," she whispered. And it was true.

Though she was no longer a virgin, it was the very first time she'd made love. She now knew why they called it that. The act was so different when it was experienced between two people who cared.

Jacob began to move again, this time at a more frantic pace. His face was a study in concentration. She clung to him and silently urged him on, loving the feeling of him inside her. A moment later, he tensed and groaned and thrust one more time before falling still.

After a while, he lifted his head and looked at her. She smiled shyly. "Good?"

His face filled with tenderness and love. "Better than good. Amazing."

CHAPTER 24

Dear Diary,

I had such plans for my nephew. I took out a policy on his life for the sum of one million dollars. It was to be my final paycheck, a clearing of his debt. An overdose of heroin, or even crystal meth—whatever his drug of choice at the time—it hardly mattered to me.

But now, he's gone and ruined it all. He's brought the police to our door. I've had to change my plans. He can no longer be my windfall, the sweetest pot of gold, but I can still make use of him; there's still a way I can collect on my debt.

I've been thinking it over for the past few weeks and it's a good and decent plan. Young Bobby will rue the day he treated me with so much disdain. He's going to be my scapegoat. That will more than repay his debt. The police will be none the wiser, until it's far too late.

But now time is of the essence. I need to act fast. Toby will have to die sooner than I expected. The police will have Bobby in custody sooner rather than later and when that happens, my plans will be stopped in their tracks. I can't risk doing away with another employee while the prime suspect is warming his ass in jail. It just won't do.

No, my final act of brilliance must be set in motion tonight...

Toby continued walking blindly, his thoughts in turmoil. He scuffed at the uneven pavement with the toe of his brand new boots. He couldn't remember the last time he'd worn new shoes. It must have been back when he was a kid. He certainly hadn't had the money or the inclination to buy new shoes over the last ten years.

He thought of the shock on Jake's face when he'd come across him in the emergency room. His fingers were twice the size they should have been and were throbbing with pain. He'd done his best to defend himself. His attacker had eventually taken off, but not before inflicting considerable damage.

Toby hadn't realized his brother was a doctor. He hadn't seen or heard from his family since he'd left his hometown just months into his brother's incarceration. The knowledge that Jake was in prison because of him had eaten away at him until he couldn't stand to live an easy life anymore. He'd had to escape the ever-present reminders that his brother was doing time when it should have been him.

He'd kept the pain of their deception bottled up for so many years. He realized the only way he'd be able to deal with it was to remove himself from society as he'd known it. A week after Jake pleaded guilty, he'd walked out of the modest apartment his mom had helped him find and he hadn't looked back. He hoped she'd received her security bond back after he'd breached the lease. Not that it mattered now.

Jake had told him their mother died two years before. It saddened him to know that he wasn't there during her final days and that he'd never get to see her again. But even two years ago, he wasn't ready to return to his family. Life on the streets had been hard, but it was no less than he deserved. He was sure Jake had endured worse in jail.

It was only the chance meeting with Max, shortly after he'd reunited with his brother that Toby felt the stirrings of a yearning he'd long ignored. He wanted to reach out to his family again, he wanted to be the Toby Black they'd grown up with and loved. His two older brothers had made something of their lives and even Rusty was well on his way to being a success.

Toby wanted his family to be proud of him. He wanted to be worthy of their respect and love. When Max came along and offered him a job, he was ready to accept it. Having Hannah Langdon work at the same place had come as a lovely surprise. It brought back, of course, the sad memories of that time, but she'd always been kind to him and right now, he needed a friend.

It was different, accepting her offer to move in with her than it had been when Jake and Lane had extended the same invitation. Hannah was a friend and could help him through the transition to when he'd be worthy to stand shoulder to shoulder with his family again.

He'd noticed the way Hannah had been looking at Jake and he'd always known how his brother felt about her. The truth of what had happened that fateful night had been blocking their path to finding love and he couldn't stand by another minute without opening Hannah's eyes.

But now, he'd gone and spoiled it by blurting out the truth. The shock and horror on Hannah's face would forever haunt his dreams. He didn't know if she'd ever forgive him or Jake, for not telling her sooner. Or forgive him for what he'd done that night. There were no winners and he couldn't bear the thought he might have made the whole sad situation worse.

He stumbled on an uneven piece of concrete and fell down on his knees. His cotton pants tore on the rough surface as it cut into his skin. Blood seeped from a gash on his knee, but he pushed himself back to his feet. Looking up, he realized he was outside the door of the funeral home.

Feeling around in his pocket, he found the key Hannah had given him the week before. She'd had a morning appointment and had told him to let himself in. Max didn't usually appear downstairs until a little after nine. The embalming crew were expected to start work at eight.

He fitted the key into the door. The knob turned under his hand and he sighed softly in relief. He'd go into the embalming room and sit there, in the peace and quiet. The solitude of the place had always appealed to him. After the night he'd had, it was the perfect place to escape with his thoughts and pray that the morning would bring an improvement and somehow remove the strain between Hannah and his brother.

———————

Max placed the final set of clothing in his suitcase and closed the lid with a sigh. There. It was done. Two suitcases stood beside his bed. Another four suitcases were downstairs by the front door. Six suitcases that represented his life—his old life, at least. There would be plenty of time and even more money to create a new life after tonight. The life he'd looked forward to for so many years. The life he deserved.

The claim on Christopher Lowery's policy had already been paid out. Even now, the money was sitting in an account somewhere in the Caymans, ready and waiting for him. He'd left instructions with his bank to transfer the rest of the insurance money to the same offshore account. With a bit of luck, the money from Edward Sutton would be transferred before the police made their findings public. He'd called Andrew Bloomberg at General & Life just the day before and had been assured by the claims officer that everything was in order. The only thing left to do was to bring an end to the life of Toby Black.

It saddened him a little to cut short the young kid's life. He was a good lad with a heart of gold and, unlike the other two, he had a supportive family who cared. At the time Max chose him as his next victim, he didn't have a clue that the homeless man had family, but that fact didn't really matter. He'd made sure his nephew would take the blame.

He'd phoned Bobby only an hour earlier. His nephew had sounded drunk or high—or both—but he didn't say anything about the police or an imminent arrest, so Max could only assume the detective still hadn't tracked his nephew down. That was good. He needed Bobby free for just a little while longer—long enough for him to do away with Toby.

Today, he'd hoped to invite Toby out for a drink after work, but his plans hadn't worked out. The kid had already accepted a lift home with Hannah and had declined his invitation. Max had wracked his brain in an effort to come up with a plan to entice Toby out alone, but time had almost run out. It was time to resign himself to the fact Toby, and his payout, weren't meant to be. Better to escape with a million than get caught and spend the rest of his days in jail. Nothing about that scenario was appealing.

A sound from downstairs caught his attention and he frowned. It was getting late. At least eight o'clock. There shouldn't have been anyone downstairs. *Perhaps Bobby had come back, looking for somewhere to sleep?* In addition to his other faults, last Max had heard, his nephew had defaulted on the rent and had been kicked out on the streets.

Taking his flashlight from the hook by the door, Max made his way downstairs, switching on lights as he went.

"Bobby? Is that you? What are you doing here?"

His questions bounced off the silent walls. He paused and then heard another sound. It was coming from behind the door that led to the embalming room. It sounded like a chair scraping across the floor. A little more cautiously, he approached the door and eased it open.

The room was windowless and dark. Max felt along the wall for the light switch. He blinked at the sudden illumination and was even more surprised to see Toby Black seated in a chair with his legs propped up on the counter. At the sight of his employer, the boy dropped his feet to the floor and hastily stood.

"Toby! What are you doing here?"

"I… I'm sorry, Max. I had an argument with my brother. I walked out of his apartment and I… I found myself here. I thought I might spend the night in the embalming room. It's peaceful here, among the dead. I hope you don't mind?"

The last was said a little anxiously and Max hurried to reassure him, hardly able to believe his good luck. He'd been wracking his brain to come up with a plan to get the boy alone—and here, he'd fallen into his lap. Life couldn't get any sweeter.

"Of course, not, Toby. My place is yours. I'm sorry to hear about your brother. Stay as long as you like."

Relief flooded the younger man's eyes and Max felt the tiniest twinge of guilt.

"Thank you, Max. I... I really appreciate it. I'm sorry I disturbed you. I promise I'll be quiet as a mouse."

"Don't be silly, Toby. You didn't disturb me. I was just upstairs having a drink." He smiled kindly at the boy. "Why don't you come up and join me? I hate to drink alone."

"I'm not much of a drinker, Max. Coke and lemonade is about all I do. Alcohol makes me feel funny in the head. I don't like it."

Max laughed in a friendly manner. "Of course, and it's probably best that you don't drink. But I do have Coke in the fridge upstairs, if you're interested."

The boy continued to look doubtful. Max tried harder. "I also have some cookies and milk and my housekeeper baked a key lime pie. Are you hungry? There's plenty to share and I hate to eat alone."

Toby's eyes lit up with pleasure and it was all Max could do to hold back his grin.

"I love key lime pie," the boy said. "I haven't had it since I was a kid. My mom used to bake it on my birthday. I've almost forgotten the way it tastes."

"Then that's settled then," Max replied. Slinging a friendly arm around the boy's shoulders, he added, "How about we go upstairs?"

———————

Lane rubbed his eyes with his fists and drew in a deep breath. Pushing open the door to the interview room, he dug deep to find the energy to conduct the final interview of the day. It was way past the end of his shift, but he couldn't help the feeling that he was on the cusp of a breakthrough with the case against Robert Grace.

They still hadn't been able to find the asshole. He wasn't in any of his usual haunts and he'd been kicked out of the last place he rented. The chase would start again tomorrow. In the meantime, Lane intended to find as much evidence as he could to link Max's nephew to the crime.

Diandra Robinson had already confirmed she'd paid the first claim into a bank account in the name of Robert Grace. Lane had traced the details back to a branch in Ashfield. A few more telephone calls had located the bank teller who had attended upon Robert Grace when he opened the account. Lane had asked her to come to the station.

She was waiting for him now. He'd get her to confirm the details and the amount deposited and then he'd head for home. Zara had been expecting him hours ago. The twins had come down with another bug. He'd hated to phone her and tell her he was going to be late.

"Mrs McInnes, I'm Detective Sergeant Lane Black. Thank you for coming in."

He extended a hand in greeting to the middle-aged woman who sat in the chair. She shook it with barely a smile. Apparently, he wasn't the only one who was keen to get home.

"I'll be as quick as I can, I promise," he reassured her with a smile. "I need to tell you this interview will be recorded. Is that all right with you?"

The woman nodded. "That's fine. Let's just get this over with. I have a cat that needs to be fed."

Lane acknowledged her comment with a brief nod and then got down to business. In short order, he established the woman's full name and address. She also confirmed she was a teller at the National Bank in Ashfield and had attended upon Robert Grace.

"What can you tell me about him, Mrs McInnes? What was his demeanor like?"

"I don't know. He appeared just like any other customer. He was there to open an account. I explained the procedure and he provided me with the required documentation. I was pleased that he'd come prepared. Many of our elderly clients don't realize the paperwork we need. It's a requirement of the law, you see, that we sight original documents that add up to one hundred points of ID."

Lane frowned. His attention had snagged on something she'd said. Something about the elderly…

With his elbows on the table, he leaned forward. "Mrs McInnes, I'm curious. You mentioned your elderly clients, almost as if they had something in common with Robert Grace."

The woman looked bemused. "I don't understand why you find that curious, Detective. Mr Grace is a man well past his prime. Granted, he looks pretty good for his age, but still, he's not a young man."

A growing knot of suspicion filled Lane's gut. He opened the file in front of him and pulled out a recent photo of Robert Grace and showed it to his witness. "Is this the man you know as Robert Grace?" he asked.

She frowned in genuine confusion and shook her head. "No, that's not him. I've never seen that man before. Robert Grace is elderly, like I said. He has a wonderful head of snowy white hair. He's in his seventies. I can't remember his exact date of birth, but I recall thinking at the time he was around my mother's age. She'll be seventy-eight this summer."

The noise of Lane's blood rushing through his ears almost drowned out the sound of the woman's voice. *It wasn't Bobby at all.* This had all been an elaborate set up, even down to the concern and resignation Max had exhibited earlier, when Lane and his men had attended the funeral home for the purposes of arresting Robert Grace.

It was now clear it was his uncle they should have been after. Max Grace was the mastermind behind the murderous plan. His nephew was nothing more than a patsy.

"Mrs McInnes, could you describe the Robert Grace you met?"

The woman frowned. "Well, he had a head of thick snowy white hair and the sweetest face you've ever seen. He reminded me of my dear old Dad who passed away a couple of years ago. He—"

A sense of urgency rushed through Lane and he pushed abruptly away from the table. The woman stopped, mid-sentence and stared at him in surprise.

"Detective? Are you all right?"

"I'm sorry, Mrs McInnes, I'm going to have to cut this interview short. I promise we'll talk again tomorrow, but right now, I have to go. I'll send someone in to see you out."

With that, he opened the interview room door and strode back into the squad room. It was early evening. The night shift had begun, but very few officers were scattered around the open concept office. Lane tugged out his phone and dialed Jacob. At the same time, he yelled out to anyone within hearing distance to gather close.

CHAPTER 25

Jacob heard the sound of his cell phone ringing from out in the other room. Hannah lay asleep beside him. He glanced at the clock on his nightstand and noted the time. It was barely eight-fifteen. He felt like he'd been asleep for hours.

The lamp was still on, filling the room with golden light. With an effort, he dragged himself from the bed. He pulled on his boxers and padded down the hall. Locating his phone on the kitchen counter, he checked the screen and frowned.

Lane.

"Hey, bro. What are you up to?" he said quietly, in deference to Hannah.

"Jacob, we were *wrong*. It isn't Robert Grace. The one behind the murders is his uncle. It's fucking *Max!*"

Jacob frowned in confusion and tried to make sense of Lane's words. "What the hell are you talking about?" he said.

"I interviewed the bank teller who attended Robert Grace when he opened his bank account."

"Right. And?" Jacob prompted.

"She referred to him as being elderly. It was then that something clicked. I questioned her further and showed her a picture of the nephew. She'd never seen him before. It wasn't Robert at all. I'm still trying to track down a photo of Max, but I'm sure she'll identify him as the man who opened the account. Her description fits. It's Max, Jacob. I *know* it."

"Shit," Jacob muttered. "Max? It's Max?" He shook his head back and forth as the information finally sunk in. "How could it be Max?"

"He's got the perfect cover. He's a sweet old man who wouldn't hurt a fly. In fact, to the contrary. He's gone out of his way to portray himself as generous and kind, to a fault. He takes in homeless men. He gives them shelter, gives them a job. Treats them like they're human, like they mean something to him. Yeah, they mean something to him, all right. They're another life he can insure and then do away with."

"Shit," Jacob said again, unable to believe it. Never in his wildest dreams had he suspected Max was a killer.

"Where's Toby?" Lane asked, breaking into his thoughts.

"I think he's in bed."

"You think?"

"We... We had an argument after dinner. He... He told Hannah the truth about Luke."

"That the prick was sleeping with anyone who'd let him?"

"Yes, well, that came up, but the worst part was the bit where he confessed to—"

Jacob stopped midsentence. Lane didn't know. He didn't know the truth of that fateful night.

"What the hell did he confess to, Jacob? What are you trying to say?"

Lane's impatient questions hammered into Jacob's brain. His mind spun in circles. A moment later, his shoulders slumped on a heavy sigh. *What did it matter if Lane finally knew the truth?* It was time to come clean and put it behind them, once and for all.

"Toby confessed to Hannah that…that he was one the behind the wheel that night. The night that Luke was killed."

"*What?*"

Lane's shocked response didn't come as a surprise. For more than a decade, the twins had kept the secret. Not even their mother had known. Jacob hadn't seen the point. He'd pleaded guilty, he'd served the time. As far as he was concerned, it was over with.

"*Toby* was the driver that night? Are you *kidding* me? It was Toby who caused the accident?" Lane asked, aghast.

"Yes. I tried to stop him from saying anything to Hannah, but he was insistent. He… He told her everything."

"Forget that, why the hell didn't you tell *me?* I'm your brother! How could you have kept this from me?"

"I'm sorry, Lane. I don't know what you want me to say. I thought it was the best thing to do."

There was silence on the other end of the phone. Jacob could tell Lane was struggling with the recent revelation. He wished he could help him, but he'd spoken the truth. What was done was done. There was nothing Jacob could do.

At last, Lane sighed heavily on the other end of the phone. "This isn't over, Jacob. We're not done discussing this, but right now, I have more important things on my mind. Just answer me this: Why the hell would Toby tell Hannah? After all this time?"

"I don't know, but the fact is, he did. She knows the truth."

"How did she react?" Lane asked somberly.

"About as well as you. She was shocked, of course, and angry, but I think she'll come around."

"What about Toby? How's he doing?"

"I haven't spoken to him since his confession. I'll go and check on him now." Jacob walked down the hall toward Toby's bedroom. The door was still open. He peered inside. Even in the dimness, he could see the room was unoccupied. A shaft of concern went through him.

"He's not here. He mustn't have come back," Jacob murmured.

"What do you mean? Where did he go?" Lane asked, a note of urgency in his voice.

"Nowhere. He... He left after the argument. He went outside for some air. I... I thought he'd be back by now. I'll go outside and look for him. I'm sure he's not too far away."

"Call me when you find him. I want to know he's all right. I've had men out all day looking for Robert Grace and all along, the perpetrator's been right under our noses."

"So, have you arrested Max?" Jacob asked curiously.

"Not yet. I've only just put the pieces together. I'll talk to the boss in the morning and get another arrest team together. The man's so confident we're looking at his nephew, I doubt he'll be going anywhere."

"Yeah, you're probably right. Max is the last person I suspected. I knew The Bobster better than anybody. I can't believe I didn't give him the benefit of the doubt."

"Don't beat yourself up about it, Jacob. I'm trained for this kind of shit and I didn't see this coming."

After exchanging good-byes, Jacob dropped his cell phone onto the breakfast bar and padded back to his bedroom. His gaze fell on Hannah. Her golden hair was spread across the pillow. She looked so beautiful, like an innocent angel, sound asleep. Tugging on jeans and a T-shirt, he switched off the lamp and quietly left the room.

The night was cool and he shivered a little. The sound of the occasional car passing by broke the stillness. The smell of parsley, sage and thyme teased his nostrils as he walked by his neighbor's herb garden. Her apartment was dark. She must be visiting her grandson again. He lived two hours to the south.

The front garden that faced out onto the street

was empty. Jacob walked around the building to the back. It was darker there and the shadows of the tenants' communal clothes lines looked like racks of thin, ghostly fingers in the night.

"Toby?" he called out, peering into the darkness. There was no reply. He stubbed his toe on a rock that bordered the path that led back to the building and cursed. He should have brought a flashlight. This was stupid, walking around blindly in the dark.

"Toby! Can you hear me? It's time to go back inside. I'm sorry, mate. I know you're upset. Let's go and talk about it."

Nothing moved, not even a breath of wind. The night remained silent. Jacob frowned. *Where the hell was he?* There was no way his brother had left the apartment complex. Toby was terrified of the dark. Jacob had been surprised when his twin had stormed out—testament to how upset he'd been.

With a faint stirring of panic swirling low in his gut, Jacob turned and headed back the way he'd come. He spied his phone on the breakfast bar as he entered. He picked it up and dialed Lane's number. His brother answered on the first ring.

"Did you find him? How is he?" Lane asked without preamble.

"No, Lane. I didn't find him. He's not outside the building. He's not anywhere."

"What the hell do you mean, he's not anywhere?"

Jacob bit back an impatient retort. It wouldn't help matters to get into an argument. Lane was just trying to find their brother, like Jacob was.

"I mean, I walked around the building. He's not here. He must have gone for a walk, or something."

"At this time of night? He hates the dark!" Lane retorted.

"Yeah, he does," Jacob agreed. "Or at least, he used to. It's been a long time since we had anything to do with him, remember? It's my guess he's spent many nights in the dark since he left home. Perhaps he's gotten used to it?"

Lane growled something indistinguishable under his breath and then sighed. "What about his cell phone? You told me Hannah bought him one. Have you tried calling him?"

"No, but I'll do that now. Hold on." Jacob found Toby's number and dialed it on his home phone. The call rang out. Jacob walked around the apartment, but couldn't hear the phone. He guessed that unless Toby had it on silent, he must have taken it with him. Eventually, the call went to voicemail.

"At least we know it's still switched on," Lane said when Jacob reported back to him.

"Yeah, I wonder how much battery he has left? I don't know how many times I've reminded him to put it on the charger."

"Let's hope he followed your advice for a change," Lane replied, his voice dry.

"What are we going to do if he doesn't answer?" Jacob asked. "I can't let him disappear again, Lane. I've only just found him."

Jacob heard the quiet desperation in his voice, but there was nothing he could do. What he said was true. Over the years, he'd missed his twin like he'd miss an arm or leg. It was a hole that was always there, bearable for the most part, but never going away. The moment he'd spied Toby in the ED and had realized it was his twin…well it was one of the happiest days of his life. He couldn't simply let his brother up and walk out of his life a second time.

"How long are we going to wait before sending someone out to look for him?" Jacob asked quietly.

Lane sighed. "How long's he been gone?"

Jacob glanced at the clock. "I'm not sure. A couple of hours?"

"That's not long. Especially when we're talking about an adult. And you did say you'd had an argument. The police won't be interested in a missing person's report at this stage."

Jacob was flooded with irritation. "So we're just going to leave him out there, wandering around for God knows how long. Is that how this is going to work?"

"Calm down, Jacob," Lane replied with a trace of annoyance. "I didn't say I wasn't going to do anything. Just that your average cop wouldn't be interested. Call his phone again. I'll do a triangulation on his phone signal and see what tower he's bouncing off. It will give us a rough idea of his location. Do you know which phone company he's with?"

"Yes, he's with Optus."

"You're sure?"

"Yes. I re-charged his prepaid account only two nights ago."

"Good. That should speed things up. Give me a few minutes. I'll call you back."

Jacob ended the call and sighed. He wondered where the hell Toby could be. It hadn't occurred to him that his brother would leave the apartment complex. He'd been upset, but not, he thought, uncontrollably so. Jacob would never have left him alone, if he'd thought his brother needed immediate consolation.

Instead, he'd let Hannah kiss him and he'd been more than happy to kiss her back. No, not happy. Delirious. He'd made love to her with his heart and mind and body and it had been all so amazing and great. He couldn't wait to do it again. But Toby was missing and he needed to be found—and Max Grace was a murderer.

Lane's revelation struck him anew and he wondered if he should wake Hannah and give her the shocking news. The thought had barely formed when he decided against it. Nothing would be gained by waking her tonight. The morning would be soon enough. The phone rang in his hand and he answered it immediately. "Lane, how did you do?"

"Great. His phone's pinging off a signal in the Balmain area."

"He's gone to the funeral home," Jacob guessed.

"Why the hell would he do that?"

"I guess he's looking for somewhere to spend the night. He knows the funeral parlor."

"How would he get in? I assume the building's locked."

"Yeah, I wonder if he'd knock on the door," Jacob replied. "Maybe he has a key. I'd ask Hannah, but she's asleep."

"Well, the phone signal puts him in that location. It makes sense that's where he's gone."

"I'll go over and fetch him. Let's just hope he lets me in. He's not answering his phone. I don't want to wake the neighbors."

"What else is in the vicinity?" Lane asked.

"Mostly warehouses, a couple of small businesses. Hairdresser and a coffee shop, if I recall. And of course, the residence upstairs."

Lane's voice sharpened. "Who lives upstairs?"

Dread formed an icy ball in the pit of Jacob's gut. "I don't know for sure, but I'm guessing it could be Max."

CHAPTER 26

Toby blinked and tried to clear his vision. It was weird. He'd barely drunk half a glass of Coke and yet he could see two of everything. Max sat across from him, smiling and telling him stories from when he was young. At least, he thought that's what his boss was saying. It was a little hard to stay focused with his eyes playing tricks and his brain not keeping up.

"Drink up, lad. Don't let it get warm. Nothing worse than warm Coke," Max joked.

Toby tried to laugh. He didn't like warm Coke, either. But his efforts came out in some sort of garbled moan. He wondered if Max had noticed. He did his best to look over at his boss, but once again, his eyes refused to cooperate. And now his head had begun to thump.

A piercing pain behind his eyes left him gasping and wondering what was going on. He'd been fine when he first came upstairs. Max had shown him around the small apartment. It had a nice view over the roofs of the other buildings to the water. He'd spied a collection of suitcases lined up neatly by the door. Max had explained he was going on a holiday. He wasn't sure for how long.

Toby frowned. He couldn't remember Hannah telling him their boss was going on a holiday, but then again, he was new on staff. He wouldn't be told everything. He was still so grateful for the opportunity Max had given him and he told his boss as much. Max merely smiled and looked even more like the guardian angel he was—or at least, that's how Toby thought of him.

"How are you doing, Toby? Are you feeling all right over there?"

Max's voice held a note of concern. Toby began to feel worried. If Max had noticed that he was looking poorly, perhaps he was really sick? He felt beyond awful. He felt worse than he ever had in his life.

"I… I think I need to see a doctor. I… I don't feel well."

Max's face immediately creased in concern. At least, that's what it looked like, but it was a little hard to tell. Toby was still seeing everything in twos. That made it hard to know what was real and what was not.

"How about we go outside and get some fresh air?" Max suggested and pushed away from the table.

Toby tried to nod, but even the slight movement was beyond him. "I… I don't know if I can make it down the stairs, Max. My head feels like it's going to split open."

"Oh, don't worry about that, Toby. I'll help you. We'll go down slowly, side-by-side. I promise I'll hold on to you. After all, I'd hate to see you fall."

Jacob pressed his foot against the accelerator until it was almost flat on the floor. Lane had promised to meet him at the funeral home with a team of officers. They were only guessing Toby had gone to the funeral home, but with their recent discovery of what Max was capable of, they weren't taking any chances.

Jacob glanced across at Hannah where she sat white-faced in the front seat. He hadn't meant to wake her, but she'd overheard him talking and when she came out into the kitchen dressed in sweat pants and a T-shirt. Catching a glimpse of his expression, she worked out straight away that something was dreadfully wrong.

As quickly as he could, he'd told her about her employer and the possibility that Toby had gone to the funeral parlor. She was as shocked as he was about the discovery her boss was a murderer, but she insisted on accompanying him to Balmain.

"Turn left at the next intersection," she said and he shot her a quick look.

"It's a shortcut. Trust me. I know these roads better than anyone."

Without argument, he made the turn and once again, hit the gas.

Toby stumbled awkwardly and fell heavily against Max, crushing him momentarily against the wall. Max grunted in pain. Edward Sutton had weighed about half as much as Toby. This wasn't going to be easy. Not for the first time that night, Max wondered if he should simply abort his plan.

The police were on Bobby's trail. It was only a matter of time before they arrested him. If they did so prior to Toby's "accidental" death, Max's carefully laid plans would be torn asunder. Questions would be asked. The insurance policies might be scrutinized more closely, including the bank account where the money was transferred. It could get tricky. More than tricky. It could interfere with the grand retirement he'd planned.

Toby stumbled again and Max wondered if he should simply push the man down the stairs. It had worked once. There was no reason it wouldn't work again. But Toby was bigger than Edward and he was inside Max's home. The police would ask questions and wonder. Toby's family would do the same.

It was too risky. Best stick to the original plan. He'd take Toby down to the Harbour where the boy would "accidentally" fall in. With the amount of alcohol and LSD Max had put in his drink, it wouldn't take long for Toby to drown. A very sad end to a man who'd largely lived a very sad life.

As far as Max had been able to ascertain, Toby Black had lived most of the last decade on the street. He ought to be grateful for the charity Max offered him the night he came across him hunched over a bench in a bus shelter. But charity had its limits. Nothing came for free. It was time to collect on his debt.

It seemed to take forever to reach the bottom of the staircase, but finally, they made it. With Toby leaning on him heavily, Max struggled to make it to the front door. With an effort, he got it open and then awkwardly negotiated the front steps. Not long to go and he'd have Toby in his car and then the deed was as good as done.

———————

Jacob took the last corner wide and with a squeal of tires. He was less than two blocks away from the funeral home. The streets were dark and relatively quiet, which aided their progress. Coming to a halt at a red light, he tapped the steering wheel impatiently.

"I'm sure he's all right," Hannah murmured and Jacob couldn't help wondering which one of them she was trying to convince.

"Yeah," was all he said and then hit the

accelerator the second the light changed to green.

———————

Max made it down the front steps with Toby in tow. His heart rate had picked up its pace. His Jeep was parked beside the curb, only a few feet away. The sound of squealing tires caught his attention and he looked up in time to see a pickup truck bearing down. It was moving fast and looked like any second the vehicle would mount the curb and wipe them both out.

The street was poorly lit and there was no one else around. In a split second, Max aborted his original plan and maneuvered Toby across the narrow sidewalk and onto the road, in line with the oncoming truck. The sound of the engine drew nearer, roaring with impatience. Max had time to capture Toby's startled look before he bent low and using his head and shoulders, pushed with all his might.

Toby was caught totally unawares. With a shout of fear, he reached out blindly, grasping at air, then hurtled into the path of the oncoming vehicle.

———————

"Watch out!" Hannah screamed, pointing to the road in front of them.

Jacob swerved and hit the brakes. At the same time, he spied a familiar shock of white hair disappear into the night.

Max.

The truck went into a slide. Jacob fought against the wheel, finally bringing it to a halt. Throwing open the door, he bolted from the truck, at a run. Hannah caught up to him.

"Did you see him?" she panted.

"Who? Max?"

She frowned. "You saw Max?"

"Yes, at least, I think it was him. Who did you see?"

"I'm not sure. It was a man with dark hair. I only caught a glimpse before he fell onto the road. It was like he'd overbalanced."

Jacob immediately thought of his brother and picked up his pace. If it *had* been Max he'd spotted, Jacob could have just aborted Max's attempt to throw another employee under the tires of a vehicle. He was puffing by the time he saw a figure lying prone on the side of the road.

"There he is!" Hannah shouted, at the same time. They ran to the man's side and slowly turned him over.

"Toby! Oh, God! It's Toby!" Jacob gasped. "Stay with him and call an ambulance! I'm going after your employer."

"You don't know—"

"Yes, Hannah, I do," he cut her off. Anger flooded through his veins. All of a sudden he was certain it was Max who'd pushed Toby into their path. If Hannah hadn't seen him fall, Jacob might very well have run over him. His own brother. It didn't bear thinking about.

Hannah pulled out her phone. Jacob jumped to his feet. Satisfied that the ambulance would soon be on its way, he took off at a run in the direction of the funeral parlor. Max Grace had a lot of explaining to do.

Max's heart pounded. He felt like he was having a heart attack. *Perhaps he* was *having a heart attack?* His chest felt tight and he was panting like he'd run a marathon wearing concrete boots.

It was the fact that he'd turned tail and ran the moment he'd given Toby an almighty shove that had his heart thumping so hard. He hadn't waited to see if his last-minute change of plan had been successful. He'd heard the squeal of brakes seconds after he pushed Toby into the path of the oncoming vehicle. He knew better than to be found at the scene of the crime.

It hadn't been like that with the other two. He'd met with Christopher Lowrey in a bar on the corner of a busy intersection. He'd waited until the early hours of the morning before suggesting they leave the bar and go for a walk. He'd checked the street in all directions for other passersby. There had been nobody.

The semi had been visible from some distance, even in the dark. Max timed it perfectly. Keeping to the shadows, he'd supported Christopher's drunken form until the very last minute. The cab of the truck had already passed them by when he threw the man under the back wheels.

And nobody had been the wiser. Even the truck driver hadn't seen a thing. Max had dissolved into the shadows, just another anonymous figure making his way home. Then there was Edward Sutton. His death was even easier.

The man was already a hopeless drunk. It didn't take much convincing for him to agree to meet Max after work for a drink. Edward wasn't shy about alcohol. Max plied him with rum until the man could hardly stand and had then escorted him home to the dingy hostel where he'd been staying. It was way past late. Not a soul stirred in the house. He managed to half-walk, half-drag Edward up the stairs. It had been a simple matter to exert a little pressure and watch the man fall.

All the way to the bottom.

Max had winced at the thud of the man's head. The concrete floor was so unforgiving. He'd calmly walked by his former employee, pausing briefly to check for a pulse. There was none. His plans had gone better than he'd expected.

Then Toby Black had dropped into his life at a most fortuitous moment. Max had waited years to call in his "investments," but the sight of his growing bank account proved too hard to resist. He got impatient and that was a mistake. He'd chosen Toby and had sent him for the medical right away. The boy had gotten curious. Max had overheard him discussing it with Hannah.

Still, it had all worked out in the end. The boy was dead and Max was positioned to inherit a final, tidy sum. All he needed to do was get his things and get on the road. His yacht was packed with all the essentials for his journey, full of fuel and ready to set sail.

A noise from downstairs caught his attention and he froze. Two visitors in the same night. It couldn't be a good sign. Unless it was his nephew. Max eased open the door to his bedroom and stepped quietly out into the hall. Plastered against the wall, he peered around it to see who had come inside.

A tall figure who looked terribly familiar stood in the entryway, as if deciding which way to go. It sent a shiver down Max's spine to see the brother of the boy he'd just killed. They looked so much alike. It was like staring at a ghost. But he was being stupid. The man was the identical twin. Of course he looked like his brother.

Thinking fast, Max moved back toward his bedroom as quickly and as quietly as he could. Reaching for his bathrobe, he tugged it on over his clothes. He pulled back the bedcovers and climbed into bed and then switched off the light. A sound from the stairs alerted him that the man was close.

A moment later, a knock came on one of the outer doors. Max ignored it. When it came again, followed by a loud and impatient hello, Max switched the light back on and climbed out of bed. Taking his time, he made his away across the room to the door that led to the top of the stairs.

Toby's brother called out a third time before Max opened the door.

He frowned at the man and took his time rubbing the sleep out of his eyes. It wasn't all that late, but Jacob Black didn't know what time Max usually went to bed. It suited his purposes to make the fellow believe he'd woken Max from a deep sleep.

"Hello? Is there something the matter?" he asked. To his annoyance, his voice trembled from the strain of pretending. He cursed silently.

"I'm here about my brother," Jacob stated, his eyes hard.

Max pretended to be confused. "What are you talking about? Toby left for home hours ago. He won't be back until the morning."

"Try again, Max. Toby's downstairs. He's lucky to be alive. Someone pushed him in front of my truck. It's a miracle I didn't hit him."

Max fought to keep his expression from revealing his frustration. *Of all the luck!* Not only did he fail in his attempt to do away with Toby, his brother was the witness. And that same brother was watching him with eyes narrowed with suspicion. Max thought fast.

"Oh, my goodness! Is he all right? Where did it happen?"

"Cut the bullshit, Max. It happened right outside your building. I saw you with him at the same time he fell onto the road."

Max's heart began to pound and the blood rushed through his ears. He had to do something to distract the man, to move the focus of his attention.

"You must be mistaken. I've been asleep for more than an hour. Your brother's downstairs, you say? Come, let us go to him. I might be able to help. Have you called an ambulance?"

"Yes, of course we have, and I'm a doctor," Jacob snapped.

Max frowned. "We?"

"Hannah and I. We traveled in the same vehicle. We were out looking for Toby."

Max forced himself to nod, but he wasn't pleased to discover Hannah was also nearby. She knew him far better than Jacob. She'd notice anything amiss. All he could do was get Jacob out of his house and distract him from his suspicions. Tightening the sash of his bathrobe, he made a point of locating his slippers and then led the way down the stairs, Jacob on his heels.

They'd made it across the entryway. Max was already at the front door when Jacob spied the suitcases. Max cursed under his breath. He'd meant to load them into his car earlier, but then Toby arrived and his packing had been interrupted.

"Going somewhere?" Jacob asked, fresh suspicion visible in his eyes.

"Just a little holiday. I've had it planned for a while," he responded lightly and hoped the man would leave it at that.

"You're taking a lot of luggage. How long will you be gone?"

Max forced a laugh. "Yes, I told myself to pack lighter. I just can't seem to manage it. I'm only going for a couple of weeks; can you believe it?"

To Max, his voice sounded shaky, but he prayed Jacob wouldn't notice. He pulled open the front door and debated making a run for it. His car was parked where it usually was, right outside the building. The keys were still in the pocket of his pants, concealed beneath his robe. No doubt Jacob had called the police, along with the ambulance. There would be more questions to answer.

And then he noticed the blue and white strobe emergency lights and the stern face of the detective who'd attended upon him. *Had it only been earlier that day?* It felt like a lifetime ago. The man strode toward him with intent. Max's gut stirred with fear. Was it too late, already? Had he miscalculated?

The detective reached for the handcuffs that were attached to his belt and Max had his answer. With nothing to lose, he made a dash for it.

Running harder than he had in his life, he raced toward his car. Tugging out the remote, he unlocked it and kept running. His heart pumped. His breath came fast. Three yards to go. Two... He dived toward the driver's side and reached for the handle. His fingers scraped the door. He was almost there. And then the wind was knocked out of him from behind and his lungs were screaming for air.

The detective had flattened him against the side of his car and was holding him still with his weight. All the while, he had Max's arm in a death grip, twisted behind his back.

"Going somewhere, Max?" the officer growled low against Max's ear.

Max strained against the hold, but it was of no use. The man held him fast. Max went limp. The game was up. He was filled with a feeling of despondency... He'd come so close to fulfilling his dream. So close... And now it was over.

CHAPTER 27

Jacob stared at his brother, lying still and silent on the white sheets. Toby had been brought by ambulance to the Sydney Harbour Hospital and was in the emergency ward. Jacob had already checked him over and couldn't find any injuries other than a gash on the back of his head, but he was still only semi-conscious and Jacob wasn't sure why.

"Toby? Can you hear me? Tobes? Please, open your eyes. Tell me you can hear me!"

A faint moan came from Toby's lips and Jacob nearly collapsed with relief. Tears streamed down his cheeks. He'd been separated from his twin for more than a decade, not knowing whether he was alive or dead. Not knowing *anything*. He couldn't lose him again.

"How's he doing?"

Jacob looked up in time to see Hannah parting the privacy curtains and moving closer to Toby's bed. He was relieved to see her.

Jacob nodded cautiously. "I think he's

improving. I can't find any injuries, other than a scratch to his knee and a bump to the head, but something's not quite right. He's in and out of consciousness. If I didn't know any better, I'd hazard a guess that he's drunk. Either that, or he's been drugged—maybe both. We'll know for sure once the doctors get back the results for the blood tests."

Hannah shook her head in disbelief. "Do you think Max…?"

She left the question hanging, as if she was unable to complete the thought. Jacob could only imagine how it would feel to discover the boss she had liked and respected was a murderer. But, he refused to sugarcoat it, even for her.

He nodded grimly and answered. "Lane's convinced Max is behind it. I think so, too. Lane's questioning Max as we speak. I hope the bastard confesses and saves us all a lot of time and money."

Hannah continued to look shell shocked. "I just can't believe it! I mean, how did he do it? It must have taken considerable planning. These crimes didn't happen on the spur of the moment."

"You're right about that," Jacob replied. "Lane believes Max took out the life insurance policies in his nephew's name. He opened a bank account using fake ID. Everywhere the police looked, the trail would lead to The Bobster. Max almost got away with it."

Hannah crossed her arms and shivered. "If we'd been a few moments later… If it had been another vehicle that had come along… Toby might have ended up dead, like Christopher and Edward and nobody could have proven it wasn't an accident."

Jacob moved closer and put his arm around her shoulders in an effort to provide her comfort. "You saw Tobes on the sidewalk. You saw him fall. You saved his life."

She stared at him, her eyes wide. "You saw Max. You helped get him arrested. If not for you, he'd still be out there, free to do the same thing to someone else. He's already gotten away with it twice. He must have been feeling rather confident."

"Yes, well, we've taken the confidence out of him. Lane assures me he'll be behind bars for a long time to come. Likely for the rest of his life."

Hannah remained silent. She rested her head against Jacob's shirt. He enjoyed the feeling of having her in his arms, of protecting her and keeping her safe. He pressed a tender kiss against her hair and was gratified when she tightened her arms around his waist.

"Jake? What happened? Where am I?"

Jacob released Hannah and rushed to Toby's side. His twin stared up at him, his eyes shadowed with pain and confusion.

"Tobes! Oh, thank goodness! You're awake! And you know who I am! You don't know how happy you've made me, bro."

"My head hurts," Toby complained and reached up to touch the bandage that was wrapped around his head. "Why do I have a bandage?"

"You hurt yourself when you fell into the street outside the funeral home," Jacob explained gently.

"The funeral home? What was I doing there?"

Jacob stared at him. "You went there after dinner. You were upset."

Toby's frown deepened. "I went to the funeral parlor? In the middle of the night?"

"Well, it wasn't the middle of the night when it happened, although it was certainly dark. Don't you remember?"

Toby shook his head slowly back and forth. "No. The last thing I remember was telling Hannah about..."

"That's it?" Jacob asked. "Nothing else?"

"No, nothing," Toby replied and then added, "Do we have to do this now? My head hurts."

Jacob hurriedly reassured him. "No, mate. We don't have to do this now. Lane's all over what happened. We'll talk about it later, when you've had a chance to rest. How does that sound?"

Toby's eyes lit up with a smile. "That sounds great."

———————————

The clock on Jacob's nightstand showed it was almost midnight when he and Hannah finally made it home. They crawled into Jacob's bed and collapsed against the mussed sheets, exhausted. *Had it only been a matter of hours since he'd made sweet love' to her? If felt like a* lifetime. Rolling to his side, he reached for her, needing to feel her close.

"What a night," he murmured, pressing a kiss against her lips.

She kissed him back and even though he was tired, his body immediately responded. Her lips were warm and inviting. Her arms crept around his neck. He pressed her to him and she tightened her hold. Need, immediate and explosive, flooded his veins.

He wanted to take things slowly, but his body was having none of that. His cock throbbed, hard and pulsing. In record time, they divested of their clothes, not pausing until they were both naked and pressed together, skin to skin. Jacob sighed at the exquisite feel of her against him.

"I shouldn't be thinking about how much I want you when my brother's still lying in a hospital bed," he muttered and nuzzled her neck.

"At least we know there's been no permanent damage," she replied, a little breathlessly.

"*Mm*, I was relieved when his CT scan came back normal. I'm guessing whatever drugs Max used have resulted in the memory loss. Still, Lane's confident he has enough to make a case."

And with that, Jacob turned his attention to more important matters, like loving the woman in his arms as thoroughly as he could. He started with pressing kisses along her jawline and then moved lower, across her neck. His hands cupped the fullness of her breasts and squeezed gently. She moaned.

"Do you like that?" he murmured, continuing the onslaught.

His tongue flicked at her earlobe and traced the curve of her ear. She smelled of vanilla and spice and every now and then he caught the scent of her shampoo. The strawberry stuff. His favorite. Until now, he hadn't been close enough to take advantage of the delicious smell.

He buried his nose in her long, thick hair and breathed in deeply. She smelled clean and spicy and wonderful. She smelled like Hannah, the woman he loved. Finding her lips, he kissed her again, slowly, lovingly, tenderly. Moving lower, he kissed his way to her breasts.

Her nipples were small and puckered and slipped easily into his mouth. He suckled gently, first one and then the other, loving the breathy little gasps that elicited.

He continued lower and pressed kisses against the soft skin of her stomach. Pausing at her belly button, he dipped his tongue inside the shallow hollow, before moving to the nest of curls between her legs. Once again, he breathed in her sweet scent. His tongue stole out for a taste.

"Jacob!"

He lifted his head and stared at her. "You don't like it?"

"No! No! It's... It's just that...no one's ever...done that before."

Light from a nearby street pole leaked through the half-open blinds. He looked up at her and caught her blush. His heart swelled with tenderness.

"Then I'm unbelievably lucky," he said and meant it.

He parted her soft lips with his tongue and lathed the silky skin until she stirred restlessly beneath him. Her hands reached down and tangled in his hair. He wasn't sure if she was trying to get him to stop or hold his head in place. From the murmurs of want coming from her mouth, he guessed the latter and continued his sensual investigation.

"Jacob, I... I need you. Please."

The whispered plea filled him with quiet satisfaction. A surge of eagerness quickly followed. His cock was so hard it was painful. He couldn't wait to bury himself in her warmth.

Lifting his head, he stared at her, loving the desire that filled her eyes. He moved and reached for a condom. Quickly sheathing himself, he kneeled between her thighs. He meant to take it slowly, but the tip of his cock was barely inside her when he lost the battle with his self-control.

He plunged all the way inside her and her eyes flew open in surprise. He paused, but she reached for him, drawing him down hard against her and clinging to his shoulders. His strokes lengthened and he slowed his pace, luxuriating in the feel of her surrounding him. Her scent, her taste, her murmurs of desire. He loved everything about her. He wasn't sure how she felt about him, but it was clear they had a connection. He was hopeful that one day, she'd care for him as much as he cared for her.

Her mewls of excitement became more frantic and he opened his eyes and stared down at her. Her color was high and her face was tense. She was on the cusp of an orgasm. He stroked harder, pounding into her. Her nails dug into his skin.

And then she reached the climax and was toppling over the edge. She cried out and clung to him, while her body convulsed around him. He stilled, enjoying the feel of her pleasure. When it was over, she stared up at him, her expression filled with delight and wonder.

Jacob locked his gaze on hers and slowly began to move once again. In and out, he stroked her tight warmth until he couldn't stand it a moment longer. With a low growl, he thrust inside her, faster and faster until he'd also reached the peak. With a guttural moan, he collapsed against her. They both groaned their relief.

He was still catching his breath when she whispered the words.

"I love you, Jacob."

He tensed. Propping himself up on his elbow, he stared down at her, hardly daring to believe what he'd heard.

"You… You *love* me? Are you sure? Because, I understand it might take you a little while to reach the place I am, but I've been in love with you for years. Just because we've made love, doesn't mean I expect—"

She placed a finger against his lips and smiled. "*Shh*. Don't say anything more. It's got nothing to do with the fact we've just shared the most wonderful experience of my life. I think I've been falling a little in love with you ever since we reconnected. You're good and kind and generous. Your love for your brother melts my heart. To top it off, you're incredibly sexy." She gave him a cheeky wink. "What's not to love?"

EPILOGUE

Six months later

Hannah smoothed down the white satin fabric of her wedding dress and tried to suppress her nerves. It wasn't like she hadn't been looking forward to this day for the whole of her life. She was getting married to the man of her dreams.

Jacob Black was the man of her dreams in every sense of the word and it wasn't until she'd experienced love as an adult that she could look back on her childish infatuation with Luke Parker and see it for what it was. She could only shake her head now, all these years later, and be grateful that things hadn't worked out the way she'd prayed. Not that she'd ever wanted Luke to die, but she could see now sometimes there was a reason God didn't answer all her prayers.

"You look beautiful, Hannah," Samantha whispered, smiling softly at her friend.

Hannah smiled back at her. "Thank you, Sam.

And thank you for being here, supporting me as my matron of honor. You've barely dragged yourself out of the birthing suite and I'm sure you're desperate for some sleep. I really appreciate it."

Sam's eyes welled up with tears and she hurriedly wiped them away. "Look at me, getting all emotional! As if the pregnancy hormones didn't wreak enough havoc!" She moved closer and took Hannah's hand in hers and gave it a reassuring squeeze.

"There's no need to thank me, Hannah. No matter how much I love and adore Rohan Junior, I wouldn't be anywhere else in the world. After all you've been through—you and your future husband—I wouldn't miss this day of happiness for anything."

Hannah felt the burn of tears behind her eyes and quickly blinked them away. She didn't want to smudge her makeup before Jacob had seen her in her finery.

"We're lucky things worked out so well," she admitted quietly. "Out of such evil came some remarkable things. Bobby's finally cleaned up his act and he's the best boss I could ever have. Toby's starting to like him and Bobby thinks a lot of Toby, too. I think he reminds Bobby of Jacob and the time they spent in jail."

She sat down on the bed and pulled on her five-inch, white satin heels before continuing. "They were good friends. They looked out for each other. That kind of bond is hard to break and I think it's nice the two of them have renewed their friendship. I think it's helped Jacob, too. He's able to look back on his incarceration and remember that something good came out of it."

"What happened with Toby?" Samantha asked softly. "Did anything come of his confession?"

Hannah shook her head. "No. Jacob and Lane and I agreed not to say anything to the authorities. There was no need. What was done was done. Jacob had repaid the debt. These past months have given us all time to come to terms with our past and forgive each other. I'll always feel a little sad I never saw the truth all those years ago, but Jacob's helped me to stop beating myself up about it and to let it go.

"He's such a good man," Sam said quietly.

Hannah stared up at her best friend and smiled. As she thought of the future, her heart filled with hope. "Yes," she replied, "he is. And best of all, he's mine."

Note to Readers

I do hope you have enjoyed reading Hannah and Jacob's story. If you've enjoyed this book, please feel free to leave a review for The Debt Collector at Goodreads and your favorite digital retailer. Every review is very much appreciated.

If you would like to receive news on upcoming stories, release dates, book launches and other snippets, please feel free to sign up for my newsletter. You can do this by visiting my website at www.christaylorauthor.com.au and clicking on the "Subscribe to my Newsletter" link on the right.

The Lab Test is the next book in the Sydney Harbour Hospital Series. Here's a sneak peek:

As a teenager, Danielle Porter was a wild child. The product of a broken marriage and parents who never wanted children, she did all she could to live up to her reputation, despite the desperate urgings of her younger sister, Sabrina.

Ten years later, Danielle has finally gotten her life together. Working as a respected pathologist at the renowned Sydney Harbour Hospital, she's come a long way from the turbulence of her youth. Sabrina couldn't be more proud.

Now married to a successful lawyer, Sabrina's also done well for herself. She's living the dream with a husband who loves her and a baby she adores. To Dani, Sabrina has the perfect life.

And then Sabrina and her daughter are brutally murdered and nobody knows who's responsible. Is it the maintenance man who was in the apartment or someone far closer to home?

Detective Constable Jett Craigdon of the State Crime Command catches the case. Angered by the senseless deaths, he's determined to catch the killer. With thirty-seven stab wounds to Sabrina's body, it's obvious this attack was personal, but is it the grieving husband who has done this awful thing, or is Sabrina's beautiful, enigmatic sister the one to blame?

The Lab Test will be released on 28 August, 2016 and is available for pre-order from your favorite digital retailer.

ABOUT THE AUTHOR

Chris Taylor grew up on a farm in north-west New South Wales, Australia. She always had a thirst for stories and recalls writing her first book at the ripe old age of eight. Always a lover of romance and happily-ever-afters, a career in criminal law sparked her interest in intrigue and suspense. For Chris to be able to combine romance with suspense in her books is a dream come true.

Chris is married to Linden and is the mother of five children. If not behind her computer, you can find her doing the school run, taxiing children to swimming lessons, football, ballet and cricket. In her spare time, Chris loves to read her favorite authors who include Richard North Patterson, Sandra Brown, Kathleen E Woodiwiss and Jude Devereaux.

You can find out more about Chris and sign up for her newsletter at her website:

http://www.christaylorauthor.com.au

www.ingramcontent.com/pod-product-compliance
Lightning Source LLC
Chambersburg PA
CBHW062016190726
48284CB00012B/284